A VAMPIRE'S LIFE

"I'm Michael Bowman," I said. She nodded, an elegant gesture of encouragement. "Who—how—"

"Let's just say I'm here to help you find Adam," she said. "I'm an old friend of his."

"You know where he is?" I asked stupidly. She gave me a smooth, pitying smile.

"No, I don't. I think maybe we can help each other with that. What can you tell me about his whereabouts?"

"I think William—you know William—" She nodded, smile gone. "I think William's got him, and maybe is controlling him somehow."

Celestine clicked the briefcase shut, set it aside and cocked her head a little to the side. Her face was smooth and unlined. Youth caught in the amber of vampirism.

"Then we don't have a lot of time left," she said. "I'll need to see you tomorrow evening. Here. My card."

She handed it to me, and our fingers brushed. Hers were as cold as mine, soothing, not like the touch of hot human flesh. I glanced down at what she'd given me.

CELESTINE VAUGHN, it read in thick raised type. There were numbers for a telephone, and a fax. In modest letters in the lower right corner, ATTORNEY AT LAW.

"I guess you get a lot of jokes about bloodsucking lawyers," I said. She laughed.

"Not from my clients. Tomorrow evening, Michael. Seven o'clock?"

"Fine," I heard myself say, and she smiled at me again. This time, because I was looking for it, I saw a faint glint of fangs.

She walked out the way she'd come. I watched her go. She got into a waiting Mercedes with smoked glass windows.

Just another night at the JiffeeMart.

ROXANNE LONGSTREET

ZEBRA BOOKS
KENSINGTON PUBLISHING CORP.

To Theresa Patterson,
Team Pegasus,
and Sue McMurray—
for reminding me why I write.

It's because of folks like you
who believe I can.

ZEBRA BOOKS are published by

Kensington Publishing Corp.
850 Third Avenue
New York, NY 10022

Zebra and the Z logo Reg. U.S. Pat. & TM Off.

First Printing: January, 1995

Printed in the United States of America

One

Having a Wonderful Time.
Wish You Were Here.

So there I was, on the cracked, dingy apartment steps, heading down toward my car. Dallas lights glimmered yellow-orange on the clouds overhead like spilled sherbet, and traffic growled on the freeway seven blocks down. My Volvo was parked on the street next to beat-up Toyotas and rust-red Camaros and a Jeep missing most of its upholstery.

In retrospect, I guess the Volvo looked pretty darn out of place. I wasn't thinking of that as I came down the steps—three at a time—and saw the taillight of my car wink redly. Just one taillight. The other was out. *Gee,* I thought. *Need to get that fixed.*

It took a few seconds for me to get the obvious point. *My car was driving away without me.*

It wasn't until the son of a bitch was half a block away that it all hit me, like a hammer to the forehead. My *car.* He stole my *car.*

"Hey!" I yelled. The thief's hand came out of the window and gave me a friendly little share-the-road wave. He hit the gas, spun the tires, and drove away into the cool, whispery distance.

Leaving me there, in the predawn dark, with a body over my shoulder.

I dumped the body on the sidewalk and spent slightly more than a minute running after the car, running back to the body, picking up the body, throwing it down again in disgust, picking it up again. It slowly penetrated to me that the theft of my Volvo was not an inconvenience. It was a life-threatening problem.

The sun was coming up in—a quick glance at my watch— thirty-five minutes. Since I am a vampire—had I mentioned that?—sunrises are not my favorite moments of the day. This particular sunrise was looking more and more menacing.

And I still had a body balanced like a beanbag over my shoulder.

Son of a bitch, what a night.

Options. I needed options. My favorite: I could try to find a store-it-yourself place. *Vampire In A Can. Bring your own key.* But that idea was pretty much moot, because I didn't know of a storage place close by and I didn't have time to go shopping.

Option two. Well. I couldn't think of anything under option two. That meant I'd have to dump Mr. Dead. Upsetting, considering all the trouble I'd gone through to get him, not to mention the trouble I'd have getting rid of him without awkward, unpleasant scenes.

Option three, then. I went back up the stairs, into the crumbling apartment house. Three stories, a pay-by-the-night sort of place that made the "$19 per couple" specials look like a Hilton. It was still what most non-vampires considered early, but I heard people stirring, light switches clicking, water running. Somewhere on a floor above me, somebody was running a blow-dryer. Somebody else was making coffee. Just another Tuesday morning, for the breathing population of Dallas.

I, on the other hand, had developed a little tight ball of panic somewhere around my belly button. Every second brought the sun closer.

Thirty-three minutes left, while I stood and considered nonexistent possibilities. There was a door down to the basement, it was locked. I didn't want to break it down, since it was in plain sight and even the dimmest wino would have noticed, so I went on to the fly-specked apartment listing taped to the wall next to the stairs.

No vacancies. Then again, it was a piece of paper that went back to Eisenhower's days and probably didn't represent the current state of rental affairs. But I couldn't exactly go door to door looking for a place to crash for the day.

Just not done.

The apartment where I'd originally located Mr. Dead belonged to an S. Johns, who must have been female, considering the clothes I'd seen in the closet. Mr. Dead did not look to be the cross-dressing type. I figured S. Johns, God rest her soul, was probably in a shallow grave or floating in a pond. Mr. Dead did not look to be the considerate type, either.

Mr. Dead—or rather Mr. Undead, Esquire, fellow vampire—mumbled something and tried to shove my hand away from his neck. I bashed his head against a convenient wooden post and put him out again. It wouldn't kill him, because the varnish on the wood cushioned the blow—I'd done some experimenting on that. Just call me the Mr. Wizard of the undead. Mr. Dead wouldn't be shuffling off his immortal coil until I found out what I needed to know.

Back to the apartment of S. Johns, then, cool brass knob

turning in my palm, door creaking inward. The sweet smells of powder and scented soap and lingering perfumes puffed out—the powder my wife liked, the perfume I'd given her for our last Christmas while I lived. *No fair,* I thought, and pushed it away. *No time for Maggie now. Work to do.* I sucked up the burning sensation of pain in my chest and closed the door behind me. Just in time. Somewhere down the hall a door slammed shut and someone tip-tapped past in high heels.

Out the south window, the heavy sherbet clouds looked like dawn, only colder. Still some time left. I dropped Mr. Dead on the unmade bed where I'd first found him and went to the kitchen.

S. Johns had a big roll of aluminum foil. I papered the window with it, drew the curtains and hung a heavy quilt on top, just to be sure. There was only one other window in the place, a little tiny one in the bathroom. I blocked the room off and shoved towels up against the crack in the door, and did the same for the front door after bracing it with a chair.

Thirteen minutes to go.

S. Johns still had a working phone. I dialed a number from memory.

"Hello?" Maggie said. Such a neutral voice, these days. Used to be so warm. I wished I could see out the windows, because I could feel dawn coming. The clouds would be ember-red, burning. The pain was back in my chest, stabbing deep. I closed my eyes and smelled Maggie's powder, Maggie's perfume.

"It's me," I said.

No thaw on the other end.

"Where are you?"

"Trapped. Listen, somebody boosted the Volvo, I didn't get a good look at him. Report it as stolen, okay?"

"Sure," she said, and I heard the scritch-scratch of a pencil. "What's the address there?"

I gave it to her, feeling a little bitter because she hadn't even sounded worried about the "trapped" business. Her pencil scritched again.

"Want me to come get you?" she asked. I leaned back against the wall; my bones felt gray and heavy as concrete, pulling me toward the center of the earth. My lungs had begun to ache.

"No time," I answered. My voice sounded slurred. "Going down now."

"Sleep tight," she said, and the line clicked and hissed, disconnected.

Why did this happen to us? I had gotten tired of asking the question, but its ghost hung around. I heard it whispering to me every time I heard her voice.

Across the room, on the bed, Mr. Dead's eyes gleamed at me as we both started to sink down in the dark. We were going to be staring at each other all goddamn day. I was drowning, water clotting in my lungs. I wondered how Mr. Dead felt when he died every day. Had he overdosed? Been shot? Been stabbed?

Did it matter?

I wanted to close my eyes. I couldn't.

If I dreamed, I don't remember.

TWO

In Which Michael Meets A Friend.

Nightfall. The usual waking-up kind of stuff, water draining out of my lungs painfully, stiff muscles convulsing, eyes blinking away dryness. I secured Mr. Dead with a double set of handcuffs on each arm and leg, connected to the bed frame. I was sitting slumped in a chair, still trying to think away my headache, when he blinked his dry open eyes— slowly, lizard-like—and came alive. It took him a few seconds to figure out where he was; I let him think about his predicament while I turned on a few low lights and took the quilts and aluminum foil off of the window. Kept the curtains closed, though. Privacy for this kind of thing was usually preferable.

His name—at least the one he gave me when I asked him nicely—was Harold Gerhardt. Nicknamed, for some unfathomable reason, Dicky. Dicky had breathed his last in 1976, a bicentennial poster child for vampirism. Jet-black hair, probably dyed that way, hacked off unevenly around his shoulders and falling over his too-pale face. His eyes were green. He dressed like he'd seen *The Lost Boys* too many times.

I went on over to the window and looked out. The sky was gold-orange-red, colors layered like a strong Tequila Sunrise. The freeway seven blocks away was a metal parking lot; I heard the rumble of engines vibrating through the thin glass. If I listened really hard, I'd probably hear the curses.

"Hey," Dicky said from behind me. Fake tough-guy bravado, learned from bad television. I left the sunset to do its thing alone and went back to my chair. "Hey, asshole, who the hell you think you are?"

He was hungry. I saw it in his nervous, jerky pulls against the handcuffs. Junkie nervousness. I knew how it felt, the jitters, when I hadn't had my rich, red drug.

I shook out a cigarette and lit it from a lemon-yellow lighter. My hands still shook when I did it, but I held onto the cigarette, put it to my lips, pulled smoke into my lungs. Managed not to choke on it.

It was an effective demonstration. Dicky's eyes got very wide, and he stopped struggling.

"Don't burn me," he whispered. "Oh, man, don't burn me, please don't."

"I'm not going to burn you, Dicky," I said, and took another drag. The heat of the smoke made me feel uncomfortably claustrophobic. "Not if you answer some easy questions. Ready?"

"Oh, man, who the fuck are you?"

"Frosty the Snowman. Do you know Adam Radburn?"

Blink, went the green eyes. And again, blink.

"No."

I considered the glowing red tip of my cigarette and scooted my chair closer to him. Springs squeaked as Dicky tried to cringe away. His eyes were wide and unfocused, right on the edge of panic. I let him hang there and get a good view from the drop-off.

"Dicky, Dicky, Dicky," I said. "You just aren't catching on to the game. You aren't scared, are you?"

"I ain't afraid of nothin'," he snarled. His canines flashed white as they came down. "Sure ain't afraid of *you*. Fuckin' faggot yuppie. Think you got some shit just because some faggot asshole bit your neck. You don't scare me."

I tapped some ash from the cigarette.

"You're making me blush. Let's talk about Adam."

"Don't know him," he declared. "He a breather?"

"You know exactly who he is. And I'll bet you even know where he is, don't you?" I breathed smoke out of the cigarette, blew it gently back in his face. He turned his head and closed his eyes. "Look, Dicky, I'll make you a deal, okay? You tell me where Adam is, and I let you go and give you the parting gift of a set of Ginsu steak knives."

"Fuck you, man," he said. I guess he thought I wouldn't do it.

I put the cigarette close to his arm, just close enough for him to feel the heat, no contact. He screamed. I jammed one of S. Johns's white scarves into his mouth and let him scream. The bed rattled like a xylophone, jumped into the air with his thrashing.

When I took the gag out of his mouth, he tried to bite me. His eyes were hunting-red.

"Clock's ticking, Dicky. Where is he?" I asked again. Dicky's lower lip quivered where his white canines touched it.

"Man, William's gonna fuck you up for this," Dicky whispered. "Swear he will. He's the *man* around here, you're nobody."

I waited. The cigarette was getting warmer now, and I was fighting to hang on to it. My fingertips felt like they were on fire, though there was an inch of unburnt tobacco between them and danger.

I remembered the first time I'd struck a match, in my vampire days. I'd torn the door handle off of Adam's convertible, trying to get away from it. It had been a bad night for control. I'd put a blind woman in the hospital, too. Had almost put her in a grave.

Poor Dicky.

I stuffed the scarf back in his mouth and went to work.

The smell was terrible, sickening. It brought back memories of my flesh cooking in the dawn light, of an enemy's crispy black skin, smoking and popping as the fat boiled underneath.

Poor Dicky. He kept screaming for quite some time. The handcuffs bent, but they held him. I watched the blackened hole I'd put in his arm slowly turn red and then white as it healed. My cigarette had gone out. I relit it.

I left the gag in for a while, until his eyes looked a little more sane. When I took it out, he didn't say anything, just stared at me with shimmering bloody eyes.

"Want to go for door number three now?" I asked.

"He's with William," Dicky said. His voice was fast and rough, a cat's tongue licking words.

"Yeah, I know that. I want to know where."

"I don't know, man, seriously, I don't know. I seen him sometimes, hanging around. No place special. Saw him once or twice down at the bus station. He's William's pet rat, now. Does what William tells him to."

"Meaning?"

"You know, do this, get that, kill this. That stuff."

I flicked the cigarette onto the floor and crushed it out. My fingers felt sunburned. My lungs were leathery from the smoke.

"Yo," Dicky said. He rattled his handcuffs, attempted an appealing smile. It didn't really work. "Yo, man, I told you what you want. When you gonna let me go?"

"What, before you go for the grand-prize round?" I asked, and went back to the window. A car pulled up to the curb, a basic black sedan. A blond woman got out.

Maggie.

She tilted her head up and looked for me. I waved. Her face barely changed as she recognized me, nothing warm, nothing happy.

Never mind poor Dicky. Poor Mikey.

Michael Kevin Bowman. Formerly *Dr.* Bowman. Formerly human, formerly breathing, formerly a loving husband to a loving wife. Except now I was a vampire, and my wife was not, and that made things more than a little strange between us.

Not to mention the little problem of Adam Radburn, my friend and fellow vampire, now enslaved by *another* vampire who met every qualification I could think of for being an evil bloodsucking freak. Maggie wasn't handling that little problem very well, either.

Poor little Mikey. Neither was I.

I listened to her quick, light steps as she ran up the stairs. She gave a one-knuckle knock at the door, and I swung it open.

"Jesus, it's gloomy in here," she began, and saw Dicky. All the expression drained out of her face. "What the hell are you doing?"

"Never mind," I said, and took her arm and guided her away from the door. I shut it behind us. "Anything on the car?"

"No, nothing yet. Michael, what are you—"

"Just don't ask, okay? You don't want to know. Can I put something in your trunk?"

Her skin felt hot in my fingers, even through the layer of her thick cotton shirt. She yanked her arm from me and took two steps away, creating a space that we'd never needed before. Her wide blue eyes were hard, now. She'd put on her cop face.

"You crazy bastard," she said. I tried to reach out to her, but she wasn't having any. "Do you really think I'd help you kidnap somebody? What the hell's wrong with you?"

"He's a vampire—"

"Jesus Christ, what do you think *you* are, anemic? Are you crazy? What's happened to you?"

I thought about reaching out for her again and decided, from the look on her face, that I'd better not try it. I might be faster, but faster wasn't always better.

There was another reason not to exercise my aggressive instincts. I was getting hungry.

"Maggie—"

"Don't start."

"Sweetheart—"

She opened her mouth to say something really, really hurtful, but I was saved by the bell, so to speak.

Dicky's scream split the night, a horrendous, terrified shriek. I leaped for the door and threw it open.

He was still moving, weakly, though his green eyes had rolled back in his head and I figured the tremors were just the last instinctive jerks. It would be impossible for Dicky to survive the stake that had been hammered through his chest, not to mention the bloody ruin somebody had made of his throat. I reached out, automatically, tried to pull the stake out from his ribs. The lightest touch raised blisters on my fingers. Hawthorn or ash.

Something was going out the window, just a flicker. I leaped for it and slipped on the discarded aluminum foil, the wadded quilt. I leaned out into the night and onto an uninformative, deserted street.

A flash in my peripheral vision made me look up. There, just disappearing over the edge of the roof, was the figure of a man.

The moonlight splashed on his face when he looked back to see if I was watching.

Sensitive, fine-boned, pretty-boy face, eyes flickering red behind the round John Lennon glasses.

I stood, rooted, unable to follow him.

Because Adam was not the friend I remembered. I could tell by the blood on his mouth, and the grin.

When I turned back, Maggie was standing in the doorway, gun drawn, looking from me to Dicky's trembling corpse. Her eyes were wild.

"He's dead," she said. "Jesus."

"What do you think I should do?" I asked her quietly. She froze, staring at me. "I'll do what you think is right."

"Jesus," she breathed. "Go. Get out of here. Go!"

She came all the way in and kicked the door shut behind her.

"Out the window," she ordered. I must have looked stunned. "I hope to hell nobody's called the cops yet."

"Should we do something with the body?" I said, just as the fire started. It started from his chest, burning white like phosphorus. The stake, I thought. Burning. Some kind of biochemical reaction. I covered my eyes against the white glow—

—and then I was outside on the fire escape. I'd ripped a chunk of wood out of the window sash in my hurry to get away. Maggie climbed through carefully, touching nothing with her fingers, bracing herself with her forearms and elbows. We started down the iron staircase, her steps light, mine almost undetectable.

At the bottom, we looked back up. The room had an eerie glow, getting dimmer as we watched. A little smoke drifted out.

"We should call the fire department," Maggie said. She sounded shaken.

"No," I said. She leveled a look at me like a .45. "Sure."

I jogged half a block away to a phone booth and dialed 911. By the time I had dodged the "and your name, sir?" question, she had the car idling at the curb. I got in. Maggie gunned it and we drove away. No sirens, not yet. Maybe not ever, knowing this neighborhood.

After a while, Maggie said, "Let's go home," and I put my head back against the slick plastic headrest and tried not to think about Dicky, dying.

All I could think about was Adam, blood on his mouth, grinning at me. Like William. I clearly remembered that grin on his evil white face. Sweet William liked killing a lot.

But he liked pain more. I wondered where that left Adam.

Interlude:

Adam

He ran blindly, eyes shut. Thinking of nothing. It was the only way—

Adam.

—the only way to—

Adam.

—to be free, even for a second. He might be blind, he might be mindless, but he was *free.* The longer he could run, the stronger he was. The closer to revenge. Where was he? In a tunnel; the water dripped loudly, his footsteps were whispers.

A few more feet—

And then his body went out of his control, spun around, pressed his face hard against a rough wet wall. His hands stretched out flat on the bricks, but he couldn't push away. All he could do was endure the acid burn of William's presence in his head.

Adam, it don't do you no good to run.

Oh, but it did. It did.

You come on home now.

No threats, no promises. Just the command. Adam's body

spasmed under the whip of his master's will. He screamed, but it came out a strangled grunt, airless. The pain twitched in every nerve ending, robbed him even of his anger. There was only one way to end it.

He fell away into the distance as William took control. His body stepped away from the wall. His feet walked in the direction of a distant glimmer of streetlights. He had run farther, this time. Almost two blocks.

He walked to a car and slid into the back seat. William, behind the wheel, turned and grinned at him, white face, white icy eyes, white teeth glistening.

"Let's go home," his master said, and Adam was allowed to close his eyes. It did not help. He knew he would always see the boy's face as he plunged the stake into his chest. And even now, hating what he had done, he remembered the taste of Dicky's blood.

Soon, he thought. *It has to be soon, or I am lost.*

"Thinkin' about little Dicky?" William asked. Adam opened his eyes, tried not to twitch at the intrusion. "Your buddy Michael ain't doin' so bad, these days. Used to be a real baby about trouble, but he's gettin' used to it, looks like. He's fast, I'll give him that. And real determined."

He'll find me, Adam thought. It made him colder. *What then?*

"Then," William said, picking the thoughts out of his head like delicious little morsels, "then I guess we'll see just how determined he is, Johnny Reb. You never were very strong. Always runnin'. Always hidin'. You and that Injun woman of yours—what was her name?"

"Sylvia," Adam whispered aloud, to keep William from picking at those memories, too. Her heart had felt cold and heavy in his hands.

"Yeah, Sylvia. Too bad about her. You should'a stopped fightin' me, I might'a let her go. You never know."

"I knew."

"Ah," William said, and grinned. He turned around and put the car in gear. "Your buddy Michael's got a wife, don't he? A pretty little china-doll wife."

"Not so fragile as that," Adam answered. He had the feeling William glanced at him from the front seat, but the rearview mirror didn't reflect anything but empty upholstery.

"They're all fragile," William said. "Just blood and skin."

Adam felt his master's insect-like scrabbling in his head again, and closed his eyes.

"Yep," he heard William murmur. "They all come apart when you pull hard enough."

Three

Irreconcilable Differences

The radio was playing "Radar Love." Maggie turned it up to a conversation-stopping volume as she took a right onto the freeway. Her fingers tapped the steering wheel, random clicks of fingernails out of rhythm with the song. I waited for her to say something, anything, but she just stared straight ahead, concentrating on traffic that wasn't there.

I put my hand on her knee. She gave the kind of jerk a mule gives right before he kicks you in the *cojones*. I took my hand back, while I still could. She glared at the road ahead as if waiting for somebody to make her day.

"Radar Love" faded into the distance. Aerosmith started wailing about "Home Sweet Home." Home was a burnt-out hole in the ground where my old life was buried, and here we were, me and my widow, staring at the future with confused eyes.

It had been four months and seven days since I died.

Maggie reached out and turned the radio down. She flicked her eyes toward me, a quick blind glance that didn't really see me. Smudged shadows under her blue eyes, scars of late nights and long days.

"Did you find out anything?" she asked. I looked away from her, out toward the streetlights and neon signs that said things like *welcome* and *open all nite*.

"Nothing much." Just that vampires could die twice, messily. Just that my friend had turned into a hunting animal.

And that he was watching me.

The car, as always, smelled like overripe sweat and mold. I rolled the window down and let the cold February air rush in over my face. Maggie cursed softly and flicked the heater on HIGH. The smell of hot metal was almost unbearable. I clicked the control down to LO.

She should have complained about my inconsiderate attitude. That might have been healthy. But she didn't. She just kept driving.

"I saw Adam," I said. The car jerked as she took her foot off the gas, then jammed it back on.

"Where?"

"Back there." I gave her the opportunity to ask some questions. She didn't. "I think William's controlling him somehow."

"Great. Peachy. Puts you in a really great position, doesn't it?" she asked, and I didn't miss the "you" part. *Well, Tonto, we're surrounded by all these Indians.* "Do you think he's after you?"

"No," I said, and I sounded more certain than I actually was. Not sure enough to fool the cop sitting beside me, though. She just looked at me. "I don't know. Maybe. Maybe it was just a coincidence."

"A coincidence. Yeah, he was just walking by a second floor window, looked in, saw this guy handcuffed to the bed, pulled out a stake he had tucked in his back pocket and stabbed him. Why don't we just call it fucking accidental death, Mike? Maybe your guy got depressed and cut his own throat. Why not?"

"Calm down."

"I am completely fucking calm!" she screamed. I looked at her, sidelong; her fingers were so white on the steering wheel I thought her knuckles would pop through the skin. The hiss of the tires sounded very loud. "There's something wrong with you, Michael. Really wrong."

I turned and looked at her, straight on. She had tears glittering in her eyes, glassy panic tears.

"You used to be a doctor," she continued. The words were pushing up from the pit of her stomach, low and bitter. "You *never* would have hurt anyone, you *never* would have done what you've done these last few months. Maybe you need somebody to help you. Help you remember how you used to be."

I drew in a lung full of cold air I didn't actually need; it tingled like a mouthful of Alka-Seltzer. I let it gently back out again.

"Do I scare you?" I asked.

"Maybe," she murmured. She sounded ashamed. "Maybe you *need* to find Adam. Maybe he could show you what's happening to you. I don't think you'll believe it from me."

And the truth was, I didn't. Maggie was cold, distant, angry at me and our shattered life. I still loved her. I wanted to stay with her.

But damned if I knew how I was going to do that.

She turned the radio back up to cell damage levels. The conversation was over.

Aerosmith went away. Melissa Etheridge began singing about chrome plated hearts.

* * *

I had an apartment, nothing fancy, in a lower-middle-class complex. There were no neighbors, just a loose association of strangers who didn't look each other in the eye when they passed on the sidewalk. People who communicated by banging on walls and ceilings when TVs or fights got too loud. People who turned over at the end of every six-month lease.

It was perfect for somebody who didn't want to be noticed or remembered.

"Home sweet home," I sighed, and turned on the lamp beside the door. It didn't do a lot to make the place look homey. The couch had been a loser even when ugly furniture was in; the velvet blackout curtains (my own) clashed with the puke-green shag carpet. At least I had a decent TV set, with all the cable trimmings, so that I wasn't forced to watch Thighmaster reruns in the wee hours of the morning.

Maggie closed the door and locked it, sat down on the couch. I went to the kitchen and poured her a tumbler of scotch, added two ice cubes, and came back to offer it to her. She stared right through me for a second, then took the glass and sipped.

"Christ, I can't believe you live here," she muttered. I looked around in mild surprise—it wasn't going to be in *Architectural Digest,* but it wasn't *that* bad—and glanced back to see her rubbing her eyes with trembling fingers. "I can't believe this is real. Does that sound stupid? I mean, there we were—"

"And here we are." I sat down, too, an arm's-length away. "Did you like it better when you thought I was dead?"

She jerked so hard the scotch slopped over, making little wet circles on her blue jeans.

"No!" she snapped, and for just a minute she looked straight at me and really *saw* me. Her eyes widened. "No. Of course not. Please don't believe that, Mike."

"I'm trying not to." I looked down at my empty hands, rubbed them together. They felt like real human hands. But without touching hers, I couldn't tell how cold they were. They were pale, and would get paler the older I got. And my eyes . . . I knew that my eyes were different now, even though they seemed the same to me. Maggie didn't enjoy looking at them anymore. I was halfway glad I couldn't see myself in the mirror well enough to tell what was wrong.

I was hungry, and I had a plastic baggie half-full of blood in the refrigerator, but I knew it was not a good time to get it. She couldn't help but ask where it had come from.

"You want to stay?" I asked. Her pulse beat like the bass of a stereo three apartments away. "We could, you know, watch a movie. Or something."

She stared into her scotch, waiting for it to tell her what to say.

"Or talk. We should talk, Maggie."

"Why?"

She knew she'd hurt me, but she didn't look up to gloat. She tilted her glass to one side, then to the other, watched the amber liquid slosh. She took a hard slamming gulp of it.

"There isn't a lot to talk about anymore, is there?" she asked. She didn't really want an answer. The last of the scotch disappeared. Blue eyes flashed at me, just a peripheral look. "I'm sorry, Mike, but it's the truth. I can't pretend to be— I—"

"I love you," I whispered. Helplessness bled out into it from the clot in my chest. "Swear to God, I've never stopped loving you. Not for a minute."

She didn't say anything. She turned the tumbler around and around in her fingers, and the dim 60–watt light glittered

on her wedding ring. *Til death,* the inscription said. Too bad
we hadn't thought past that.

"Please keep trying," I said. She nodded. A wisp of blond
hair came free from behind her ear and brushed against her
cheek, and I wanted to reach out and smooth it back, yet
knew better than to try. She set the tumbler on the stained
coffee table in front of her.

"Thanks for the drink," she said, and stood up. She walked
to the door. I got up too.

Please look back, I thought. It hurt so bad, and I wanted
her so much. *Look back, Maggie. Look back. Goddamn you,
look back!*

I wanted it so much that suddenly I *knew,* in one bright
second, that I could make it happen. I could make her turn
around and look at me, and love me, and stay with me forever.

"Maggie," I said. She stopped with her hand on the doorknob and I saw her knuckles turn white. "Turn around."

Her head turned, slowly. Her muscles were trembling all
over, uncoordinated panic jerks. Her eyes were wide and vacant. Waiting.

I had made her turn. Oh, God, I had *made* her.

I let go of her—whatever part of her it was I held—and
stumbled backward as her eyes filled up with rage and fear
and loathing. She yanked the door open and ran away, out
into the night, without bothering to close it behind her.

I sat down where I was, in the middle of the floor. Bone-
less. Stunned.

What would I have done? What *could* I have done to her?

God, I was so hungry.

"You," Rajala said, "are late, Joseph."

I zipped up my red-and-green JiffeeMart jacket, adjusted

the fit of my JiffeeMart cap, and tried an apologetic grin. We were jammed in together in what was politely referred to as the office—actually, it was a storage room, stacked with Styrofoam cups and plastic bags, barely big enough for the two of us to move. Not enough air in here for two, so it was lucky I didn't breathe.

"Actually, I'm ten minutes early," I said. Rajala was too serene to frown. She tallied her cash drawer with quick, efficient moves while studying me from under her long eyelashes. She hardly ever looked at me directly; I wondered if she thought my too-pale skin was unusual. Next to the rich bronze of hers, it looked startling.

Whatever she thought, she just smiled. "My father always said, 'To be early is to be on time, to be on time is to be late.' "

"Yeah, well, your dad never worked here," I shrugged, and she gave me a little slow smile. She counted ones, a blur of fingers and green bills. "Any trouble?"

"Not so far," she said without even slowing her count. "You're lucky, the lottery machine is working tonight. Oh, and don't forget to pull your time card out and put it in the envelope when you go. Hassan says if we do not do it we will not be paid."

I pulled my time card out of the slot. Employee #93, Joseph A. Vico. I slid it into the machine and got a satisfying *clunk*. Rajala offered me the tallied cash drawer, and I recounted it and signed off on her sheet.

"Joseph?"

I looked up from breaking open a roll of quarters. Rajala stared at me for a second with her big chocolate-rich eyes, and her golden-tan skin darkened a little. Blushing. She busied herself with clocking out.

I waited. Eventually, she looked at me again.

Rajala was one of the most beautiful women I had ever seen. A tiny doll with silky black hair and sharp cheekbones, skin that should have been on magazine covers. I had noticed that a lot, lately. More than I should have. She unzipped her red-and-green jacket and hung it up, then bundled up in a thick gray coat. It was sleeting outside, and the radio had predicted an ice storm for the weekend. She added a thick red scarf over her head.

"Joseph, do you go to the movies?" she asked. I blinked. She worried the knot she'd tied in the scarf and tried not to look at me.

"Yeah, sometimes." Not recently, though. It hadn't seemed important, in the last few months. Not to mention extravagant, on my present salary.

"I—you are not married—and . . ." She took a deep breath and stared hard at the concrete floor. "Would you go with me to the movies, Joseph? Sometime?"

"Uh—sure," I said. The sane part of me caught up with my tongue, too late. *Idiot*. What about Maggie?

Rajala's eyes went wide and bright, and I was glad I had been stupid. Nobody had been happy to be around me for a long time.

"I would be honored," she said, and blushed again. She bobbed her head. "Perhaps we can discuss it tomorrow."

"Okay. See you then."

She fled. I lost count of my quarters and rubbed at my forehead. What *had* I been thinking?

The worst thing was that Maggie probably wouldn't even care.

I carried the tray out to the register, and loaded it in. Just in time. The electronic door sensor ding-donged the arrival of another customer.

On my shift, I got the weird ones.

The guy was squatty, measuring only about to five-five on the height scale by the door. He had the vacant look of somebody who'd watched a lot of traffic go by, but he was still functional and reasonably clean. He shuffled over to the junk food and picked out Twinkies, on sale three for a dollar.

I was almost afraid to touch the bill he slid across to me, but it was still green and spendable. I shoved it into the cash drawer and vowed to wash my hands after he was gone.

And then, with two of his three Twinkie packages clutched close to his chest, he did the strangest thing.

He held one out to me.

"Uh . . . thanks, man. But I don't need it," I finally said. His skin was brick red from months on the street, his eyes almost white by contrast. Could eyes fade in the sun, like photographs? His fingertips were dirty yellow calluses, cracked open like desert dirt. The skin underneath was a fresh baby pink.

He slowly retracted the Twinkie. I reached in my pocket and found three quarters, rang up a sale and dropped the change in the cash drawer.

"Get a Coke to go with those, man. On me," I said. He looked at me a long time before he shuffled over to the cold drinks and took out a red-and-white can.

He left without a glance back.

Just another night at the JiffeeMart.

I sold a six-pack of beer to a kid who looked thirteen but was, according to his authentic-looking drivers license, twenty-one. I refused to sell any to a fifteen-year-old whose license looked like he'd put it together in shop class. I called an ambulance for a man who said he was having chest pains. I sold about six hundred dollars worth of gas to weary travelers, some of whom were actually nice to me. I gave directions to six different strangers, one of whom told me I was an idiot.

Around four o'clock, things reached what we in the convenience store trade call the Dead Zone. Nobody came. I amused myself by figuring out the difference per hour between what I made now and what I used to make as a surgeon. It quickly got depressing, rather than amusing.

Poor Rajala. What the hell was I going to do now? Maybe I could take her to a vampire movie and, at an opportune moment, mention that I knew a lot about the living dead. Yeah. That was suave.

Maybe it was time for Joseph A. Vico to vanish and find another job.

Ding-dong.

I put my magazine aside and stood up. Good employees always stood up when a customer was present.

What a customer.

She matched the little line on the door that said 5'11". Here it was the black hole of night, and she was wearing a hunter-green business suit with a silky pale blouse underneath and a discreet little pin that gleamed real gold, a poster child for corporate America.

No coat. No umbrella. Sleet had made little snail-trails over her suit, but she didn't seem to care. Her shoes—high heels, high enough to qualify as fuck-me shoes had they not been worn with the suit—were an unwise choice for ice.

The briefcase in her left hand made her look very much like a lawyer, except this was the pro bono side of town. Her sunglasses seemed a little dramatic for the hour until I saw the white cane in her right hand. She hardly seemed to need it, steering herself so expertly through the aisles toward me that I had trouble believing she was blind.

She stopped in front of the counter. I said something appropriate to the moment, like "Can I help you?"

"I suppose you might," she said, and her voice stroked me like a fall of silk. "Joseph Vico?"

Right about then I felt a tingle at the back of my neck.

"Yeah," I admitted. "Who's asking?"

She reached up with smooth white fingers to slide her sunglasses down her nose. She was blind all right. Her eyes were dead white.

She smiled. Her eyes shifted color, from white to a deep blood-red.

Eyes I knew.

Vampire eyes.

"Celestine Vaughn," she said. The sunglasses slid back into place, having made their point. "Now, is it Joseph Vico? Or Michael Bowman?"

Oh Jesus, I thought, and couldn't get past that. I felt frozen in place. Fear felt different, as a vampire. No heart hammering. No adrenaline pumping. Just an icy sensation spreading over my body.

"Come on, Michael," she said. "Much as I'd love to chat, I really don't have time just now. You *are* Michael Bowman."

"You got the wrong guy, lady. Like you said, I'm Joe Vico."

She sighed. Then she lifted the briefcase and set it on top of the counter and opened it. Her fingers took an inventory of the contents and came back to hand me something.

A picture. I glanced at it, glanced back at her, then stared. I took another look.

Celestine Vaughn, in the costume of the antebellum South, standing stiffly next to a young, awkward-looking Rebel soldier in his grays. His face was faded, but recognizable.

I knew him as Adam Radburn.

"I'm Michael Bowman," I said. She nodded, an elegant gesture of encouragement. "Who—how—"

"Let's just say I'm here to help you find Adam," she said, and retrieved the picture. She wrapped it carefully in a swatch of black cloth and stowed it in a pocket of the briefcase. "As you can see, I'm an old friend of his."

"You know where he is?" I asked stupidly. She gave me a smooth, pitying smile.

"No, I don't. I think maybe we can help each other with that. What can you tell me about his whereabouts?"

"I think William—you know William—" She nodded, smile gone. "I think William's got him, and is controlling him somehow."

Celestine clicked the briefcase shut, set it aside and cocked her head a little to the side. Listening, I thought. Listening to things maybe even I couldn't hear. Her face was smooth and unlined. Youth caught in the amber of vampirism.

"Then we don't have a lot of time left," she said. "I'll need to see you tomorrow evening. Here. My card."

She handed it to me, and our fingers brushed. Hers were as cold as mine, soothing, not like the touch of hot human flesh. I glanced down at what she'd given me.

CELESTINE VAUGHN, it read in thick raised type. *9212 LAUREL ROAD.* There were numbers for a telephone number, and a fax. In modest letters in the lower right corner, ATTORNEY AT LAW.

"I guess you get a lot of jokes about bloodsucking lawyers," I said. She laughed. It sounded honest, healthy and unselfconscious. She must laugh a lot, to be that good at it.

"Not from my clients. Tomorrow evening, Michael. Seven o'clock?"

"Fine," I heard myself say, and she smiled at me again. This time, because I was looking for it, I saw a faint glint of fangs.

She walked out the way she'd come, moving as quickly and accurately as a sighted person. I watched her go. She got into a waiting Mercedes with smoked glass windows.

Just another night at the JiffeeMart.

Interlude:

Maggie

Sleep wasn't coming. Maggie watched the shadows move restlessly on the ceiling and thought about the precious few pills she had in the drawer. Sandman in a bottle. And no dreams.

Six left. No refills, not without seeing the doctor again, and she didn't want to do that. He'd take one look at her and send her to a shrink to work out her unresolved conflicts.

Maggie turned over and buried her face in her pillow. She felt heavy and bloated, too uncomfortable to sleep. She took a deep breath and the clean sheets smelled like Mike, and that hurt like a body punch. Imagination. He'd never even slept on these sheets. She'd bought them new and washed them twice before using them, and still—

Need to buy new sheets, she thought, knowing it wouldn't help.

Six little pills. When had she taken one last?

Oh, yeah. Two nights ago.

Another turn, and she was on her back again, staring. From next door she heard someone talking, a dim mist of words she couldn't understand. People carried on their lives all around her.

What is this, Maggie, the self-pity hour?

She had almost finished listing all the reasons she had to feel sorry for herself when the sheets started to feel softer, the bed warmer. Sleepytime, after all. Just took a while, some nights . . .

The phone shrieked. She jerked herself upright hard enough to feel twinges in her stomach and had the hard plastic to her ear before the echo of the ring died.

She started to say something, then stopped. It might be Mike. She couldn't stand to talk to him just now, couldn't stand to—

"Bowman? That you?" Not Mike. Maggie's muscles unlocked, and she leaned back against the headboard. It bumped the wall gently, not even enough to incite the imaginations of her neighbors.

"Yeah, Andy. What's up?" She closed her eyes and saw her partner's seamed face, brilliantly real. He was smiling now, she thought. He had that sound in his voice.

"Just thought you ought to know, Frank's got a boy. Named him Andrew Patrick. How about that?" Definitely smiling. Grinning.

"Jesus, how could they do that to the kid? Just kidding. That's terrific. Congratulations." She ought to sound happier, she thought.

A baby. What did people ask about babies? "How's Melanie? What did he weigh?"

"She's fine. Um—" The sound of pages flipping. "Seven pounds, seven ounces. Lucky seven."

"Andy?"

"Yeah?"

"You didn't write the kid down in your notebook, did you?

In between corpses?" Maggie asked. She drew her knees up and rested her chin on them. Andy McDonnell cleared his throat.

"Of course not. And if you tell Frank I did—"

"Would I do that?" she asked innocently, and was surprised to realize she was smiling, really smiling. "Hey."

"What?"

"Are you off duty?" There were phantom voices on the phone, whispering indistinctly to each other. She listened to them while he hesitated.

"Yeah. I'm just catching up on some files. Why?"

Good question, she thought. Why?

"I need a drink," she said, and that was a half-truth, at best. "Want to meet at M.L.'s?"

"Sure. Be there in—twenty. Okay?"

"Twenty. I'll be there," she promised, and hung up. Her heart was hammering and she hugged her knees closer to shut it up. Her hands felt weak and cold; she rubbed them on the flannel of her nightgown and frowned at them.

She was breathing in acrid nail polish remover and scrubbing at chipped Peach Blush lacquer when she realized what she was doing. Worrying about her fucking fingernails. When was the last time she'd cared about something like that?

On a date.

She stared at herself in the mirror, the dark circles under her eyes, the limp hair, and looked for the truth. *On a date.*

She reached for her makeup.

M.L.'s was a cop's bar, but a quiet one. Maggie nodded to the two or three guys she knew, exchanged an arm squeeze with Gabriella Danforth from Vice, waved vaguely to a couple of women in the corner who she thought were from Internal Affairs. McDonnell was holding court over by the pool tables. She couldn't remember seeing him relaxed like this, and when he looked up and saw her, his smile was as bright as a spotlight. She was smiling back before she could stop herself.

McDonnell stood up to welcome her with a hug. Warm. The smell of aftershave and male sweat, something she'd missed so much it scared her. She was afraid to let him go, afraid he wouldn't let her go, but he did. She sat down and he signaled the bartender for a beer she didn't really need but would drink anyway.

"You look great," McDonnell said warmly, and slapped her on the shoulder. "Hey, smile, partner. It's a party."

She smiled. She saw the reflection of it in his face. He stared at her for longer than he should have before he looked away and said something to the guys standing around. They drifted off, not even glancing back. Maggie wondered how he'd done that.

Her beer appeared in front of her, big and frosty. She took a sip and let the thick flavor settle on the back of her tongue. McDonnell wasn't looking at her anymore; he was scanning the bar, an old habit, looking for anyone near enough to overhear. Somebody across the room dropped quarters in the jukebox and a country song started; somebody else, half-drunk and belligerent, yelled to get rid of the music.

"You didn't need a drink," he said when his eyes settled back on her.

"Yeah? How do you know?"

"Don't kid a kidder, Maggie. Something's been eating at you ever since we were assigned together. You want somebody else?"

"No," she said instantly, and closed her eyes. "No, Andy,

that's not it. We get along great, don't we? I mean, we really click as a team. Maybe I'm not as good as Frank was—"

"Frank," McDonnell sighed, and waved it aside. "Listen, kid, Frank never should have been with me. We never could read each other—not like you and me. He's better off with somebody else, and so am I. Nothing wrong with that."

Funny, how partners were like spouses. Good marriages, bad marriages, ugly divorces, parting as friends. Maggie thought about the ugly split with her old partner Nick, and felt sick to her stomach. She took a hasty sip of beer to cover it.

"Sure. I mean—Frank, he's great, I'm glad we're all friends. But—yeah, okay, maybe you should hear this. Maybe I—I can—" She took a deep breath. "I'm pregnant."

Released, she felt as if she were rolled over by a steamroller. She struggled against the tears, and lost. The sobs hurt deep down inside, right around the fetus—no, the baby. She folded her arms over her belly and tried to cry quietly.

Andy McDonnell watched her, unmoving. A lot of men would have tried to reach over and do something stupid, like pat her on the hand. He just sat. She wiped at her eyes and got her breath back. A quick glance around told her some of the others were looking at her, but they looked away. Everybody understood privacy here. The right to cry.

"You're going to hate me for the question, but is it Michael's?" he asked. She blinked and nodded. "Jesus, kid."

She almost said something stupid, like *he doesn't know,* but stopped herself in time. She couldn't think straight anymore. *Michael's dead,* she reminded herself. *Michael's been dead for four months.*

"You going to have it?"

The question took her by surprise and she didn't know why. It was so obvious, she'd asked it so many times. She took a gulp of beer. *Shouldn't be drinking,* she thought, and pushed the glass away.

"I don't know," she finally answered, and it came out weak and timid and totally unlike her. She scrubbed at her face and remembered too late that she'd put makeup on. She looked around for a napkin to wipe mascara from under her eyes.

"You want free advice?" he asked, and picked a pretzel out of the bowl that sat between them on the table. He didn't eat it, just began picking flecks of salt from it.

"Better than paying for it."

"You drinking that beer?"

"No, I shouldn't—" She stopped, caught, as he gave her an ironic one-sided smile. "Okay. So maybe I've kind of made up my mind, but how the hell am I going to manage it? What kind of mother would I be, never there, running around all day and night? Shit, I've taken kids *away* from better single mothers than I'd be."

"But?" he prodded. She nodded and stared down at the table. It was late February but they hadn't changed the tablecloths from hearts and flowers, Valentine's Day cupids. She'd spent Valentine's day all alone.

"It's all I've got left of him," she whispered. The tears came back, quiet and painful. "I can't just—dump it. It would be like losing him all over again, and I don't think I can survive that."

"Bullshit," McDonnell said, and she looked up to meet his eyes. "You're strong, Maggie. You've always been strong. You'll survive, whatever you do."

"Alone?"

She hadn't meant it to be an invitation, but she knew it sounded that way. His eyes flickered in recognition. He broke off a piece of pretzel and let it drop to the tablecloth, stirred it with a fingertip.

"You're not alone," he said quietly. "Jesus, Maggie, you're part of the biggest goddamn family in the city. You think we won't stick by you? You think *I* won't? You're *never* alone."

She thought of Mike, his eyes turning red, his hunger.

"No," she said. "I'll never be alone."

Four

The Refuge

I hoped the trip would be worth it; a twenty-minute cab ride on my salary was an extravagance I couldn't afford. The ride wasn't a treat, either; last night's vomit still lingered colorfully in the upholstery, and my chauffeur had eaten enough garlic to kill off more vampires than just little old me. It made me wheeze if I breathed, so I tried not to do a lot of that until I paid him off and escaped into the freezing evening air.

At least it had stopped sleeting, and the day I hadn't seen had roasted away most of the snow. A thin rime still clung under the trees and around the bushes, but the night was clear. The stars glittered like chips of ice above me. Even with the distracting glare of streetlights, I could see more stars now than I ever had in my human life. Galaxies, like a white frost across the sky. The light tingled on my skin like the touch of ghosts.

Laurel Road was in a nice, exclusive sort of neighborhood. There weren't any houses visible from the street, just wrought-iron gates and the occasional wandering security man. The gate with 9212 on it was atypically plain, just straight black bars that ran on an electronic track. I walked up to the intercom in the stone fence and pressed the button. The metal speaker looked freshly polished.

"Your name, sir?" a voice answered. I had to think, briefly, whether I was Joseph Vico tonight, or the other guy.

"Michael Bowman," I said. A brief electronic pause.

"Thank you, sir. Please follow the path to the house."

The gates hummed and slid away—only wide enough for me to walk through, I noticed. A camera squatted on top of the fence and whirred softly as it tracked me. I resisted the urge to wave to it.

Celestine Vaughn had grounds, not a yard. The expanse of grass stretched out under the trees looked like a golf course. Winter flowers bloomed in the correct colors, in the correct places. A fountain burbled off in the distance, tastefully lit with pastel spotlights. The night smelled thickly of pine needles and freshly mown grass, and of wood smoke from fireplaces going in every house in the neighborhood.

I'd forgotten how the rich lived. My stomach twisted up, and I wasn't sure if it was envy for what I'd lost, or just plain disgust. Michael Bowman, last of the red-hot communist vampires.

The house was a long, low Austin stone affair that didn't so much stand as ramble. The more I looked it over, the bigger it got. A couple of million spent here, between the stone facing and the grounds upkeep. I thought of Rajala, suddenly, working for five bucks an hour at the risk of her life.

She'd never see this kind of wealth. Never.

The front door looked homey, warm dark wood burnished to a shine. I didn't show up as so much as a blur in it. I knocked once with the polished gold loop on the door, and had the presence of mind to let go before I was pulled. The door opened and I stood there with most of my dignity intact while a middle-aged woman looked me over. Not a vampire, this one. She wore a pair of sturdy black pants and a white shirt, and if it wasn't a uniform it should have been. Her eyes were dark. No expression I could read, either on the face or in the eyes.

"Mr. Bowman?" she asked.

"Yeah, I'm supposed to see Ms. Vaughn—"

"Yes sir," she said, and stepped back to invite me inside. Did I really want to do this? Yes, I did. "Ms. Vaughn is in the back. Would you follow me, please?"

Her footsteps echoed in the narrow entry hall. Mine didn't. The air smelled of expensive vanilla potpourri and the faint ghosts of wood polish and dust. The front hall was probably dimly lit for human eyes, and not even vampire eyes could pick out details in the soft black shadows of the corners. But, of course, there was nothing in the corners. Just old, weary air.

The echo of the woman's footsteps changed and broadened. We passed under a low ornamented doorway and into a room kept warm by a fire burning in a long, low fireplace. Couches looked as black and lumpy as coals in the flickering light. My guide didn't pause, just walked briskly over the hardwood floor and through another low doorway, and another hall, this one even narrower. A telephone alcove painted an antique ivory-white crouched to one side; the sleek modern phone in it looked jarringly out of place.

The hallway led into another echo chamber, this one furnished with a slablike table layered with decades of polish. Someone had burdened it with a hideously wiry candelabra and a white bowl full of fruit, mostly oranges. From the walls old portraits glared, dim with time. The one nearest the door was of a woman in panniers and lace, her hair pinned into a confection and powdered like a donut. Her eyes were the striking amethyst color of Elizabeth Taylor's, but the face— the face was Celestine Vaughn's.

"Sir," my guide murmured. I nodded and followed her through six more rooms, all dimly lit, and onto a horizon of glass windows broken by sliding patio doors. The windows, I noticed, faced west. So as to get a good view of the sunset, if one awoke in time for it.

The back was better than the front. The terrace was the size of my old house. Marble steps wandered down to a swimming pool and a separate hot tub big enough for a football team and the cheerleaders, too. I think I glimpsed the end of the grounds, in the distance. It might have been a trick of the horizon.

Celestine Vaughn sat in a white lounging chair near the pool. There were six or seven others with her. I couldn't see them all yet. I concentrated on them and heard three separate heartbeats, nothing from the others. So. Humans *and* vampires. Interesting.

I went down the steps. The crowd stopped talking as I approached. Celestine turned her head toward the sound of my footsteps, and smiled. She wore a plain little black dress that set off her marble skin to advantage, and her long legs and feet were bare. She had her sunglasses on again, and her hair was tied back with a white scarf.

"Michael," she said, sounding so glad to see me I shivered. There was power in that voice, conscious or not. "Welcome. I presume you met Lilly?"

It took me a minute to realize that Lilly was the woman who'd met me at the door. She offered her hand. I shook it; her skin felt hot enough to burst into flame, though she was shivering with the cold.

"Nice place you have here," I said, and Celestine

shrugged. Her shoulders were thin and fine-boned, like her hands.

"Well. It isn't mine, exactly. Meet some of the others, Michael. People, please introduce yourselves."

After a brief awkward pause, an older black man stepped forward and shook hands with me. Cold skin. No pulse. He looked grandfatherly.

"I'm Carl Keenan, Michael."

"Mike," I said hastily. We smiled at each other like we were pleased to meet, and he gestured to a younger man sitting nearby.

"This is Jerry. Jerry's my companion."

Companion. I wondered. Jerry was human. He smiled at me, but made no attempt to get up. He looked wan and thin, huddled against the cold air in his thick coat.

"Are you joining the Society?" he asked me, and I stumbled over that, wondering. Celestine reached out, and I took her hand, as naturally as if I'd done it all my life. It was only after I realized what I'd done that I felt uncomfortable, and then it was too late.

"Don't worry about all this, Michael. We'll go through all the ins and outs of it later. Suffice to say that Carl is a very successful architect. Diane?"

A vampire in her late forties got up, and for a heart-stopping moment I thought I knew her. She was tall, beautiful, elegantly boned. Her hair, black shot with silver, reached to the small of her back.

Oh, God, she looked like Sylvia, Adam's dead lover. I couldn't help remembering how she'd looked that last terrible time, lying red and gutted. Adam had almost gone mad.

I remembered his smile, Dicky's blood smeared over it. Maybe *almost* wasn't quite right.

"Pleased to meet you, Michael," she said, and our eyes

met for one brief second. Dark eyes, not like Sylvia's after all. In spite of everything I felt my stomach lurch a little in disappointment. "My companion, Keith."

Keith was just a kid, really, twenty at the most. He looked better than Jerry. He had the same simple smile, though, and the same eager look in his eyes.

The introduction circle went around to another vampire, Paul Sheffield. He reminded me of a banker from the 1920s, right down to the wire-framed glasses and round little face. His companion was Ciaran, a young waif-like woman with close-cropped red hair. She was the only human, besides Lilly, who offered me her hand. Hers felt perceptibly cooler.

"Have a seat," Celestine invited. I took the one that Lilly indicated. "Isn't it beautiful out here? The nights are so peaceful. That's why we call it the Refuge."

"You all live here?" I guessed. Two or three of the others smiled.

"No. The Refuge is owned—well, I don't want to get technical so early, but we belong to the Society, and the Society owns it. We use it for—getaways. Or meetings. Or other things." Celestine sat up and leaned toward me, all earnestness. "We're here to help you find Adam, right now."

"All of you?"

"Well—Diane and Paul and Carl and I, yes. The others wouldn't be of much help, I'm afraid, with the kind of problem we face here. I told you, I'm an old friend of Adam's. Paul has known him for many years, as well. And Carl and Diane—"

"We don't know him," Diane interrupted, "but we know about William. We'll gladly help get rid of him, once and for all."

I had no problem with that, but I'd just gotten used to the idea of Celestine, and here I was facing three more vampires and four humans, all staring at me with the kind of look I associated with hunger. I shifted uncomfortably. Celestine noticed. She cocked her head a bit to the side and smiled.

"Lilly, would you be good enough to get Michael something warm? I'm sure we have enough. And the rest of you—could we have a few moments of privacy? I think Michael has had enough of social nicety for one evening." She was laughing about it, but I noticed that Lilly immediately turned to go back into the house, and the others stood up and wandered away, some toward the house, some out into the dark. Celestine didn't appear to notice their departures. "There. Better?"

"Uh—yes. Thanks."

"All too sudden, I know. I felt the same way, back when I first came here. All so new, so different. It can be very frightening." She fell silent for a moment, and reached up to remove her glasses. Her white eyes looked empty. She fiddled with the frames as she stared off into nothing. "Shall I tell you about it?"

"Sure," I said. I didn't know what else I was supposed to say. She folded her hands together, one over the other, sunglasses underneath. A cold night wind blew through her hair and teased loose some long strands. They whispered over her cheek.

"I was a vampire before Adam, by about seventy years. We came to the Society together—when was it? Hmm. Before the Crash, but after the Great War. 1924 or 25, I suppose. It was all very strange to us, we'd lived wild for so long; it took years for us to trust anyone, and I suppose Adam never really did trust. He was too—scarred." The wind hissed over the grass around us, making white ruffles in the swimming pool. "So, in the end, we argued and he left. He came back periodically whenever he got too lonely. The last time was in the seventies, I think, when he brought Sylvia into the Society."

"Sylvia?" I blurted. She didn't seem to mind the interruption, but her eyebrows furrowed.

"They didn't stay long. Foolish, really. He shouldn't have done it, it was all over some silly little difference of opinion, but that's how he is. Unbearably stubborn."

I could believe that. Across at the other end of the pool, red-haired Ciaran stripped off her clothes and slipped naked into the hot tub. Paul Sheffield joined her, sitting close. I heard a door slide and saw Lilly coming back across the terrace with a glass in her hand.

"So, alone, he was vulnerable to whatever William wanted to do to him," Celestine finished. I watched Lilly descend the steps and approach.

"If he'd stayed with you—"

"If he'd stayed with us, Adam would have been safe. William doesn't mess around with the Society."

The William I knew wasn't scared of much, human or vampire. The Society didn't seem to be anything that would make him think twice.

Lilly stopped a step or two away and offered me the glass. I took it and, for politeness' sake, sipped at it.

I knew it was blood, of course. I could smell that much. But what shocked me was that it was warm and fresh, as if I'd drawn it directly from—

I couldn't stop drinking. I felt my eyes shifting to red and struggled to stop them. On her lounger, Celestine smiled lazily.

"Thank you, Lilly," she said. "That will be all, I think."

"My God," I finally murmured, as I turned the empty glass in my hands. The warmth flowed through me like an electric current. "Where—"

"It's my pleasure to offer you hospitality, Michael. Did you enjoy the drink?"

I stayed quiet, because I had no idea what to say to her. Enjoy it? How could I not have enjoyed it?

"Lilly doesn't mind," Celestine said, and rested her head back against the cushions. "If you want more, she can provide it."

Provide it. I looked back toward the house, my hunger fading; *Lilly hadn't been asked,* I thought. *She had been ordered.*

But she hadn't protested, either.

"No, I'm okay," I lied. "Listen, about this Society—"

"It's simple enough. It's an association of vampires and humans. We support them, care for them, educate them. In turn, they give us their blood. Nothing sinister about it. Most human members raise their children within the Society as well. Lilly is—oh—third generation, and so is Jerry. Ciaran is rather new to all of it, but she's adapting well." Her head tilted slightly toward me. "You can bring anyone you like with you into the Society. Friends. Relatives. We encourage that."

"What if I don't want to be in the Society?" I asked. Celestine stared off into the distance a moment more, then unfolded her sunglasses and slid them back on.

"Do you kill, Michael?" she asked. I looked down at the glass in my hands. "Have you killed for blood?"

"Sometimes."

"How often? One a month? Every two months? Maybe, if you're careful, once every six months. You're going to live a long, long time. Multiply it out. If you live another, say, hundred years, that's two hundred people. Two hundred lives you've ended. The Society shows you a new way. A good way. No killing."

If it was so good, I wondered why Adam hadn't stayed with it? Stubbornness, as she'd said? Or something else? Celestine turned her head straight toward me, sunglasses reflecting the starlight, the blue pool.

"You're either in the Society, Michael, or you're living wild," she said. Her voice was very even, very cool. "We don't approve of living wild."

"Is this disapproval passive or active?" I asked. She smiled.

"Passive," she said. "Mostly. In William's case, we must take it further. You understand that, I think. You've seen him."

Over at the hot tub, steam rose and obscured Ciaran and Paul. I found myself watching, waiting for a glimpse of them. My mouth felt dry.

Celestine's fingers touched mine and lingered, stroking my arm through my shirt.

"Who's in the hot tub?" she asked. I had to swallow to answer. I could still taste blood, faintly.

"Paul and Ciaran."

"Ah." Her fingers moved to the bend of my elbow. "Would you like to join them? Paul won't mind."

Oh God, I thought. I had to shut my eyes and grab for control. Sex and blood. I'd tried to separate the two, but together they were—

"Would you like me to go, too?" Celestine's voice whispered close to my ear.

—overpowering.

I opened my eyes. The mists whirled away in a gust of wind and showed me Paul, nuzzling Ciaran's neck. His tongue was lapping at a place that ran red. Her head was thrown back, and from time to time her body shuddered.

"I'm sorry," I heard myself say. My voice sounded like somebody else's. "I've got to go to work."

Just for a second, she looked contemptuous, and then it was smoothed away by a smile. She sat up, still holding my hand; her fingers slid up to lock around my wrist.

"Come back tomorrow," she said. I stood up, and she continued to hold me. I had the impression, right or wrong, that it wouldn't be as easy as it looked to get free. "Promise."

"I promise," I said.

"Bring Maggie."

I stared at her, stunned. Her grip tightened on my wrist, though her smile remained content and gentle.

"I know all about you, Michael. You used to be a bright young surgeon. Your wife Maggie is a homicide detective. Your house was burned shortly after you took up The Life." She squeezed a little. "Bring Maggie into the Society. We can protect her better than you ever could."

It was no use telling her that Maggie didn't want protecting, and didn't want much to do with me at all. I murmured something that sounded affirmative and Celestine hesitated, then let me go. I walked over to the stairs and up to the terrace.

I was still fighting my hunger when I met Lilly inside. She gazed at me with dark, cool eyes.

"Thanks for the drink," I said. She shrugged and led me to the door.

"Will you be coming back, sir?"

I looked around at the rich beautiful rooms, at Lilly's placid face.

"I don't know," I said. "I just don't know."

Interlude:

Maggie

Morning. Her head hurt. There were still shadows crawling around on the ceiling, or maybe it was just a trick of her aching eyes. She rubbed her face and sat up. The room spun one more quarter turn and stopped, as if she'd caught it doing something naughty.

The doorbell rang. She fought her way out of bed and to the closet for a white robe. She belted it tight, then picked up her gun on the way to the door. There was a round in the chamber. She clicked the safety off with a gentle glide of her thumb and looked through the peephole. Sunlight burned like a flashbulb popping; she blinked to resolve the hazy image of the man standing outside.

McDonnell.

She unlocked the door and shuffled aside to let him in. He took in the robe and grinned when he saw the gun.

"Expecting company?" he asked, and parked himself on the couch. "It's nine a.m."

"Not according to my clock." She sighed, and dropped into a chair. Her hair was a fuzzy mess. She brushed it back from her face and gave up worrying about what she looked like. "It says seven."

"It's wrong."

"Yeah?" She found her watch lying on the coffee table and squinted at it. "Seven. Look."

McDonnell took it and studied it seriously, compared it with his own watch. She wasn't fooled for a minute.

"Frank said you'd do this."

"What'd he say?"

"You show up at all hours of the morning, bright-eyed and bushy-tailed, and pretend it's later than it is. Well, I'm not falling for it. I'm going back to bed. Let yourself out." She stood up and made a shooing motion toward the door. "If I hear another knock, I'll shoot."

McDonnell raised his eyebrows and kept grinning. He had on a freshly pressed pair of gray pants, and a black zip-up jacket that looked like leather. He didn't look much like a cop, today.

Except for the eyes.

"Maggie," he said. She waited. "I had a thought about the Two-Pack case. Want to hear it?"

"No."

"I think his friend popped him and made it look like a drive-by."

"His friend was shot, Andy."

"Flesh wound. Could have been self-inflicted."

Maggie sat down in her chair again, thinking. She clicked the safety on the automatic, on-off, on-off, finally put the gun down on the coffee table.

"It's workable. He gave us all the details on the car and the gang members—"

"And nobody else saw anything. Only corroboration we got was four shots fired. Three holes in Two-Pack, one real minor one in his buddy." McDonnell picked up her week-old TV Guide and leafed through it. "I say we take a closer look at him."

"I say I go back to bed and *you* go."

"You wouldn't let me go out there naked. Come on, Maggie. Get dressed. Time to fight crime."

Maggie glared at him and tried to look cynical. She *was* cynical, but not around McDonnell.

"You're a lunatic."

"It's a gift. Got any eggs? I'll make us omelets."

She shrugged and awarded him the kitchen with a wave of her hand. Seven o'clock. She'd had—what? Four hours sleep? She must be getting old, to feel this beaten over it.

"There's ham in the meat drawer," she said. "Don't touch the coffee maker. I'll make the coffee."

She forced herself to move faster down the hall, to walk with the long confident stride of a woman in charge of her life. No more shuffling.

As she bent over to pull on her underwear, she felt a twinge that wasn't quite pain. She straightened up with a gasp, but nothing happened. Muscle strain, she thought. Nothing to worry about.

She put on makeup, for the second time in twenty-four hours. Her second-best tan suit, with low-heeled shoes and smoke-gray hose. The skirt was getting snug; she'd have to buy some drop-waisted stuff for the next few months. She took one last look at the woman in the mirror, added one dab of perfume behind her ear. At this rate, the bottle would last longer than she did.

McDonnell had made omelets, all right. Big ones. She ate about half of hers before her stomach started lecturing, and drank only a half cup of strong coffee. She had an incredible, embarrassing craving for blueberry pop-tarts with ice cream on top.

"You know where to find the kid—what's his name, Gerald?" she asked. McDonnell nodded.

"School. If he's not blowing somebody else's brains out. You remember what we're looking for?"

"Nine millimeter, modified barrel. Andy?"

"Yeah?"

"Good breakfast. And thanks for the ear last night."

He gave her a slow, one-sided smile.

"Yeah, I'm a big-hearted son of a bitch," he said. "You done?"

"Done."

"Let's roll."

She dumped the plates in the dishwasher, and found the cooking utensils already neatly racked. Oh, God, he was neat, on top of everything else.

She tried to remember Mike. The only thing that remained vivid in her mind were his eyes.

Red eyes.

"Hey," she said as McDonnell started the car. "You always this intuitive?"

"No," he answered soberly. "If I were, Gerald wouldn't have walked out of the station the first time."

She reached for the radio and checked them in; she had an uncleared message from last night waiting, and she gave the dispatcher her code. The phone number he read her didn't ring any bells.

Neither did the name, Kurt Cadell.

"Who's he with?" she asked the dispatcher. A brief, crackly pause.

"Fidelity Insurance. That's all I got here. Dispatch out."

"Twelve-seventeen out," Maggie said automatically, and hung up the handset. McDonnell frowned at her.

"Something wrong?"

"Don't know," she murmured. Fidelity Insurance. Fidelity *Life* Insurance. Mike's policy.

Five

Hearts and Flowers

It came to me like a white-light religious conversion while I pushed my cart down the aisles of my neighborhood Tom Thumb. My basket contained dish soap, sponges, paper towels, shampoo, and soap. You can tell a lot about people by examining the contents of their shopping carts. If you had a cart full of virtuous goodies like fat-free cookies and fat-free dinners and, hidden deep down in the shadows, a big frosty carton of Rocky Road, you had an obvious conflict going on. And if you got to the checkout and said something like "oh, that's for my wife," you had a real problem.

My basket was the most boring one I'd ever seen.

I stopped my cart and looked at the racks. Potato chips. I used to love potato chips, layered with French onion dip. Tortilla chips, topped with gooey melting cheese and jalapeño peppers. Popcorn—the caramel kind.

I looked back in my basket.

I no longer had a life.

Standing there with the Muzak washing over me and the heartbeats of a hundred other shoppers thudding in my ears, it hurt. No wonder I found it uncomfortable to sit in my apartment. Human lives are built around rituals of eating and drinking.

I had lost all of that.

Just for the hell of it, I reached out and picked up a bag of Lay's. *Too Good To Eat Just One.* The Mylar packaging crackled in my fingers, and there must have been a tiny hole in it because I smelled oil and earthy, gritty potatoes. Or imagined I did, the way a man with an amputated arm will sometimes feel it tingle.

I dropped the chips in my basket.

The next aisle held glittering plastic racks of bottles. Orange drinks. Clear drinks. Brown drinks. Red drinks.

I stared at the red drinks a minute. Not really red, after all, just a muddy shade of pink.

I pushed past.

A kid wearing so many layers of coats and scarves he looked like the Pillsbury Doughboy careened around the corner and flattened himself on the front of my cart like a bug on a windshield. I skidded to a stop, and he pressed his round pink little face against the chrome bars and giggled.

"You look funny," he said. A genius.

"So do you," I replied. "Want to get off my cart?"

"No." He wiggled himself into a more comfortable position, hands gripping the sides, sneakered feet braced on the bars above the wheels. "I want a ride."

"Didn't your mom ever tell you not to talk to strangers?"

"You're not a stranger. We live in the same place. We're in number 717. I'm seven. How come you work at night? Can I have a potato chip?" He blinked his blue eyes up at me over the silver bars of the cart.

I stared at him for what seemed like a long time. The details finally sifted together. He lived in my building complex, apartment 717.

He'd noticed me.

I opened the bag and handed him a chip. He gobbled it up, oily flakes dusting his lips, and held out his chubby hand for another. I wiggled the bag in front of his face. A matronly lady, her cart piled with frozen dinners and cat food, pushed past me and gave the kid a scowl that should have unraveled his scarves.

"You can have another one if you get off my cart," I said. He regarded me seriously for a minute, then put his feet back on terra firma and let go.

I gave him another potato chip. He ate it with a solemn expression, never taking his eyes off me.

"How come you're so white?" he asked. I glanced down at my hand where it gripped the bright yellow potato chip bag. It was fish-belly pale.

"How come you ask so many rude questions? Hey, why don't you go find your mom?"

"She's not here," he said indifferently. "Why don't you have any food in here?"

"I'm on a diet. Where's your dad?"

"In Hawaii with his girlfriend. If you're on a diet how come you're buying potato chips? My mom says they're full of fat."

I was rescued by the arrival of another shopping cart, this one loaded to the gills with sugars, fats and a lonely bag of broccoli. The girl pushing it—she couldn't have been more than sixteen—shoved it impatiently off to the side, where it caromed off a concrete pillar with a loud scrape. She swooped over to the Pillsbury Doughboy and grabbed his oily hand.

She looked like a vampire. White makeup, dark eyeliner, hair dyed a dead shiny black. She had on a black T-shirt and leggings, and a thick silver necklace with a pentagram swinging from it. Whatever she wanted to look like, though, her annoyance was pure teenager.

"Teddy, I *told* you not to run off. How'm I supposed to keep track of you and do all the shopping? Jeez, you are such a pain." She let go of his hand and rubbed her palm on her T-shirt. *"Iccchh. What is that?"*

"Frog guts," he said happily. "This is my sister."

She glared at him and, then, for variety, glared at me.

She didn't glare for long. Her black-lipsticked lips parted in amazement. She was looking at my skin, whiter than hers in spite of her makeup. *Makeup,* I thought. Interesting idea.

"Hey—" she said, and her voice just faded into a whisper when I smiled. She was pretty under the thick pasty crust. Not quite as bored with life as she wanted to seem.

"Bye, Teddy," I said, and pushed my cart past her. He waved cheerfully at me.

Their argument disappeared into the haze of Muzak as I rounded the corner and went to inspect the makeup aisle. I picked something at random—it said Ivory Blush—and smeared a drop on my skin.

Almost made me look human. I checked the price and realized why women were always broke. *Seven ninety-five?* For a little bottle of pink-colored paint?

I dropped it in.

The last aisle on the end was stocked with cards. Birthday cards, anniversary cards, cards for get-wells and sorry-we-forgots. I picked up one that said simply, in flowing bold script, *I'm sorry.*

The verse was stupid and saccharine. I started to put it back, then picked up the envelope to go with it. I went back to the candy aisle and found a sampler that only held chocolate-covered nuts. I wheeled up to the checkout counter.

I saw some flowers I couldn't afford, but bought them

anyway. The checkout clerk, a pimply kid of about eighteen, smirked at the card, and the candy, and the flowers. Forty-seven dollars and eight-nine cents for the whole shebang. I accepted my handful of change and declined help with my groceries.

The air outside was cold and waiting. Low thick clouds. The night smelled of sour milk and ripe garbage, blown downstream from the dumpster, and over that a thick haze of sharp wood smoke. I thought about fires, about Maggie, curled up in front of one, a glass of wine in her hand, laughing at something I'd said. Long ago. So long ago.

Less than a year.

I started the long walk home.

People didn't walk in this part of town. Every house had two cars, or three if one of them was up on blocks. I had developed a new appreciation for walking, after all those years of tooling around in my luxurious Volvo. Walking took time, time to think, to remember, to feel the cool wind on my face and my muscles flexing, time to try to be Michael Bowman again.

A dog barked at me in a deep-throated frenzy that sent his spit flying over the fence to speckle my jacket. Every house I passed had an identical blue glow in the window, the technological campfire. I tried not to listen too closely to what was happening in the houses—listening to other people's arguments and lovemaking and laughter left me feeling even more alone than before. Better to pretend I couldn't hear that. That I was just another guy, walking home with his groceries.

Only I was going to have to eat soon.

From the last house on the corner drifted the unmistakable sound of crying. I slowed a little, listening. A woman. Alone.

Not here. Not now.

I kept going, turned left at the corner and started past a condemned apartment building, fenced off with chain link and razor wire and signs warning CRIMINAL PROSECUTION. Its broken windows and gaping doorways looked hungry. I caught something strange out of the corner of my eye, just a flicker that wasn't anything more than a shadow when I looked at it straight on. There were noises inside, but that was only to be expected—a breeding ground for rats and roaches, at the very least.

The sign said HOPEWOOD. Or it had, under all the graffiti. The place was home to vagrants and gangs who wanted to prove how tough they were before heading home to watch MTV. I had nothing to fear from anybody who might be lurking around, but that didn't stop the prickly feeling on the back of my neck. Was somebody watching me? Following me?

Funny, I had figured I'd stop being afraid, having become immortal. Instead, fear seemed to have crawled in my bones—so many enemies, so many years stretching ahead of me. I was already tired, and I hadn't even lived a year as a vampire. How tired could Adam be, or even William? Centuries worth. Maybe all the fear just made us more and more insane until one day it just tore us apart.

Something scraped in the bowels of the apartments, metal on concrete. I should have been able to see inside, but I couldn't; too many conflicting shadows—that *might* have been a man, moving, or not. I came even with a sagging doorway leprous with old paint. The window next to it was a toothless hole. Glass on the ground made a spray of stars.

Nothing there, I told myself. But I knew there was.

A car turned the corner behind me and slowly cruised up to the curb. A dark sedan, dark windows. The fear in my bones turned sick and cancerous. *Please,* I thought. I don't even know who I was asking it of. *Please, no more.*

One of the windows rolled down. Teddy stuck his pink Doughboy face out at me and crossed his eyes. I kept walking. The car crawled along with me, tires crunching over sticks and rocks in the gutter.

"Hey!" That was Teddy's sister, the wanna-be vampire, who leaned over and called to me. "Hey, mister!"

"What?" I asked. The car stopped with the sharp metal squeal of bad brakes.

"You want a ride? It's a mile or so, and it's awful cold—"

She was blushing under her white pancake, nervous enough to tremble a little. Teddy uncrossed his eyes and scrambled over the hill of upholstery to the back seat. His sister popped the door handle, and it swung out toward me along with a warm breath of air and the inevitable moldy stench of a car.

"Please?" she asked. Pretty little teenager, didn't know what she was asking.

I got in, balanced my bags and slammed the door.

"Thanks," I said, and looked back out the open window toward the decaying ruins of the apartments. Nothing stirred. Nothing attacked. She stepped on the gas and we left it behind.

"No problem. Hey, nice flowers! You—um—you buying them for a girlfriend?" I remembered being that subtle at the same age. I kept myself from smiling.

"Sort of."

"The blond lady?" Teddy asked from the back. I twisted around to give him a look, and he grinned. "She's pretty."

The smell of the girl's perfume was thick as fog in the car, a supermarket brand of no particular pedigree. It wrestled the mold from the heater into submission.

"Yeah, she is," I remembered to say. "Thanks for picking me up. My name's Joseph, by the way."

"Hi," she said, and smiled. The corners of her mouth trembled. "Um, my name's Whisper."

"Is not." Teddy's voice came up from somewhere around the floorboards behind me. "Her name is Jody Lynn."

"Shut *up,* you little brat!" Jody Lynn hissed, and slammed her elbow into the seat for emphasis. "My *friends* call me Whisper."

I could see why. Her voice was soft, when she wasn't yelling at Teddy, and she had a frail look under all that paint and powder. Vulnerable.

"It suits you," I said, and was rewarded with a smile that didn't tremble. "How old are you?"

"Eighteen," she said, so quickly that even without Teddy's inevitable contradiction I knew she was lying. "Okay! *Almost* eighteen."

"Almost *seventeen,*" called a voice. It sounded like he'd crawled under my seat.

"Bear, if you don't shut up, I'm going to stick you out on the side of the road and let you freeze solid. Play with something back there, okay?" She heaved a sigh too heavy for her age. "Kids."

I nodded sagely.

"Um, we live in 717. You're in Building 2, right? On the second floor?" She must have thought that crossed the line into prying, because her skin flushed and smelled warm and redly delicious, a thick undercurrent to the perfume. "Sorry. I just thought I could, you know, drop you by the door . . ."

"That'd be fine, thanks." The driveway loomed up out of the dark black asphalt and fading yellow stripes. She took a too-quick left and pumped the brakes as we lurched past rows of parked Dodges and Chevys.

Whisper convinced the sedan to grind to a halt near Building 2. I opened the door and stepped out into the cold, then leaned down to give her and Teddy a polite smile.

"Thanks again," I said, catching myself before I said "kids." "Get inside and get warm."

Whisper—no, Jody Lynn suited her better—nodded and looked at me with dark puppy eyes, and Teddy stuck out his tongue. I turned around and walked up the sidewalk toward my apartment.

The management, in their infinite wisdom, had decided to plant thick bushes next to the sidewalks. They might have started as bushes; but now they were higher than my head. Thick spiky sculptures that thrust into the right-of-way and put too much wood in my path for comfort. I was used to dodging them; it had taken on a rhythm, lean left, lean left, lean right, hop, one long step and you're free.

Only this time, as I leaned right, a hand came out of the bushes and grabbed my shoulder and pulled. Not a human hand. Not human strength.

I toppled. My shopping bags fell, impaled on branches; soap and sponges and shampoo rained out. A branch tore through my skin and as I tried to jerk free another one stabbed at me. Branches everywhere, reaching for my skin, my eyes, scratching and clawing.

"Hey," a voice whispered next to my ear, and I turned my head to look at him. "Hurts, don't it?"

William stood there, wrapped in wood. One sharp branch bored into his cheek, and blood dripped lazily from the hole and down the curve of his jaw. Another piece of wood pierced his neck, like some strange piece of jewelry. As I watched, smoke stirred sullenly in the wound, and white fire flickered.

And he *smiled*.

He had a rank smell of old blood and ancient cruelty. His

hair was white and thin and matted with dirt. His sharp face was slashed through with a smile that showed fangs like little exclamation marks. His eyes were white, like his skin, only not so pure.

He was so *old,* the years of killing thick around him.

He wore an old army trenchcoat and a thick fleece sweatshirt that said MISKATONIC U and a pair of battered work pants and tennis shoes.

And he felt no pain from the wood, or the fire.

"Ain't ya goin' to say hello?" he asked me, cocking his head to one side and frowning like a concerned parent. I didn't dare push him away. One shove in this maze of wood and he could impale me, maybe kill me.

"Hello," I managed to say. He smiled.

Nothing about him was right anymore, not the jerky way he moved, not the way his eyes widened, not the rubbery smile. His face was a cheap Halloween mask, and what was underneath was horrible.

"Where's Adam?" I heard myself ask. I wasn't really thinking of Adam at that moment, I was thinking of myself, pinned like a butterfly to a wall four months ago while William drove stakes into my hands and tried to drive one through my heart. *Why wasn't he dead?*

"Around," William answered. "I been lookin' for you, boy."

"I haven't made myself hard to find." Stupid bravado. "What took you so long?"

He stared at me, and the wind drifted through the holly bushes. It smelled of smoke and burnt leaves. It blew hair over his face like a wedding veil, and he didn't bother to push it away.

"I was waitin' for the other shoe to drop, Michael. But it 'pears to me that you were a one-legged man. Why you been diggin' around for me? Couldn't leave well enough alone, could ya?"

"I want you to let Adam go."

"Who you think you are? Moses come out of the damn wilderness? Naw, boy. I'll let him go when I'm damn good and ready. Maybe never." The wind whipped again, blew hair back from his face. His eyes never blinked. "You shoulda forgot about it."

There wasn't any forgetting, he knew that. He'd as much as told me that when he tired of Adam he'd be coming after me—and even if I didn't value Adam as a friend and something of a father, I *needed* him.

A car door slammed. Footsteps rapped on the path, hesitant, two quick ones, then one more slowly.

"Mr.—um—Joseph? Are you okay?"

If I'd had a heart, it would have stopped.

"No," I whispered, too softly for her to hear. I said it to William. "No."

His expression had gone rigid, distorted. He still stared at me but he was hearing *her.* Her pulse pounding, her breath puffing fast and warm. His nostrils flared to catch the smell of her blood and cheap perfume.

"No," I whispered again. *She was just a kid.*

"Hungry?" William asked me, just like he was scanning a menu at McDonald's. "Yummy. Well, I'll be seein' you, Michael. Soon."

The branches rustled and I grabbed for him and got a single white thread of hair that curled possessively around my fingers.

He was gone.

"No! Jody!" I shouted, and the branches whipped at me, stinging. I covered my face and pushed through. The slashes burned like acid. "Jody!"

I came out on the sidewalk. The apartments' security lights glowed whitely, turning concrete to marble. The shadows were very dark.

I had been in the car with her. People had seen me talking to her at the grocery store.

Teddy could describe me. Completely.

With one stroke, William could wipe out everything I'd built for myself.

And her life, I reminded myself. *Don't forget her life.*

A strange numbness settled over me. I reached down and mechanically began fishing my toiletries out of the grabbing branches of holly.

"Joseph?"

I looked up. Jody stood there trembling. Scared half to death.

"I saw you—" she tasted the word *disappear,* I saw it on her lips. "I saw you fall. Hey, are you okay?"

I looked at her neck. Pale vulnerable neck, veins pulsing quietly under the skin.

No wounds.

"I'm okay," I said.

William stepped out of the shadows behind her, hair blowing like a halo around his head, eyes wide and fixed. He smiled, but I wasn't sure if the smile was meant for me or her.

And then he was gone.

I fumbled the bottle of shampoo I'd picked up. Jody, ever helpful, bent over and pulled it out for me. I felt dizzy with fear and relief.

Close. So close.

He'd be back.

Interlude:

Maggie

"Gerald Trent?" The school administrator flipped through her notebook. "Do you know his ID number?"

"Excuse me?" Maggie asked. Even to her own ears she didn't sound particularly apologetic. The administrator glanced up and away, a blush blotching her cheeks. She was an older woman, severely perfect hair, wearing what Maggie figured was the power suit circa 1950. The pearls really made the outfit. She knew she was being catty, but her feet hurt and she wanted to sit down and she wasn't in a particularly good mood, anyway.

McDonnell, she found as she glanced over her shoulder, had taken up a casual leaning position in the doorway.

"Oh," the administrator said. Her mouth worked, forming little fissures in her twenty–years-out-of-date lipstick. "I see. Well, I'll have to use the *computer.*"

She weighted that with the ominous significance of a priestess going to consult a hostile oracle. Maggie shifted her weight from left to right and tried to keep smiling.

The administrator, now that she was sitting at her desk, had a name. MRS.CULLEN. The nameplate sat sandwiched between a photo of a tired-looking man squinting into the sun, and another of a tiny little dog caught amazed and red-eyed by the flash. Mrs. Cullen typed like a bird pecking at its food. Maggie shifted her weight again and looked back over her shoulder. McDonnell crossed his eyes at her.

"Oh," Mrs. Cullen said, in a voice dark with discovery. "Oh, *Gerald* Trent. Yes, ID number 76349."

Maggie wondered if she was expected to write it down so she wouldn't forget it. She could see it now: *Halt, 76349! Police!*

"Mr. Trent," Mrs. Cullen continued, disapproval ripening, "is not at school today."

"He call in sick?" McDonnell asked. Mrs. Cullen looked beyond Maggie and must have received one of McDonnell's brightest smiles, because she almost smiled in return before she caught herself and cleared her throat.

"No, no, he didn't. We tried to call his home and received no answer. We have a truant officer scheduled to go by but—"

"Don't bother, we'll go," Maggie broke in, and managed to get a smile out onto her lips. "Thanks, Mrs. Cullen. You've been very helpful."

"Oh. Well," Mrs. Cullen said. The door swung shut on her before she thought of anything else to say, and Maggie breathed a long, disgusted sigh of relief. McDonnell shoved his hands in his jacket pockets and took shorter steps than usual to let her keep up. The halls in the school were deserted except for the occasional teacher cruising for class-dodgers.

"Metal detectors," McDonnell sighed, just as the next turn of hallway revealed them. A security guard in a smartly pressed khaki uniform stood at his post with a cud-chewing look of absolute boredom. McDonnell presented his badge and beeped through. Maggie followed. "Christ. Life's pretty shitty when we have to have these in schools."

"Ought to have them at the mall," Maggie said. She pushed open the glass door and the chill hissed in around her like a second skin, raising shivers. "At Christmas."

Christmas had been especially energetic.

"Yeah, well, fifty thousand people a day, it's tough to organize security. Too many entrances. Maybe everybody'll start carrying and then it'll just be one big shoot-out at the Hallmark Corral," McDonnell said. "Maybe that'd be okay. Teach everybody some manners for a change." Three teenaged Hispanics in matching leather jackets stared glass-eyed at them from the bus stop. One of them saw Maggie watching and gave her a flash of his middle finger.

McDonnell steadied her as she slipped on a frozen patch of ice on the pavement.

Gerald Trent lived in a neighborhood that tried hard. His house was a plain baby-blue trimmed with white, complete with a postage-stamp sized yard and one leafless tree. There was a metallic flake green Camaro parked on the street, jazzed down to wire wheels and a chrome chain-link steering wheel.

Maggie, without waiting for the suggestion, radioed for backup. McDonnell tapped his fingertips on the steering wheel. Careful controlled drum rolls. Maggie watched the street. Nothing, not even a stray dog.

In six minutes, a black-and-white cruised in slowly from the far end of the street and glided to a stop on the other curb.

"Banzai," said McDonnell, and popped his door.

The green car—Gerald Trent's, Maggie assumed—had that loving-care shine to it. She leaned over to look in the driver's side.

"Nice," she said.

"Rich Corinthian leather," McDonnell grunted. "Didn't buy this with his milk money."

Maggie checked her gun, an automatic graze of her fingers over cold smooth metal. She nodded to the two uniformed officers in the black-and-white, and they opened their doors and sat there, waiting.

She and McDonnell turned up the sidewalk toward Gerald's house.

As they came up the steps, the door swung open. Gerald stepped out and stopped, feet apart, staring down at them.

Shit, she thought, and stopped on the first step, letting McDonnell jog up by himself. If it bothered him, he didn't show it.

Across the street, the two uniforms were still sitting, waiting.

McDonnell was at least six inches taller than Gerald, but Gerald was built big enough to play the Pro Bowl. Plus Maggie didn't particularly like the baggy sweats, big enough to hide just about anything short of a rocket launcher. She took a step to her right to get a better angle.

"Gerald," McDonnell said warmly, and smiled. "Good to see you. Got a minute?"

"What for?" Gerald asked. He had big hands, and they stayed close to his sides.

"Just want to clear up a few things. Normal questions, you know." McDonnell had a great voice for this type of situation; perfectly smooth, warm, no hints of nervousness. "Want to talk inside or out here?"

Gerald's face went blank. Maggie's fingers twitched.

"Don't want to talk, man. I got a funeral to go to."

"Two-Pack's getting buried tomorrow, isn't he?"

"Ain't Two-Pack. It's Dez."

"What happened to Dez?"

"He slipped in the shower. Man, you want to get off my back?"

McDonnell kept smiling.

"The way I heard it, Dez slipped in the shower and fell on his own .38. People ought to be more careful."

"Yeah," Gerald mumbled. He looked at Maggie, and she smiled. He looked away. Somewhere two or three yards away, a dog barked furiously then stopped.

"Tell you what," McDonnell said. "We'd like to pay our respects, go along to the funeral. We can talk on the way."

"No, man, I'm goin' with my boys."

Maggie didn't see anything happen in McDonnell's face but knew it had happened in hers. The door opened up behind Gerald and a kid even bigger than Gerald walked out and took up a place just behind and to Gerald's left. He crossed his arms over his chest. Another one came out to stand in McDonnell's space, too close for even normal citizens to stand. McDonnell didn't back up. He turned his head and stared, just stared, until the kid took a small step away.

"Your boys want to come with us too?" he asked. Maggie saw a flicker in Gerald's eyes, saw his fingers move, patting. A nine millimeter, maybe.

"No, man. Ain't none of us goin' 'less you want to read us our rights."

"Motherfucker," one of the other kids added.

McDonnell stared at him, smile gone. He took a pair of handcuffs from his belt and jerked his head at Gerald.

"Turn around. Now. Unless you want three more fucking funerals, don't fuck with me, you got that? You're pissing me off. Maggie."

"Yes?"

"Are you prepared to bury all these assholes?"

"I'm prepared," she said.

"Then I would suggest to you gentlemen that you not piss us off anymore."

Gerald stared at her. Maggie stared back until she thought her eyeballs might freeze from the cold. Gerald blinked.

He turned around and put his wrists behind his back. His boys exchanged a long, considering look and stepped back. One of them sat down in the white lawn chair next to the door.

"Good," McDonnell murmured as he snapped the cuffs shut. "Very good choice. You may get to see Dez's funeral after all."

Gerald had a nine millimeter stuck in the waistband of his sweats. Maggie bagged and tagged it and let McDonnell wrestle Gerald down the steps and over to the car.

"Wait," Gerald said as McDonnell started to guide his head down under the doorframe. "Wait! Right front pocket, man."

McDonnell reached in and found his car keys. He looked back at Gerald.

"I ain't leavin' my car here with no protection, man," Gerald said. He nodded toward the black box on his keychain. McDonnell shrugged, pointed it at the green Camaro, and pressed the button. The alarm blooped shrilly and settled down to wait for its prey.

Three detectives were having a shouting match by the coffee machine with Belinda Brown, who kept the supplies stocked. Maggie hadn't listened to the whole thing, but it clearly had to do with nondairy creamer and the difference between EQUAL and Sweet 'N Low. As she watched, Belinda threw a package of something blue in the air and walked away into the women's restroom. One of the male detectives followed her in, still arguing.

"Ballistics won't be back until tomorrow, but the powder test is positive," McDonnell said over the uproar; he tossed her the folder over their joined desks. Maggie nodded and finished chewing her Twinkie. Sugary filling squirted mushily over her tongue. "He isn't talking," McDonnell added.

"He won't until we get a match on the gun," she mumbled, and wiped white foam from her lips with one finger. The shouting continued in the women's restroom, muffled by walls. One of the other female officers walked out, shaking her head, and for the second it took for the door to close behind her Maggie clearly heard Belinda Brown say something about "make it yourself."

"Probably won't then. Dez slipped in the shower. Yeah, sure. Gerald is clearing out his buddies, that's all. Those two assholes on the porch ought to be watching their backs. They've got targets pasted on." McDonnell sipped at a cup of coffee. "What else we got?"

"In the Virginia Cleary case, nothing. The plate search came up a big fat zero. I think we need to reinterview the neighbors tomorrow."

"And?"

"And we've still got six uncleared folders. I think we're going to have to put LaDonna Bedford in the box. We've got nothing at all, and it's been twelve weeks."

Maggie flipped open the folder. The edges were dirty and ragged. On the right side she'd clipped all the photos, the statements, the forensics. A lot of paper, all leading nowhere. The photos showed a seven-year-old girl, lying on her back in a thick tarry pool of blood. Her hands were folded over her chest. The killer had put a quarter on each of her eyes.

Used to be pennies, she'd remarked to McDonnell. *Inflation,* he'd answered.

She still felt sick, looking at it. Weapon was a knife, not found at the scene. No prints lifted from the body. No trace evidence from the alley where she'd been dumped. No signs of sexual molestation. No, no, no.

She closed the folder and wrote a note on the outside. It went into her out box.

McDonnell didn't say anything at all. He reached over and took the next folder, a carjacking in North Dallas. He blew on his coffee as he looked it over.

"This'll be a quick one," he murmured.

"Why?"

"Car phone. Assholes can never resist a car phone. We'll have a list of his best friends tomorrow."

Maggie made neat little piles, stacks for things to do and calls to make in the morning. She finished and stretched. The muscles in her abdomen felt shorter and tighter, even though she got flabbier every day.

Belinda Brown exploded out of the restroom. The male detective—Maggie thought his name was Lazarski—followed her, red in the face. Everybody clapped, except for Belinda and Lazarski. And Maggie.

"Let's go home," she sighed. McDonnell nodded and grabbed his jacket.

It was already dark, cold enough to quick-freeze. He drove carefully—ice had formed where puddles had been during the day—and without conversation. She leaned her head back and tried to relax, shivering while the heater blew out chilly air and the car took on a burnt-metal smell. It didn't warm up. It hardly ever did.

As she got out of the car he leaned over and grabbed her

gloved hand. She bent down to look at him, met his eyes and wished she hadn't.

"Get some rest," he said. She smiled thinly.

"I look that bad?"

"Worse. I'll pick you up at nine tomorrow, okay?"

"Nine *my* time?"

"I promise," he said. She gave him a nod and he let her go. He watched her until she got the apartment door open, and then he drove away.

She fiddled with her key in the lock and, for a minute, didn't even know there was someone behind her. She tried to spin around but her center of gravity felt off. She turned too hard to make up for it, and felt a muscle twinge painfully in her side. Funny how long it seemed to take for her fingers to touch her gun.

"Maggie." A patient, soothing voice. She sucked in a huge gulp of air and felt some of the panic fall away. It left her feeling weak and sick.

"Where are you?"

"Here." He stepped out of the shadows, closer than she would have believed possible. Her eyes burned from the cold, or with tears she refused to shed.

Still the same Michael. Tall, a little awkward, hair tangled by the wind and too long over his ears. She couldn't see his eyes, and knew that was a blessing. No matter how he looked, he didn't *feel* the same, not even from this far away. Or she didn't feel the same. She didn't know what was right, anymore.

"I wish you wouldn't come here," she blurted. She was inside the apartment, one step over the threshold, door cold under her fingers. "Go home, Michael."

"Wait," he said, and fumbled inside a sack he held. She braced herself.

The flowers had a tired, resigned look of waiting too long. She couldn't stop herself from reaching out for them, the bright yellow, warm orange and fading red. Green paper crackled in her hands. She held them carefully, awkwardly, and Michael took a step closer. Inches away now. The line of the doorway between them.

"Thank you," she forced herself to say, hating the way it sounded. *Don't ask him in.*

"But that's not all you get with the Michael Bowman apology package," he said, and took out a bright yellow envelope with her name written on it, and a box of chocolate nuts, her favorite. She didn't know what to do but take them. He waited for a minute, and the light finally angled in to show his eyes.

Her heart hurt at the expression in them.

"Thank you," she said again, and it was the most awkward thing she'd ever said to him. Oh, God, the pain in his eyes . . .

"You're welcome," he said quietly, and stood there with his empty sack. "I love you, Maggie. I'll always love you. I'm sorry about that, too."

She could hardly see him for the tears in her eyes.

"Michael—" she finally managed to say, and the tears fell, sliding down her cheeks.

He was gone. Nothing there but the darkness.

She shut the door and locked it. All strength lost, she slid down to sit on the floor with his gifts clutched close. She didn't cry much.

She wondered if he did.

Six

Strange Visitors

Her partner had held her hand. I'd seen him clearly in the glow of the dome light in the car. Remembered him vaguely from a party, years ago.

Her old partner, Nick Gianoulos, I'd been jealous of him, with good reason. But I didn't even *know* this guy. Yet I wanted to drag him out of the car and beat him senseless and drink—

And drink. Sure. Oh yeah.

All because he held my wife's hand. For a moment.

You're out of control. I told myself, but it didn't matter. The pain was eating at me like a migraine, distorting everything I saw. *You have to go to work.*

Yeah, another night of selling gas to assholes and candy bars to junkies and coffee to cops I was afraid might have met me in my breathing life at one time or another. Work didn't seem like much of a comfort, just now.

So I walked.

She was standing listlessly on the side of the street, about three blocks from Maggie's apartment. About twenty-five, and tired for her age. Dressed in clothes a size too small, watching cars cruise by.

I didn't ask her name. I just looked in her eyes and told her to follow me and led her into the darkness. I paid her ten-dollars for a blow job, and before she could unzip my pants I tilted her face up until her gaze met mine. I kept holding her that way while I took her arm and exposed the thin wrist, the blue veins. It hurt her a little when I bit down, and I felt her shiver.

Then I forgot her. The blood hissed over my tongue, down my throat, thick and sweet. Her heart pumped it from her to me, life unraveling, and I drank until I heard her heart shuddering with effort.

The wounds weren't too large. I dug in my jacket pocket and found the roll of sterile gauze I always carried; while she stared blankly at me, I bandaged her wrist. I tied it off tightly and put pressure on it for about a minute, enough to allow the bandage to hold.

I let go of her, and she blinked and stepped back. I smiled at her.

"That was great," I said. She didn't remember, of course, but she wasn't about to argue with a satisfied customer. She just smiled and wandered back to the street, a little weaker.

I stood there in the dark with my eyes closed and swallowed, tasting the feast until it was gone.

Rita. The last one had been Rita. What I remembered most about her was her dark, curly, shampoo-commercial hair. Her face hadn't matched her hair. She had a perpetual cocaine sniffle and needle marks in between her fingers.

I had wanted her to be different. I succeeded in that, all right.

I bit her in the neck. Simple. Any vampire could do it. Only I didn't know the trick, Adam hadn't shown me—

I couldn't swallow it fast enough; it gushed out of the corners of my mouth, flooded down her neck and dripped away on the pavement. I tried, in my panic, to drink faster, but she just kept bleeding. Her eyes stayed open, glazed and dreaming. I held her while her heart labored, beating faster and faster to move the small amount of blood still in her body. Faster and faster and faster, until it had fluttered and spasmed.

She'd felt no pain.

Oh God. I'd left her in an alley, all alone.

I opened my eyes and looked down at my white hands. The long clever fingers of a surgeon.

Of a killer.

I called in sick to work and went home, to my apartment filled with the glow of the television set and my own frustration. I wanted to call my friend Carl Voorhees at the hospital, say *Carl, it was all a mistake, buddy. Let's forget I'm dead.* I wanted to go out and find another woman on another street corner and gorge myself on blood until a heart fluttered and stopped.

I wanted to kill.

I wanted to die.

I sat on my couch and watched the meaningless flickers of the screen and realized, at last, that there *was* nothing for me. No Maggie. No friends. No passion. I wasn't a doctor anymore. I couldn't pretend to heal people.

All I had now was a long, meaningless stretch of days while I killed, and killed, and killed. Did I want that? Did *anyone* want that?

I found myself in the bathroom, staring into a mirror that stared back and showed nothing but the white tile wall behind me. I put my hand flat on the glass.

And willed myself to be *seen*.

Slowly, indistinctly, my ghost swam in the mirror. A shadow. A shadow with my face and my body and eyes that were red and feral.

There were tears on my face, in the reflection. I wiped at my cheek with my free hand, and my fingers came away red.

Tears of blood.

The mirror exploded with a sharp vengeful snap, and pieces tinkled musically to the floor. My ghost lingered in them. Fading. Faded.

Gone.

My back was to the cold tile wall, and I slid down to sit on the glass-littered floor. I picked up a piece of mirror and snapped it in my fingers. No blood. No cut. No wound. I couldn't hurt myself with glass.

Wood. I needed wood for that.

I went to the kitchen and smashed one of the drawers. No good. The coffee table yielded a good thick piece, sharp on one end. I sat down in my threadbare chair and looked at the stake in the light from *Baywatch*. Healthy tanned women barely dressed in bikinis ran along a sunlit shore behind the point of wood.

In the heart. It has to be in the heart, I heard a voice whisper; it sounded like Adam. I could almost feel his hand on my shoulder, steadying me. *I've thought of it too.*

I set the point on my chest, medical training coming in handy at last. But I couldn't push it forward.

My hands trembled and spasmed and refused. They wanted to live.

I got up out of my chair and faced the wall. Maybe I could just fall on it—

I had just wedged the stake in place and felt the first tickle of heat from its point on my skin when someone knocked at my door.

The stake thumped to the carpet.

After the first rush of anger, I felt embarrassed. The coffee table, shattered into firewood. What was I going to say about—

I must want to live, I thought, *if I care about what somebody thinks about the mess.*

I kicked the stake under an end table and went to the door.

I'd never seen the guy before. He stood there and stared at me for a good thirty seconds or so, eyes getting wider and wider. I looked down at myself, figuring I'd gotten blood all over my shirt, but no, I looked okay.

"Can I help you?" I said. He was red-haired, young, wearing glasses. He wore an executive-looking raincoat and black leather gloves. I caught a whiff of what smelled like expensive aftershave.

"No," he said, and his pulse tick-tocked in my ears. Too fast. "No, sorry, wrong apartment."

I didn't like it, too strange, too abrupt. I took a step forward and tried to look helpful.

"Well, I know most of my neighbors. Tell me who you're looking for, and maybe I can point you in the right direction," I said. He smiled, and it looked good, considering how quickly his heart was beating.

"Sorry. Really." He walked away quickly, and went down the stairs. I came out and leaned over the railing. The moon reflected in his glasses as he looked up at me. Then, nothing but his footsteps, fading.

"We have got a problem," I said to myself. Myself agreed.

Interlude:

Maggie

In the harsh light of morning, Maggie dabbed cover-up on the circles under her eyes and tried not to think too much. Thinking was bad. Working was good.

She'd lain awake most of the night, listening to the wind. Listening to distant voices. Listening to her own voice tumbling around inside her head like clothes in a dryer. When she'd finally slept she'd dreamed of a hand touching her face, her arm, sliding gently down her side to rest on her hip. She'd snuggled closer into his warmth and heard him whisper her name.

And then she'd opened her eyes and there was only the empty bed, and the cold sheets.

Suck it up, Maggie. You'll get through. You always get through.

She dragged the brush through her hair and winced as it hit a snarl. Hair snapped with a stretchy sound like a rubber band breaking—her hair always stretched, while Mike's was more like brittle wire. She glanced at the brush and half-expected to see some of his hair in it, but of course there wasn't.

Crazy. It was *crazy.* Why couldn't he just accept that they had to be apart?

She finished brushing her hair and did her teeth. She stuffed herself into a pair of pantyhose, and a bra. She'd have to go to a larger cup size soon. A nice businesslike shirt, something washable. A pair of good dress pants. Shoes with a very small heel.

Her gun. Her jacket.

The doorbell rang. She glanced at the clock—only 8:30. McDonnell . . . At least she was dressed. She went to the door and slid the chain off and clicked the deadbolt and opened it.

It wasn't McDonnell. It was a tall young man, red-haired, dressed in a sober suit and an equally dark tie. Shiny shoes, like a salesman. Schoolteacherish glasses.

"Mrs. Margaret Bowman?" he asked. She hadn't had anybody call her Margaret in so long it took her a second to nod. The young man nodded in return. "Gosh, Mrs. Bowman, I'm so sorry to drop by this early. I tried calling you— I'm Kurt Cadell, from Fidelity Insurance."

Oh shit, she thought, and didn't let the fear that started in her stomach make it to her face. Instead, she smiled politely.

"Yes, I got your message, I just haven't had the time—"

"Of course, of course. Well, if it's okay with you, this'll only take a minute or two. May I come in?"

He had an honest face, and she had a gun. She shrugged and stepped back to let him in. He waited until she'd shut the door and chosen a seat to find one on the couch. He sat uncomfortably, feet precisely together, knees touching.

She had a stupid impulse to ask him if he'd like coffee, but managed to kill her upbringing in time. Let him be uncomfortable. She waited.

Cadell had brought the inevitable briefcase with him. He opened it and pulled out a folder filled with yellow sheets of notes. Neat, precise writing.

"Now, Mrs. Bowman, I'll try to be as brief as I can. I have some questions regarding your husband."

She was afraid of that, and buried the fear deep down so it wouldn't be evident in her voice when she answered.

"He's dead."

The flush looked genuine; it started under his collar and worked its way up his face all the way to his hairline. He was careful not to look her in the eye.

"Yes, ma'am, I'm so sorry. Really. Um—but there are just a couple of things—minor questions. Paperwork, you know."

She hadn't wanted to claim the insurance, but things had gotten out of control; she hadn't been able to think of a reason to refuse to claim. Frankly, she hadn't been able to think at all. So now she had one hundred thousand dollars in the bank gathering interest, and she drew a thousand in cash, every month, to split with Mike—or Joseph Vico.

Shit, she'd been afraid of this happening.

"Go on," she said, because Cadell seemed to be waiting for a response. He shuffled his notes.

"Um, I want to make it clear that Fidelity Insurance only carried the small policy that Dr. Bowman got through the hospital—all the doctors had it, you know. Part of their health insurance. Well, I know that you've already answered most of these questions for your primary carrier, so I'll skip the ones I already have the answers to—ah—I see here that you waited six weeks to start the paperwork on the Fidelity claim. Any reason for that?"

Sure. She'd been hiding out with a man who had been her husband, who'd become a vampire. It didn't seem like a good idea to mention that.

"I took some time off to get out of town and try to—to get my head back together. I'd lost Michael, I'd lost my house—things were—I just couldn't face any of that until I got away for a while."

He nodded reassuringly and wrote something down. He tapped the pen against his notes and chewed his lip.

"And the irregularities about your husband's burial?"

"Pardon?"

"Well—" Cadell hesitated. "He was positively identified at the scene of the accident, I see. But you requested a closed-casket ceremony for him, that was a little unusual, wasn't it?"

"Meaning what? Meaning he wasn't mutilated or decapitated or dismembered?" She fired the words like bullets, and had the satisfaction of seeing him flush again and wave his hands in wordless apology. "Meaning there's some social responsibility to look at my husband's dead body? Mister, I see enough dead bodies in my line of work. I didn't see any reason to force myself to look at his again."

"Yes," he said, and looked abjectly apologetic. He fumbled his glasses off and polished them with a precisely folded handkerchief; his face looked even more honest without them, the All-American Boy grown up. "I'm so sorry to be bringing all this up, Mrs. Bowman. Really, I wouldn't be bothering you with it if I didn't have to."

She shrugged and looked away long enough to let him refer to his notes again. She hadn't lied. When she'd ordered the closed casket, that was what she'd *thought,* but of course that had been a suggestion, placed in her head by Adam. The *other* vampire.

Try explaining that one, Mr. All American.

"The other irregularity, of course, is your request to have the body exhumed two days after the burial. Um—I know this is difficult—but you positively identified the body again. Right?"

"Yes," she said evenly, and thought to herself, *Oh, Jesus, I've done it now.*

"So the man in the coffin was your husband?"

He'd been about forty, about the same height and weight as Michael. Similar enough to pass a casual inspection by somebody who didn't have a personal knowledge of him.

"Of course."

She didn't like the fact that he wouldn't look her in the eye. He kept staring at his notes, nodding like an idiot. In the kitchen, the coffee maker burbled and reminded her that her breakfast was ready. She excused herself and went to pour a cup.

Her hands were unsteady. She'd have to watch that.

"Sorry," she said as she sat down again and blew the steam off her coffee.

"No, ma'am, not at all. Look, I'm sorry to have to ask this, but *why* did you have the body exhumed? What made you think your husband wasn't dead?"

A too-large sip burned the roof of her mouth.

A feeling in the graveyard. Someone watching. *Michael?,* she'd asked, and known in her guts that he was there, and not under the ground, either.

"Mr. Cadwell—"

"Cadell," he corrected her, with an apologetic shrug.

"Mr. Cadell, maybe you've never lost somebody you loved. I hope you go a long time until you do, because there isn't a damn thing that makes any sense except the pain you feel. I was crazy. Crazy. I kept hearing him, seeing him, feeling him. I convinced myself that because I hadn't seen the body in the casket that he couldn't really be dead." Maggie stopped and took a long, steadying breath. "And I was wrong. He was dead and in the ground, and I'm sorry I disturbed him."

He should have looked at her, after that. It was a good speech. But he kept nodding and staring at his papers.

He didn't believe her. She felt gooseflesh crawl over her arms.

"Mrs. Bowman, I sympathize with you, I really do. And I hope you understand that none of this is personal. I'm just trying to clear up the records."

Just some routine questions. Won't take a minute. Is that blood on your shirt?

"Sure, I understand," she smiled, and set her cup on the coffee table. "Anything else?"

"Just one thing," he said, and tried to be offhand about it, like *Columbo*. He failed. "I understand you're seeing a man pretty regularly."

"Are you asking me insurance questions or asking me for a date?"

He cleared his throat. *Now,* he looked at her, just a glance. She didn't like the glitter in his eyes.

"No offense meant, Mrs. Bowman. It's just, well, I have a responsibility to look into everything before we, you know, cut the check. We do owe you almost fifty thousand dollars."

"What if I told you to keep it?" she asked. He blinked and dropped his pen on the floor. His fingers were trembling when he reached down to pick it up.

"Pardon?"

"What if I said I didn't want the money?"

Cadell fooled around with his pen, shuffled his papers, put them back in his briefcase. He clicked the pen, while she waited.

"I can't imagine why you would say that," he ventured. She sighed.

"Because I'm fucking tired of it. Of the paperwork. Of the memories. Look, it isn't *worth* fifty thousand to me to have to go through Mike's death again, okay? So why don't you just keep the money."

"We can't do that."

"Then write a check to your favorite charity. Just leave me out of it. Now, if you'll excuse me, Mr. Cadell—"

"But—"

"I have to go to work now. Goodbye."

He was still protesting when she turned the dead bolt on him.

The coffee tasted flat and harsh, or maybe it was the fear.

"Nice morning outside," McDonnell said pleasantly, and looked at her over the tops of his reading glasses. He was holding a folder, pretending to read it but actually just looking at her. She wondered what the hell there was in her expression to look at.

"Yeah," she agreed, and rubbed the back of her neck. There was nothing to see in the interrogation room except McDonnell and the camera sitting up near the ceiling. The walls and ceiling were a uniform freshly-painted mint-green that made her think of toothpaste. "Yeah, it is."

Fear. That was probably what he saw. If Kurt Cadell got enthusiastic and dug hard, he'd find Joseph Vico. And then Michael would have to run or be killed.

She, of course, would lose everything. Her career. Her freedom. Michael.

"You're not worried about something, are you?" McDonnell asked. It sounded like an offhand question, but she'd seen him ask enough offhand questions to assume the worst. She smiled at him.

"No," she said. A simple, flat denial. A lie. The best ones were simple.

He looked at her. It went on too long. McDonnell, like Kurt Cadell, was too perceptive for her own good. She sat on one side of the table, he on the other, and she was beginning to feel a felon.

"Where the hell is Gerald?" she asked before he could decide how to call her a liar. He allowed himself to be distracted.

"He gave his cell mate a hard time last night. They may be having a little trouble getting him to behave."

"Wonderful," she sighed, and leaned back in the hard wooden chair. She just wanted to get the whole thing over with, but knew it wouldn't be that simple. Hours, probably. Days. Her back hurt, a deep-down muscle ache.

What would she do about Cadell? What could she do? Tell Mike?

Jesus God, what would *he* do?

The door opened silently, with a swoosh of air that smelled faintly like burning socks. Belinda Brown was exacting her revenge at the coffeepot by buying inferior brands.

Gerald Trent filled the doorway. He had about an inch clearance, all the way around. Two much smaller cops followed him with a wary alertness that told Maggie they'd already had a demonstration of Gerald's temper. He paused a couple of steps into the room and stared at her, then at McDonnell.

"I don't want to talk to you," he mumbled, and turned around to leave. McDonnell could move like a sprinter when he had to; he beat Gerald to the door and put an arm across it, chest-high. Gerald backed up, and McDonnell swung the door shut, leaving the two other cops outside.

"Sure you do," McDonnell said, and pointed to the empty

chair at the head of the table. Gerald stared at it moodily and shrugged. "What, you'd rather be sitting in your cell?"

"Rather be out of here," Gerald said. But he walked over and sprawled on the chair and glared at the table.

Victory number one. McDonnell sat down next to Maggie and looked at Gerald over the top of his glasses. He looked fatherly, that way. Warm.

Forgiving.

"How was breakfast?" Maggie asked, in as pleasant a voice as she was capable of at the moment. Gerald stared hard at the table.

"I ain't eating that shit. Full of cholesterol and shit. Kills you."

Great. A gangsta who ate healthy. He'd probably outlive the both of them. She exchanged a glance with McDonnell.

"You like coffee?" she asked. Gerald nodded. McDonnell nodded too. "Great. Why don't I get us all some coffee. Gerald, you want some sugar or cream or anything?"

"Yeah," he said, and looked up at her. There was no particular expression on his face, but she knew he was scared and trying hard not to show it. "Yeah, that's good."

She shoved her chair back and walked out, letting the door click shut behind her. McDonnell was safe enough alone with the kid; she'd seen him lay out a wrestler once, all by himself. Besides, they'd agreed that McDonnell was more likely to get somewhere with him than she would—and he had more patience, too. She was happy to be the coffee-getter, the note-taker, and, if necessary, the bad cop.

There were three messages on her desk, two from her mother. She tried to remember what holiday or birthday or anniversary she'd missed, but couldn't think of anything. Funny how seeing Mom's name on a note made her instantly feel guilty.

The other one was from yesterday, from Kurt Cadell. She crumpled that one up and tried to make a basket with it. For a three-pointer, it was a great air-ball.

She came back into the interrogation room with three cups of steaming coffee that smelled like socks. She set a Styrofoam cup in front of Gerald and put down three sugars and three creams. He still wasn't doing much looking; he fiddled with the packets while she sat back down.

McDonnell was still in friendly-professor mode.

He discussed the nine–millimeter. The unfortunate ballistics report. The fingerprints on the bullets in the clip.

He did a lot of talking. Maggie sipped coffee and watched Gerald's face, what there was of it to see at her angle. Guilty, all right. Guilty as hell.

McDonnell had pictures out now. He laid them out in front of Gerald and talked in a low quiet voice about Two-Pack, about Dez.

Maggie went out for more coffee, and then took lunch orders as the hours kept ticking. Gerald didn't have much of anything to say. He didn't want his lawyer. He didn't want anything except to go home.

Then, over the low-fat chicken sandwich he'd ordered, he wanted to talk. Two-Pack had a girlfriend.

"Bitch was after me all the time," Gerald said, munching thoughtfully. A strand of lettuce got caught in his teeth, and he dug around for it with a finger as big as a sausage. "She said Two-Pack was slapping her up, said she wanted me to take care of it."

"Did you?"

"I ain't no fucking pet dog. Told the bitch, she didn't like it, leave. She said she didn't want to, said Two-Pack told her she was dead if she did." Gerald took another bite of his sandwich and stared at Maggie while he chewed. "So me and Two-Pack, we're standing there talking, and the bitch walks up to us and she's got this gun, and she blows his ass away and throws the gun down and runs off."

"And you pick it up and take it home with you for a souvenir," Maggie murmured. He looked away. "She killed your homeboy, how come you kept lying for her?"

Gerald just shrugged, brown eyes vague, and chewed. He took his time swallowing.

"Maybe he was hitting the bitch, I don't know. He was like that." He looked at McDonnell very seriously. "He did the kid."

"Kid?" McDonnell just lifted his eyebrows and took a sip of coffee. Maggie nursed her own and wondered how long she could hold out before all this liquid made her run screaming for the bathroom.

"You know. That kid, that girl. LaDonna."

The bathroom went down in priority, pretty quickly. She sat up straight and leaned forward.

"LaDonna Bedford?"

Gerald nodded and broke up a couple of potato chips. Maggie swallowed, hard.

"You're saying Two-Pack killed LaDonna Bedford?"

"Funkiest thing I ever seen, like he was crazy or somethin'. You know, Two-Pack, he got no family, right? He starts goin' all crazy, sayin' this kid is his sister or somethin, talkin' 'bout how he was gonna make sure they didn't get her. Shit, the bitch didn't look nothin' like him," he finished triumphantly.

"They who? Why'd he kill her?" Maggie asked, mystified. This wasn't the usual run of lies. This was out of the blue, unrelated. And very odd. She knew from the tension in McDonnell's shoulders that he felt it too.

A feeling of truth.

"Hey, man, don't ask me. I just know he did it 'cause he come cryin' to my house, blood all over his hands. He was talking shit."

"What kind of shit?" she pressed.

"Voodoo shit. He said the dead folks had her. Said they was gonna' kill her and drink her blood."

Maggie sat back. She kept watching Gerald while he ate his sandwich and potato chips.

Voodoo, she thought. *Vampires.*

Michael.

Seven

Michael Loses His Job

No matter what my personal problems were—and I had at least one, a tall red-headed one—I had to earn my daily wage. Which meant getting my ass up at sunset and going to work at the JiffeeMart, like it or not.

Not.

I found out when I arrived that Big Boss Hassan was not happy. The inventory had come up short and he had left us all a sharply worded, if mostly incomprehensible, message about being more careful. I personally thought he was lucky that all that was missing were some Ding Dongs and Diet Cokes, and the occasional skip-out at the gas pump.

The bad news was the lottery machine was down again. The worse news was that the jackpot was up to twenty million, which meant that every single person who came in would want to buy a lotto ticket, and would be accordingly pissed when I couldn't sell it. We were, Rajala said, directing them to the Seven-Eleven three blocks down.

I couldn't wait.

"Joseph?"

It took me a minute to remember my name, but I hoped

it looked like preoccupation over the lotto problem. I looked up and saw Rajala staring at me as she shrugged on her coat. No sleet tonight so far, but it was coming. Big cold gray sheets of it.

"I have Friday evening for the movies." She blushed and looked away.

Jesus, I'd forgotten all about it. I tried to smile, hoped I succeeded.

"Don't you have to work?" I asked. She blushed.

"Hassan allowed me to trade."

"Great," I lied. "Friday it is. How about picking a movie at seven so I can make it here on time?"

"I—please choose—"

"You pick something," I said, and realized I didn't even know what was playing. Rajala seemed equally lost, but she bit her lip, nodded, and escaped through the back door. I clocked in and went out to glare morosely at the lotto machine. I filled out a card and slid it into the slot. Lights blinked.

It projectile-vomited the card back at me.

"Great," I sighed, and picked up the phone. There was a lotto machine hotline, that would supposedly tell me how to fix the damn thing. It was like calling 911 during a riot.

All our technicians are busy at the moment. Please hold. The next available . . .

I held. I had nothing better to do.

The "technician"—an overpaid schmo—knew even less about lotto machines than I did. He told me to turn it off and on. I thanked him for killing half an hour of my time and hoped for no lotto customers.

Fat chance.

By three a.m., I had been insulted, yelled at, cursed at and almost assaulted. The early arrival of the Dead Zone seemed a real relief, for a while. Then the ice storm arrived, a white blur outside the windows, a hiss of pellets on the glass. The parade of cars outside slowed to a slippery crawl.

At 3:15, the telephone rang.

"JiffeeMart, this is Mi—"I coughed loudly into the receiver and hit myself in the head with my other hand. "This is Joseph."

"Having an identity crisis?" A light, cool voice. Female. It took me a minute to place it.

"Celestine?" I guessed, and was rewarded with a low laugh. "I guess I am."

"I'm afraid that part of it doesn't get any easier as time goes by. How are you, Michael? Am I interrupting anything important?"

"Well, you missed a guy buying two packages of Twinkies and a cigarette lighter, but I think I can handle the pressure." I was ambivalent about the Society, and about Celestine, too, but there was something very appealing in having a woman call me. I liked the way she said my name, my *real* name, way down deep in her throat as if it were a secret. "It's a cold night."

"Not fit for any man, living or dead. We're having a little get-together at the Refuge. Why don't you come along after you're—finished."

"I won't be off until five."

"Sunrise is not a problem, Michael. We have some very nice sleeping quarters available. I'd like to have you as my guest."

I poked at the telephone cord and stared out the plate glass windows into an unfriendly night. "Ah, I don't have a car. Probably couldn't get a taxi in this weather."

"I'll send the car for you," she said. La-di-da. *The car.* I hoped she was sending a driver, too. "It'll be waiting for you. Be well, Michael."

"Yeah. Thanks." I listened until I heard the buzz of disconnection on her end before hanging up. I hadn't meant to do that. I hadn't wanted to go to the Refuge again.

But, obviously, some part of me had other ideas.

A half hour later, a pickup pulled into the closest parking space and a couple of men skidded their way across the concrete to the doors.

Teenagers, one white, one Hispanic. Both nervous, eyeing me in little jumps and starts. They went back to hang out near the beer cooler, talking urgently while they watched me out of the corner of their eyes.

Well, I thought with some satisfaction. *This could turn out to be kind of fun.* I'd always been a big fan of Superman.

It occurred to me, in a fleeting civic-minded moment, to press the silent alarm and summon the cops. But odds were the punks would buy their beer and go home, to get drunk and talk about what big shots they were. And if not . . . well, I had the qualifications to handle a couple of small-time robbers.

One minute later, another car arrived, this one at the gas pumps. Someone dressed in a tangle of coats and wind-whipped scarves waved at me, and I took pity and turned on the pump. Numbers rolled by. When the pump clicked off, the figure came toward the store. Another one got out of the car and followed.

The punks continued their argument by the beer. The Hispanic wanted to leave. The white one wanted to stay. I was none too pleased by the arrival of these new witnesses, who were bound to take all the fun out of things.

The door whipped open and sent a spray of ice into the store, followed by the two people from the car. A man and a woman, hardly older than the two punks in the back. She laughed breathlessly and shook the chill out of her fingers, and her boyfriend headed for the coffee.

Their license plate said Pennsylvania. College kids, clean, well dressed. Life was a big adventure.

The punks in the back had finished their argument. They picked a six-pack of Coors from the cooler and headed back toward me. They were trying too hard to look cool.

Witnesses were not stopping them. *Damn.*

I looked down at the silent alarm. The little red light above the switch had gone out. Lines were down, or something. I pressed it anyway.

"John, no cream in mine," the girl called. She was looking at a package of sunflower seeds, frowning. Her boyfriend put tops on the coffees and carried them up to me. I rang them up, along with his gas.

The punks with the beer were hanging back, hesitating. *Come on,* I thought to the girlfriend. *Come on. Hurry.*

She put the sunflower seeds back and picked up peanuts.

The Hispanic punk broke away from his friend and came up behind her. She glanced over her shoulder at him and her eyes widened.

"Nobody move!" the white punk shouted, and thumped his six-pack down on the counter. His other hand came out of his jacket with an automatic that looked, from my perspective, as big as a howitzer. He snapped the slide. Safety? I checked.

Off.

He aimed it at John, who stood there with his two cups of coffee in his hands. John looked stupid with surprise. The Hispanic punk was shoving John's girlfriend toward the counter. He had a gun, too, a revolver. The hammer was cocked.

"Put that shit down!" the white punk screamed at John. John stared at him in confusion.

"The coffee," I said, trying to sound calm. "Put the coffee down."

John tried. One of the cups fell off the counter and hit the floor with a fleshy smack. The top popped off and coffee bled out in a gurgle, steaming.

"Empty the register, asshole! And no funny shit!" the white punk—upgraded to robber—screamed. He smelled of rank scared sweat and too much cheap cologne, and his hand was shaking as if the gun were as heavy as a barbell. "Come on come on come on!"

I pushed the button, one-fingered, and the drawer zipped open. I unloaded some cash into a plastic JiffeeMart bag and set it on the counter next to the Coors. He grabbed for it, missed because he didn't want to take his eyes off of me.

Lucky for me.

"Hey, man, put down the gun," I told him. It was surprisingly easy to get into his mind, but then, there wasn't much of it. His eyes unfocused a little. "You don't need to hurt anybody. Here's the money. Just take it and go."

He blinked, swayed. I had him. The gun dipped a little.

Put the safety on.

His thumb explored the gun and slid the switch in place with a tiny click.

I'd forgotten the other robber. It caught me by surprise, the noise. I went back more out of shock than pain.

Stupid little bastard, I thought in amazement. *Shot me.*

It had surprised me, but not as much as I surprised him when I got up, unhurt and very, very pissed. He fired at me again, brown eyes wide. The bullet tugged as it passed through.

Now I was pissed.

"Put it down," I told him. He was too scared to make eye contact, just stared blankly in my direction. He turned and put the gun to John's head.

The white punk, meanwhile, had taken the safety off his gun. Instead of pointing it at me, he shoved it in the girl's face and dared me to do something.

And there was nothing I *could* do.

The door yawned open on the other side of the store. When I looked, it was flapping idly in the wind, a freezing breeze ruffling newspapers and magazines. *Cops,* I thought, and knew I was wrong. Cops would have come in guns drawn, shouting. But *somebody* had come in.

I saw him without recognizing him—a tall man, pale, long auburn hair pulled back in a ponytail. He wore ratty-looking blue jeans and a thin sweatshirt with a hole in the chest. There were dark stains on it.

Round little Lennon glasses. Brown eyes behind them, turning red.

Adam. Oh, Jesus, he looked bad. Really bad.

Somebody was standing beside him. White tangled hair. White sharp face. Pale eyes glinting like chips of ice. He was dressed in a torn camouflage coat and, absurdly, brand-new very expensive high-tops with neon-green stripes.

William. He smiled at me. It made me cold in a way that the ice storm outside never could.

He took one blindingly fast step forward and reached out with one thin, gangly arm. He turned the Hispanic punk around to face him.

The punk screamed. His body blocked my view, twitching.

"Stop! Stop it!" I yelled, and lunged over the counter. I got hold of John's arm, dragged him to safety. John's girl-friend was still tightly clutched in the white punk's grip, and from the expression on her face she had an all-too-good view of what William was doing. "Goddamn it, stop!"

The Hispanic's body hit the floor with a wet plop. A thin trickle of red snaked across the tile toward my feet.

William's white face was spattered with blood, except for his lips. He'd licked those clean.

"Howdy," he said to me, still grinning. Long, sharp teeth. "Don't be such a baby, Mikey. We just came in to pick up a little snack. Hey. Adam."

Adam took a step forward. The surviving robber made a sound that I had never heard, not even in the emergency room. It was a vibrating, keening sound of absolute terror. His pants darkened at the crotch.

He let go of the girl. I grabbed her and shoved her into John's arms, put myself between them and William.

The white punk fired, and fired, and fired. He did damage to a bag of Cheetos and the plate glass window.

Adam kept coming.

He took the gun away and dropped it on the floor. He had thin, strong fingers. They sunk deep into the punk's neck and pulled.

The smell of blood reached me, washed over me in a hot blinding wave, and my whole body shivered in response. My eyes tingled and burned as they turned red. *God. Oh my God.*

The blood was heart-hot, spiced with terror, with the feral smell of death.

Adam drank. And drank. And drank. And then William drank, too. My ears were numb from the gunshots but I heard the two survivors behind me whimpering. Too afraid to scream.

What they were seeing couldn't be real.

Adam let go of the body. It slithered wetly to the floor. So much blood, the smell flooding over me, into me, warm on my skin. A thick stream flowed downhill over the floor toward my shoes, and it would take so little effort to bend down and—and—

"No," I whispered, and shut my eyes. I imagined I could feel it through my shoes, seeping in to burn my skin like sunlight.

"No *what?*" William asked. His voice was quiet and soft and too rational. "Not hungry?"

The questions paralyzed me. The smell was so strong it painted the inside of my eyelids red, a bloody screen where I saw myself bend and drink like a dog from William's bowl of slaughter. I forced my eyes open again and saw Adam watching me. His eyes glittered like rubies, only wetter, harder.

God, I hoped I didn't look like that.

John and his girlfriend still crouched behind me, huddled together like frightened mice. He had clapped his hand over her mouth; her scream buzzed like a fly trapped in her throat. Just kids, really. From Pennsylvania. She liked her coffee without cream.

The part of me that wasn't red still cared about that.

It was quiet. Just the hissing of the ice storm outside, the dripping of blood inside.

And heartbeats, pounding like fists behind me.

"You know," William said, and looked around at the slaughter, "it's a goddamn shame. These places get robbed all the time. It just ain't safe for decent folks."

"Why did you do this?" I demanded; it came out rough and frightened. William strolled away to the ice cream case. He moved jerkily, a ghoulish Pinnochio who'd started out human, ended up something else. He opened the case, took out a chocolate-dipped Good Humor bar and unwrapped it.

"If I don't look after you, who will?" He crouched, spider-like, and dipped the bar into the blood pooling on the floor. "You're kin, Michael. *My* kin. I take care of my own. Always have."

He licked the blood from the chocolate coating; it cracked in places, showing white ice cream with red smears. His tongue made a wet sucking sound, like a collapsed lung.

"I'm not yours." That sounded right, brave and sane. He licked his ice cream and watched me. I felt Adam move behind me, just a twitch. I turned and looked up at him, saw a flash in his eyes of the man I had once known, my friend. *"We're not yours."*

Then Adam was empty. My friend had been reduced to this—this piece of *meat*, waiting for orders. His eyes pulsed red, then brown, but he wasn't looking at me, he was looking at the bodies on the floor.

He was trapped in there, somewhere, screaming.

William licked his Good Humor bar clean and dropped the stick on the floor, then crossed to me in one spiderish leap and crouched next to me. I tried to push him back but his fingers laced themselves in mine, squeezing. My bones bent.

"Adam's mine, and don't you forget it," he said. It was just a whisper, breathless, excited. "He's mine and you're next. I want to play. You a good sport, ain't you?"

"Fuck you!" I screamed, and he yanked one of my fingers out of its socket, a hot snap of agony that ended in seconds as it healed. He could do it again, I thought. Over and over and over. Never-ending pain.

He put his face very close to mine, so close I could see that the ice-colored eyes were a faint, necrotic blue with white webs. His teeth were ivory spikes, inches away.

"Don't be ungrateful," he purred. The bayou accent was

thick enough to touch. "There's worse things in this world than playin' with me."

He shoved me backward, and I reached out blindly to catch my balance. I flailed and grabbed the counter.

Hassan's notice about shoplifting slid to the floor and wicked up blood in snowflake patterns.

Behind me, John screamed, loud and full, as William reached out for him.

"William."

I had not said it. It was a female voice, quiet but holding an unmistakable snap of command. I twisted around to look over my shoulder.

Celestine Vaughn stood in the doorway, dark hair blowing wild around her shoulders, blind eyes as white as frosted glass. Her chin was raised a little as she listened; there was a look of complete concentration on her face, almost of fascination. Next to her was Paul Sheffield. He still looked bankerish, but behind the little glasses his eyes had lightened and turned a strange, unsettling pink.

"We-ee-eell, it a real goddamn bloodsucking *convention,* ain't it?" William murmured. He grinned. "Miss Celeste. Ain't you a sight for sore eyes? You got an interest in little Mike here?"

She didn't say a word. Neither did Paul.

"Boy," William said, and turned his head to stare at me. "I told you, there's worse things in this world than playin' with me."

"Stop it," Celestine snapped. Her silk voice became sandpaper. "Get out. I'm only giving you the one chance."

William lifted his arms above his head, long and gangly and disjointed, a crazy blood-smeared puppet with a homicidal grin. He danced in place, shuffling in the blood, and came back around to face her.

"Ooh, I'm so scared. I think the time's comin'," he said, wiggling his fingers like thin worms, "that I'll have to teach you a lesson, Miss Celeste. You uppity bitch, you're forgettin' who gave you The Life."

"I don't forget," she said, and just for an instant that pretty mask slipped. "I don't *forget*. And I'm going to make sure you never, ever forget *me*."

He blew her a kiss with a wet smacking sound, strolled over and picked up a glass bottle of Coke from a display. He tossed it casually from one hand to the next, eyeing me, Adam, Celestine, Paul.

His throw was blindingly fast, and unerring. The bottle hit Celestine like a grenade, knocking her backward, exploding into splinters of glass and showers of sticky liquid.

I knew by instinct that William was leaving. I was close to Adam and grabbed him, threw him bodily to the floor. He twisted under me and scrambled for purchase on the slick polished tile.

I pinned him down and bared my teeth at William, who stood in the doorway behind the counter, holding out a hand to Adam. Calling him.

"You can't have him," I hissed. "I'll fucking kill you first." William grinned.

"Well," he said. "If I can't, I can't. Guess we all have to make sacrifices. Look behind you."

I didn't want to, but the command was irresistible.

How? How could he have moved so quickly—

Blood, everywhere, pumping from their bodies. John stared at the ceiling, a puzzled frown on his face as if he hadn't actually recognized death when it caught him. His girlfriend was still alive, barely. As I watched, her eyes went blank.

Her heart stopped.

One last whisper of blood trickled out of her mouth.

Maggie. The thought crashed into me, uncontrollable. *He could kill Maggie next. No. Never.*

"Stop him!" Celestine had recovered from her shock; her furious snarl stung Paul out of his surprise, too, and he lunged after William. William gave me one last manic grin that never reached his eyes.

He was gone before Paul even reached the counter. The back door boomed.

Adam got his arms free and dragged himself to his knees. I found my voice.

"Help me!" I screamed. Paul spun, face white, eyes bloody, and snarled. "No! No! Help me hold him!"

He took Adam's legs and pulled a thick leather-wrapped club out of his pocket. The end of it was raw wood.

He hit Adam hard enough to end the fight, for a while. Celestine approached us, blind eyes staring off into the distance.

"You have him?" she asked. Paul grunted. "Good. Let's get out of here."

"What about—" I lost my voice. My God.

"We have to go, *now.* They'll be looking for you, or your body. You can't reasonably say you survived this." Celestine took a deep breath and deliberately softened her tone. "There's no coming back here for you, Michael."

"The video—" I said. Paul looked up at the whirring camera. Celestine smiled.

"Paul will take care of the videotape."

Maybe so.

But I couldn't help feeling that we'd forgotten something.

Eight

Pain

Adam's eyes flickered and snapped open, wide open. They weren't red anymore. They were black, holes in his head which seemed to look straight into Hell.

He was lying flat across the seat, shared equally on my lap and Celestine's, but his head was on my end. I had a ringside view of the suffering on his face, before it was wiped out and replaced by nothing at all.

Paul made a right turn, leaning us into a curve. The road ahead was gray and white, nearly obscured by a hissing curtain of sleet. There were no other cars driving on the road with us, but there were plenty pulled over to the sides, windows fogged over.

I felt I should say something to Adam, but some instinct kept me from opening my mouth. Celestine slowly turned her head toward me, and smiled.

"He's awake," she said. Paul watched the road, but I saw his back stiffen.

Adam just stared, blind as Celestine.

"I think he can hear us," Celestine said. "Adam, can you hear me? Adam?"

Nothing. Celestine's jaw tensed a little. She reached out one long-fingered hand to touch his face. Her fingers worked like spiders, stepping over his nose, his eyes, his mouth. Tracing the line of his cheek almost tenderly.

"Adam," she said again. No reaction. Her fingernails dug deep into his flesh. Ripped. The wounds filled sluggishly with blood and then faded. The blood dribbled away down his cheek.

Nothing. It was as if he didn't even feel it.

Celestine's lips had parted a little, and now she licked them with a pale tongue. She sat back against the smooth leather upholstery and shrugged.

"You try, Michael," she invited. I didn't want to. But her tone chilled just enough to warn me that it hadn't been a request. "Do it."

"Adam," I said. "It's me, Michael."

Just for a second—no, less than that—it seemed he was *there,* drawn by my voice, looking out of those hell-bent eyes. And then he was gone.

I wondered why he had slipped away so far, and what we were going to do about it.

Paul murmured something I didn't catch, and Celestine nodded. I looked up as the limo turned and saw we were on Laurel Road. Gates glided by like icy skeletons.

The rear wheels slid a little, gently, as he made the turn into the drive. The only sound in the limo was the distant hiss of tires on ice, the occasional crunch of gravel. No heartbeats. No breathing.

Silent as the grave.

The fountain was still working on the front lawn, but it had grown thick sharp icicles on the sides. Paul drove around to the side and into a garage. There were at least six other cars parked inside, but the limo had plenty of room to fit.

Adam took this moment to go wild. One minute he was quiet, catatonic; the next his whole body was in uncontrolled motion, arms and legs flailing, head jerking. *Seizure,* I thought clinically, and grabbed his wrists.

Until he grabbed my hand and held on. Not fighting.

Not fighting *me,* anyway. This was no seizure like I'd ever seen.

Celestine held his legs.

"What is it?" I demanded. She tilted her head in my direction.

"William's trying to call him," she answered. "Let's get him inside."

Paul came around to take Adam's head, and we eased his flailing body out of the car. It took all three of us to hold on—but it was me Adam held on to, not quite hard enough to break bones. The others cursed and tried to keep their grip.

Then, suddenly, it was over. He let go of my hand and went limp, absolutely deadweight. Paul exchanged a look with me.

"He's trying to hold it off."

"Can he?"

"Maybe. If we help him. Let's get him in," he said, and hefted him easily, like a sack of grain. Celestine stepped forward and put her hand on Paul's arm, holding him back for a second.

"Put him in the interior room. I don't want any surprises from outside."

Paul nodded, spectacles flashing in the floodlights. He walked on ahead of us. Celestine slipped her arm in mine.

"Now," she said, and her voice was velvety again, dark with promise. "I think that's a good evening's work, don't you? Deserving of a reward?"

I couldn't feel too happy with it, myself. Four dead bodies left behind. William still free, and demonstrating that he was one hell of a lot more self-sufficient than I'd given him credit for. Adam left either catatonic or violent.

"Sure," I said. Her fingers squeezed my forearm.

"I'll see what I can do to arrange one. Michael? Do you see Carl?"

I looked around, at the shadows in the garage, the ice-driven darkness outside. I had no sense of anyone present, or watching. It was a shock to finally see him standing in the deepest shadows near the limo, staring at us. He looked desiccated, ill.

"Yes," I said. I said it quietly, for fear he might hear. Celestine's head turned, first right, then left, like a radar antenna.

"Carl?" she called. "Do you need help?"

He just stood there, staring. Watching. I tightened my fingers on Celestine's, in warning.

And then he walked away, out into the dark.

"I don't think he's in a very good mood," I said. Celestine brushed her hair back from her face, and she looked wary and almost afraid. Blind a long time, but still aware of her vulnerability.

Not that *I* was much of a help to her there. I couldn't hold my own against any of them, in a real fight.

"He hasn't been well," she said finally, and produced a smile as brilliant as it was fake. "Lilly will have built a fire, I imagine. Nothing like it to warm you up."

She was speaking metaphorically, I guessed, or wishfully. We didn't warm up. Ever. I took the hint and led her up the walk toward the house, where Adam had already entered, feet first.

Lilly was waiting at the door, the cold burning bloody

circles into her cheeks. She followed us through the hall and
into the giant sitting room I'd seen on my first visit, the one
with the fireplace big enough to warm half of Dallas. The
couch was far, far away from it. Celestine settled on the thick
cushions and drew her legs up underneath her; the firelight
gave her false color and an eerie vitality, and her hair looked
rich and warm where it spilled over her dark sweater. I hadn't
noticed before, but she wore a pair of blue jeans. She hadn't
seemed the type.

"Something wrong?" she asked me, and held her hands
out toward the fire like someone starved for heat. I sat back
and drew in a deliberate breath. Wood smoke, dusty in my
lungs. The ubiquitous vanilla potpourri. Distant ghosts of
human sweat and a new perfume, coming from Celestine.
Unlike a human woman, she hadn't applied too much for
vampire sensibilities; the smell was the vaguest whisper,
faded flowers and ambergris. For all that, it smelled—lifeless. Like perfume sprayed into the air, instead of on a
woman.

Of course. Perfume was designed to work on warm skin.

"Nothing," I answered. "Just thinking."

"A useful thing to do, provided you don't do too much of
it. Enjoy the rest, Michael. I know how stressful the wild life
can be. Always thinking, always lying, always afraid. I can't
imagine why Adam prefers it to the comfort of his own kind,
in a place where he can be exactly what he is. That's what
the Society is all about. An end to fear."

"The Society seems to be about a lot of things," I said.
She rubbed her hands together. A log popped in the fireplace,
and not even Celestine had overcome her fear of fire enough
not to jump.

"Yes, I suppose it seems that way. You can't explain any

culture in a paragraph, can you? And that's what we are. We have beliefs, morality, arts, religion."

"But the same language as—"I almost said "us," but it didn't seem politically correct to put myself on the side of humanity at the moment. "Normal humans."

"Convenience," she sighed. "The Society has to exist inside human society, of course. There is no place left on earth that we could go to be alone, even if we wished to. And why would we? We evolve from humans. We need humans. Why should we leave them completely?"

A nice speech, but the first word had been the most important, for me. *Convenience.* Why travel when you could have everything you wanted at your fingertips? It was the philosophy JiffeeMarts had been based on. The Society simply liked keeping its food and pleasures within easy reach.

"You're very cynical," Celestine whispered. I bent closer to her and took a quick look over the back of the couch, into the shadows at the back of the living room. It looked empty.

I knew it wasn't.

"Practical," I said.

"Practical men don't become doctors," she countered. "They become businessmen, and work regular hours."

"Practical men like to make money."

"Lawyers make money," she said. "So do stockbrokers. They don't have to put their hands in the bloody mess of someone else's body."

Plenty of lawyer cracks came to mind, but I held them back, watching her. I could still smell blood all over my clothes, my shoes. I felt filthy and weary and sick, and somehow her presence beside me felt soothing. I wanted to keep it that way.

She tilted her head a little. Her white eyes were orange in the firelight.

"I've arranged for you to have a room in the interior. You'll be safer there in case of—intrusions."

"William," I said. She shrugged.

"No real reason to fear him. William is crazy but hardly stupid enough to come here, where we have the advantage. He has scrupulously avoided the Society for more than eighty years now. When he hunts other vampires, he hunts the wilds."

"Doing your work for you," I murmured. She said nothing. "Why move on him now? You've ignored him all this time, what makes this any different?"

She trailed her fingernails down the rough fabric of her blue jeans. Her face was thoughtful and strangely empty.

"In a sense, nothing. And everything. William is a monster, you'll hardly dispute that. But there are degrees of monstrosity. A killer is a monster. A killer of children is worse. A man who preys on his own children is worse still." She was quiet a moment. Her fingernails rasped over thick cotton. "William is destroying his own bloodline."

"And you're part of it."

"No," Celestine said, and smiled bitterly. "No, I'm *all* of it. All of it he hasn't yet corrupted."

I wondered where that left me—corrupted? Or just unimportant? Oh, yeah, I was *wild*.

Someone moved in the shadows. I heard heartbeats in the hall. Humans on the way.

"I need a shower," I said. I must have sounded sharp, because she lost her smile and all the gentleness faded out of her face.

"Go take one," she said. "Lilly will show you the way. Oh, and Michael?"

I paused. She stared off toward the fire, one hand reaching

out to the warmth. I saw skin peeking through her blue jeans. She'd torn the denim with her fingernails.

"Don't be so goddamn righteous," she whispered.

Lilly was in the doorway. Her eyes flickered with reflections of fire.

She turned and led me off into the dark, narrow halls.

My room was spacious enough to qualify for a honeymoon suite—thick pile carpeting springing underfoot, no windows, expensive-looking paintings of landscapes and quaintly dressed people frolicking under the sun. The bed was wide and inviting, piled with pillows. Lilly showed me the bathroom.

It had a tub big enough to float a battleship, and the kind of shower you used with friends. Plural. Thick white towels. No mirrors.

Lilly paused in the doorway.

"If you need some clothing, sir, I can arrange for it. There's a piece of paper beside the bed. Just write down your sizes and I'll pick up things for you tomorrow." She gave me a shadowy twitch of lips that might have been a smile. "Sunrise is in two hours and six minutes."

"Thank you, Lilly," I said. She nodded. "Hey. What do you do? I mean, outside the Society?"

"Do?" She blinked at me. "I work for Celestine, sir."

She was waiting for me to dismiss her. I nodded, and she backed out and closed the door behind her. I went and sat on the bed. Comfortable.

No surprise. I hadn't expected to suffer.

I didn't suffer in the shower, either. Hot, thick streams of water, coming from the four corners of the shower stall. Clouds of steam that smelled strangely of nothing at all. A fine-milled soap. The slide of the washcloth over my skin was soothing and sensual; I soaped my genitals and wondered if they'd ever function again, or if I was doomed to impotence the rest of eternity. It wasn't an easy question to ask anybody, especially Celestine.

There was a marble shelf inside the shower. I sat down and let the spray wash over me. For this short moment, at least, I felt warm and alive again. It wouldn't last, I knew. I'd get out of the water, towel off—

—and grow cold.

"You'll wrinkle," someone said. I jerked upright, shut the water off and eased the door open a crack.

Celestine stood there, naked. White, white skin, touched faintly blue on her nipples.

"I—" I started, and couldn't think of anything to say. She turned and walked out of the bathroom, feeling her way with expert brushes of her fingertips. Long, long legs. A model's back.

My brain was trying to tell me something I didn't take the time to hear. I found a towel and dried myself off. God*damn* it, why couldn't I have an erection?

Why the hell did I want one? I wanted Maggie. I *knew* I wanted Maggie.

Who I'd never have again.

The thought was just painful enough to sever that last little thread of resistance. Why not? Why not forget—just for a while? Didn't I deserve that?

"Michael." Her voice came from the bedroom. I stepped to the door and saw her, lying there on top of the thick velvety bedspread. Her head was turned toward me. "I want you warm."

It was like an electric cattle prod right in the spine. I dropped the towel and sank down on the bed with her, her skin cold as ice on mine, my warmth soaking into her and disappearing. She was hungry, I thought. Hungry and cold. And strong.

I kissed her. It was different than kissing a human woman. I felt the bumps of fangs under those soft lips, and it made me crazy, trembling and sick and desperate at once. Her fingers moved cold over my shoulders, my back, down my spine like the slide of a melting ice cube. Her hands cupped my buttocks and I pressed down hard on her—

—with nothing.

"No," I whispered, *begged*. "Goddamn it, no, come on—"

"It's all right," she breathed in my ear. I kissed her shoulder, tasted it. No warm perfume, but something even more intoxicating. My own kind. "It will happen. I know how."

Dry and smooth and cold, like marble. But she writhed like a real woman, gasped like one, and I kissed her and wished I had a hard-on, even a small one, anything at all to match the wildness of the feelings inside.

She tugged lightly at my hair and rolled me over flat on my back, sat astride me and arched her back. Beautiful. Cold.

"I know how," she gasped. She was trembling all over, vibrating. I reached out for her and her hands lashed out, wrapped around my wrists, smashed them back on the bed. "I know how, I know—"

She invaded me. It was so sudden I couldn't even cry out, just an overwhelming feeling of violation, of something foreign and cold and horrible in my head and I couldn't move my hands, couldn't move anything at all.

Celestine snarled and raked her fingernails across my chest. Hot spurts of pain, valleys of blood and torn flesh.

Before it healed she slashed again, bloody gouges down my arms. I tried to get control of my tongue, to tell her to stop, I didn't want this, it was wrong—

Pain exploded in my chest again. Oh, God help me, I

thought, and then the thought was gone, lost in an icestorm of nails biting into my skin, digging, twisting.

She slid down my body. I wanted to scream and I couldn't, couldn't do anything at all, just waited while somewhere inside I screamed and from a distance I heard *her* screaming like a wild creature, my blood spattered on her white body, her nails wet and dripping.

The pain was nuclear, devastating, mind-destroying.

And, hellishly miraculous, I felt my penis inflating and rising. *No,* I thought frantically. *No, I don't want it. No.*

Oh, yes. She slashed, bit, and I got harder and harder and hated myself, hated her, wished I could die and knew I couldn't.

You'll heal, I thought incoherently. *Heal.*

She slid down on me, cold and soft as an anatomy cadaver and I was terrified by the wish to hurt her and tear her and slice her apart. My hands came up, not of my own will, and rested on her breasts.

"Do it," she hissed. Her eyes were no longer white, no longer blind. Hell looked out through them, blood-red. "Hurt me!"

I threw her across the room. She hit the wall and slid down to a sitting position, crying I thought, and then I saw the wild glitter in her eyes and knew she was laughing. *Laughing.*

I stood up and swayed, braced myself with one hand on the nightstand. Celestine ran her hands through her wild hair, smearing my blood in it, and leaned her head back against the wall.

"Did you like it?" she asked. I couldn't answer her. If I could have vomited, I would have. "Of course you did. It's all we have, Michael. Pain is everything now. It makes us vital again."

"You bitch," I whispered. My knees gave way. I sat down on the bed and put my head in my hands.

"You'll heal," she said briskly. "I need a shower. Mind if I use yours?"

I heard her go into the bathroom, fingertips trailing over the walls, slicing tiny lines with those razored nails. I found my still-damp towel lying where I'd dropped it and scrubbed the blood off of my skin. I stripped the bed linens off and dumped them all in a heap on the floor.

I was fully dressed again in my stained clothes when Celestine came out, the picture of innocence swathed in thick white towels. She listened for a minute, head cocked.

"Michael?" she asked, and I didn't move, didn't reply. Her lips curled lazily. "Oh, Michael, really. You act as if it was *terrible*. It wasn't, really. Even Adam had to admit that."

A discreet knock at the door. Celestine guided herself to it and swung it open.

Lilly came in and set two steaming glasses on the nightstand. She took a quick, comprehending glance at the sheets lying on the floor, and another at my face. For a second I thought I saw pity in her eyes.

"Anything else, miss?" she asked Celestine, who shook her head. "Will you be going to your room?"

"Yes," Celestine said, to my great relief. "Yes, I think so. Thank you, Michael. It's been ever so nice."

Her smile revealed long, perfect fangs, fully extended. She upended her glass and drained it in three huge gulps. Lilly took the red-filmed empty.

I sat for a long time after they were gone, staring at the blood in my glass. I finally drank it, gagging.

I died when the sun rose. It was better than thinking.

Interlude:

Maggie

"Hello, you've reached Joseph Vico. Please leave your name and number after the beep."

Now what?, Maggie thought, and realized that her hand was aching from trying to strangle the telephone receiver. She let ten seconds or so go by, ten seconds of silence, and let out an explosive breath. She still hadn't figured out what she'd say. *I've got some good news and some bad news. The good news is, there's fifty thousand more . . .*

"Fuck," she said, and the beep cut her off in mid-*fu.*

She put the receiver down and stared at it through slitted eyes.

A warm hand squeezed her shoulder, and she looked up to find McDonnell holding out her coat. He had no particular expression on his face at all.

"Where to?" she asked; *Jesus, not another murder.* The sun was barely up.

"Somebody turned a JiffeeMart into a slaughterhouse. We've got four bodies."

Maggie stopped moving. She just stared at her telephone, fixedly. Waiting for it to say something. Anything.

JiffeeMart.

"Where?" Her voice sounded high and airless.

"Corner of Grand and Carter. You know, the upscale neighborhood; they don't have height scales on the doors, they have targets. Let's go, Maggie, they're not getting any deader but they are getting colder."

She closed her eyes. There was a weight on her chest.

Fading flowers, crinkling green paper. Michael's wounded face as she shut him out.

"Maggie?" A cool hand on her arm. "Kid, you okay?"

Grand and Carter. How many nights had she driven by there, never stopping, just looking in the windows? He'd looked like a stranger, seen that way.

McDonnell went away, came back with coffee. She wrapped her numbed hands around it and took a big sip. It brought tears to her eyes, and she was finally able to gasp for air.

The black balloon of grief shrank a little.

McDonnell's eyes were gentle and steady. She tried to meet them the same way.

"Sorry," she said. "Sorry. Won't happen again."

"What the hell happened that time?"

She slugged back another mouthful of bitterness and got to her feet. Better and better.

Please, God, no more. Don't make me see him dead.

The wind outside was almost a relief, something to think about other than the black feeling still swelling in her chest. The air was so chilled that sounds fell flat, as if they were frozen, too. The cold metal clink of keys, the thick groan of the car door, the hoarse chug of the engine grinding up. Her breath made a gray veil around her face.

She hadn't worn a veil at Michael's funeral. She'd worn blue jeans.

If he's alive, he's killed those people.

"So you got something to say?" McDonnell asked her as the heater wheezed out cold air, and the transmission clunked into gear. "Anything?"

"No."

"Okay. I figure after we do the JiffeeMart, which may take half the day, we should cruise by the foster home where LaDonna Bedford lived. What's their names? Franciscus?"

"Franischi," Maggie said absently. "Ed and Ellen Franischi. We were there before, didn't find anything."

"Yeah, but I'm curious. Big Gerald had a lot of interesting things to say. Two-Pack may have been loaded on crack and half out of his mind, but he must have gotten the voodoo shit from someplace. He wasn't original enough to think it up on his own. I'm interested to find out who told him, and why."

The car ride didn't take nearly long enough; the heater had only come up to lukewarm by the time they exited on Grand and made the left toward Carter. Maggie resisted the urge to ask him to stop; there wasn't any point in delaying, was there? No point at all.

"Uh-oh," McDonnell murmured. The JiffeeMart looked like a flea market, TV vans clustered around, lights flashing, people standing six deep to stare. The medical examiner was already there, and she counted three patrol cars, cherries spinning. "The day started early around here."

He glided the car up to a patrolman. The man nodded and touched his hat as he motioned them through. Maggie kept her gaze straight ahead and focused on nothing at all as reporters bent down to peer through the windows, mouthing questions.

A few feet farther along and they were safely in the inner

circle, cops and ambulances and the dark discreet station wagon of the medical examiner's office. It was going to be a bad one; all of the uniforms were outside in the freezing wind, rubbing their hands together and clustering in tight little blue groups. McDonnell popped his door open, and a wash of cold settled over her skin.

Don't go in, her mind whispered. But of course it wasn't an option. She got out and breathed in cold, breathed out mist. Slammed her door hard enough to knock a couple of stakelike icicles from the fender. They shattered into diamond-bright crystals on the oily pavement, and she felt like she was shattering, too.

McDonnell was watching her out of the corner of his eye. Nothing she could do but cope, which was what the world always expected of her. Husband's dead? Get over it. He's a killer? Take a pill. God, surviving was so hard.

Her ears rang with a tinny, thin whine as she followed McDonnell through the open double doors of the store. She thought for a second that she was going to faint in the sudden rush of warm air, but then a cool breeze drifted over her face and brought her back enough to open her eyes and look around. The breeze came from one of the plate glass windows, star-cracked with a funnel-shaped bullet hole through it. Other than that sign of damage, the store looked intact. It smelled of overcooked coffee and decaying meat.

Past the snack food aisle, she saw two bodies lying together.

She stopped.

McDonnell threw her a glance and kept walking. The crime scene team murmured greetings.

"What've we got?" he asked the nearest, a big-hipped, big-breasted woman named Deborah, capable of wrestling a drunken wife-beater to the ground in a pinch. Big hands clutching a clipboard and a department-issue pen.

"Three males, one female. We got two guns, one a .45 auto, one a .38 revolver."

Maggie took a long step forward, then another. The air gently tried to hold her back.

The first body was Hispanic, male. His throat was missing.

"The ME can't find any bullet wounds," the woman said in a lower tone, confidentially. McDonnell nodded. "Somebody tore 'em up good, but the guy with the .45 got off a couple of shots. Could be our perp is hurt."

The next body was male. White. Turned over on his side, away from her. Maggie took a careful step around to get a look at the dead man's face.

The relief was sweet and intense and short. There was only one reason Michael wouldn't be lying here with the others.

McDonnell left to confer with the deputy medical examiner, who was standing near the counter. He frowned at the swipes of blood on the floor. The conversation was quick, and Maggie waited until McDonnell shook his head and wandered back her way.

"Not enough blood," she said quietly. He nodded.

"Not by half, the ME says. We got us a squirrel, maybe two—looks like a couple of different people stepped in the blood. The store clerk is missing. LaGracia's already working on a warrant."

That meant a search of Joseph Vico's apartment. She knew Mike had been careful—no pictures of her, no letters, no cards. They'd agreed it was too dangerous now. Nothing to link her to him.

Thank God she hadn't left a message on his answering machine.

But they would dust for prints. And her prints were there, on the glass she'd drunk from, on the arm of the chair, other places. Michael's fingerprints weren't on file, as far as she knew—but hers were.

"I think we should take the search," she heard herself say. McDonnell nodded.

"Yeah, after we get done here."

He went behind the register and talked to the guy lifting prints. The register still had money in it: seventy-five dollars and sixty cents. The time lock safe hadn't been touched.

"What about the security camera?" Maggie asked. McDonnell looked up.

"Tape's gone. They must watch the evening news."

One problem down. Of course, they'd take a look at last shift's pictures, to get a good photo of Joseph Vico. She swallowed hard and tried to think of some way to delay that.

Hell, I should be trying to solve this, not slow it down. What's wrong with me?

Michael was wrong with her.

She just stood there, miserable, while McDonnell did his job.

The steps going up to Michael's—no, Joseph's—apartment were icy. Maggie braced herself with one gloved hand on the rail and remembered how much she'd enjoyed ice as a kid—instant roller coaster. She remembered the sensation of rushing over a long sheet of ice, out of control, arms flailing.

Funny, how her whole life had become a patch of ice.

McDonnell had found a junior detective in the apartment manager. The woman was bright-eyed and rosy-cheeked, ready to point out important clues they might miss.

"Well," the apartment manager *(call me Rose)* said as she flipped keys on her giant ring, "He's been here about three months. Signed up for a six month lease, I looked it up when you called. Paid his security deposit, but he didn't do any extras, no pet deposit or anything. So is he—um—"

"We're just trying to locate him, ma'am," Maggie interrupted. Rose flashed her a nervous look and nodded.

"Oh, of course. Sure. He was real quiet, you know. Never had any complaints about him playing his stereo too loud or parking in other people's spaces or anything like that. Some people, they're born troublemakers, but he never—"

"Do you know him?" McDonnell asked. Rose tried one key. It didn't work.

"Well, not *well,* you know. I've talked to him. Nothing personal or anything." Her face crinkled with the effort to remember. "I know he told me he was on the night shift and he slept during the day. He specifically wanted to make sure that we didn't come in during the day. Well, I told him, that's not always possible because of pest spraying and things like that, and *he* said just to let him know in advance and he'd arrange to stay someplace else for the day. That's kind of strange, isn't it?"

"Door," Maggie reminded her. Rose jumped and started fumbling through her keys again. One with a blue dot, this time. She jiggled it, with no effect.

"You need a good description of him, I can do that. I'm very observant, everybody's always said so. He had a little scar, right here, at the corner of his eye. Just a tiny one. Would you call that an identifying mark?"

"Yes ma'am," McDonnell said; Maggie could tell by the way his eyes had narrowed that he was trying not to crack up. "That's great. Anything else?"

Rose found a red-dot key and inserted it in the lock with a sound like a zipper ripping open.

"He always paid on time," she said. "In money orders, no checks. Tried to give me cash once, but I told him we weren't allowed to do that. Can you imagine? Handing somebody three hundred dollars in cash?"

She remembered to jiggle the key. It made metallic clicks, and she frowned at it and eased it out of the lock a fraction of an inch.

Maggie sighed, and her breath blew gray over her face.

"You know, I guess there was something suspicious about all that. Him having all that cash, you know. And not wanting anybody in the apartment." Rose's eyes opened wide in their thicket of mascara. "Oh my. You know, Mrs. Gonzales's cat disappeared right around the time he moved in. Yes, I think it was just about then. That's probably important."

Rose turned the key. The sound of the lock surrendering was the sweetest thing Maggie had heard in a long time.

"We're going to want to talk to all the people whose doors face his, okay? Or who are on this same block of apartments. Can you give us a list?" she asked as Rose jingled her heavy key ring and tried to fit it back in the pocket of her too-red coat.

"Sure." Rose sounded less eager now that detecting involved actual work. "Most of them won't be home right now."

"Then we'll come back."

The door swung open. Rose started to lead them inside, and Maggie put an arm in her way and held her back.

"Thanks for the information, ma'am. If you could get us that list, it would be a real help. We'll let you know when we leave."

"Okay," Rose said. She didn't mean it. She stood there simmering until Maggie closed the door on her and locked it.

"Jesus, it's dark," McDonnell's voice echoed. A click, and then a yellow light from the kitchen. "Cold as a meat locket in here. Doesn't this guy ever turn on the furnace? At least he's neat."

Maggie carefully worked the gloves off of her hands and put them in her pocket. She took a deep breath. The air wasn't much warmer in here than out there, and her fingers were already stinging with cold.

"Great. I hate looking through piles of trash." She turned on a light in the living room and tried to remember what she might have touched. The doorknob, certainly. The coffee table, maybe—what the *hell* had happened to the coffee table?

"Andy," she called. His shadow came into the room and spilled over her feet. "What do you think? Signs of a struggle?"

The coffee table had been destroyed. One sharp-ended piece lay half under a chair. *Wood,* she thought, and felt a chill.

"Looks that way. Kitchen looks clean. We got a couple of glasses in the sink, rinsed out. Nothing else."

Had he checked the refrigerator? Maggie was afraid to look, but she wandered in to the kitchen and swung the door open. Colder air puffed out.

Nothing. She pulled open the vegetable bins.

One plastic bag. half full of blood. She glanced over her shoulder and saw that McDonnell had gone down the hallway.

The bag went in her coat pocket, a cold, unpleasantly squishy lump. *Don't leak,* she thought miserably.

"He's got messages on his answering machine." McDonnell's voice echoed hollowly down the hall. She choked and tried to breathe around the lump that grew like instant cancer in her throat.

She shut the refrigerator and went down the hall.

The bathroom was covered with shards of mirror—pieces in the sink, glittering underwater in the toilet, coating the floor. McDonnell raised his eyebrows at her.

"In here," he said, and before she could stop him . . .

. . . he hit the button.

Beep.

Ten long seconds of silence. She wanted to scream but she couldn't, couldn't look at McDonnell so she stared at the answering machine and willed it to shut up, blow up, *anything.*

Her sigh sounded like a scratchy gust of wind on the tape.

Her voice said "Fu—"

And the machine beeped twice and sat there flickering its red light, well satisfied. She kept staring at it, entranced; she knew that McDonnell was looking at her, waiting for an explanation, but she couldn't do anything at all. There was nothing to do.

The machine, disappointed at the lack of response, whirred to itself and reset with a click. The red light went back to a steady blink-blink-blink rhythm.

"Well, somebody isn't too happy with him," McDonnell said, shrugged, and walked off.

He didn't know. He hadn't heard. He didn't recognize the voice.

She couldn't breathe, but somehow she had the craziest urge to laugh. She forced it down, stomped on it until it was only a ticklish giggle in the back of her throat.

"You going to work or just stand there?" he called, and she managed to swallow the giggle, too, and followed him into the bedroom.

Here, Michael was not so neat. He'd left the sheets in a tangle, blankets tossed on the floor. The windows were blocked with heavy double curtains and, under that, aluminum foil.

McDonnell opened the closet door and started poking through the meager collection of clothes. Maggie opened drawers, randomly. Underwear. Some T-shirts. Socks.

In the third drawer, she found a single Polaroid picture from years ago, a young woman who looked like her, only happier, waving at the camera from a tangle of Florida greenery. Jesus.

She slipped it into her pocket and closed the drawer.

When she turned around, McDonnell was staring at her. It felt like a punch in the stomach.

"What?" She was instantly defensive. "You told me to work, I'm working. What?"

He was quiet for a few seconds, just staring at her. She didn't like the assessing look in his eyes.

"What's with you?" he asked.

"Nothing! Nothing's with me! What?"

He'd remembered, she thought, and her stomach took a thirty-floor suicide dive. He knew. He was staring as if he'd never seen her before.

"You'd better start giving me some reasons, Maggie, because when you screw up, I screw up. Get it?"

"No, I don't get it!" She heard her voice echo off the walls and heard panic lurking under the anger. "You want to just spit it out?"

"Put your goddamn gloves on," McDonnell said, every word a nail, his voice a hammer. She looked down at her cold-pinched white fingers. "You know better than this."

"Shit," she hissed, and fumbled her gloves out of her pocket. She slid them over her skin; they felt stiff with cold.

She didn't apologize, just glared at McDonnell. He glared back.

"I'll finish in here," he said. "Go check the neighbors."

She nodded and walked away, down the narrow dark hallway, past the bright kitchen light. She opened the front door and stared out at nothing in particular, rooftops, spiky trees, blank windows and doors.

She *hated* not doing her job. She *hated* it.

There was a face looking at her from a window across the way. A girl. Jet-black hair and a white face and red lips. Too much eyeliner.

The curtains rippled back, shutting out her image. Maggie stretched a little to work out the killing tension in her shoulders, and sighed.

And started canvasing the neighbors.

The score ended up sixteen no-shows, three tenants who'd never so much as seen Joseph Vico, and one who'd passed him once coming home from work.

She started on the apartments across the way. When she got to the one where the girl was, she kept knocking until she heard the dead bolt click back.

The girl was younger than she'd looked at a distance— maybe sixteen, trying too hard to be cool. She had on a knee-length black crepe dress with pointy lace edging, and big silver ankhs and upside-down crosses. Her shoes were ugly, clunky, high-top leathers.

The picture of high fashion.

"Police," Maggie said. "I need to ask you a couple of questions."

The girl nodded, avoiding her eyes. She opened the door all the way and invited Maggie in by turning her back on her.

There was another kid at home, too, a boy. He spared

Maggie a glance before going back to his Nintendo. The
game was full of unnervingly realistic screams and wet
sounds of violence.

"Mind if I sit down?" Maggie asked. The girl shrugged
and flopped into a threadbare chair left over from the seventies. A whiff of dust and old cat piss puffed out of it. Cats.
She glanced around and spotted one, a big ginger-colored
tabby licking its balls on top of the kitchen table. It gave her
an insolent glare.

She could already feel her throat swelling.

"My name is Detective Bowman," she said, and wrote
down the apartment number, 717, in big block letters on her
notepad "And you are—"

"Whisper," the girl said, and hesitated. "Jody Lynn Whitfield."

Maggie wrote it down.

"Whisper, I'm trying to find out something about the man
who lives in 216. You can see his front door from your window, right out there. His name is Joseph Vico."

"I met him," Jody Lynn said, and pretended to be fasci-
nated with her brother's video game. Her voice was so soft
that Maggie had to listen carefully to catch any of what she
said. "He comes home real early in the morning and leaves
at night. He works nights."

"That's right. How did you meet him?"

"I gave him a ride home from the grocery store. Me and
Teddy."

"Teddy." Maggie looked at the kid lying on the floor, who
was too entranced with the game to care about his name
being mentioned. She had to clear her throat; a slimy scum
had formed in it, and now she could feel that unmistakable
tightening in her chest. Cats. Jesus. "What did you guys talk
about in the car?"

"Nothing much. He's nice." Jody Lynn looked wretched. "I didn't know you were with the police."

"But I said——" Maggie began, and stopped. Jody Lynn raised her head and looked straight at her.

"Before. When you were at his apartment before."

Nine

Captives

Trouble, I thought, and opened my eyes. I could barely hear the voices through the door, whispers like flies buzzing. But I knew something was wrong.

I sat up and thought that I ought to feel worse, considering. I didn't have a single scratch on me to commemorate Celestine's little games, but not all the clawing had been done outside. *Skin heals,* I thought. *Minds don't.*

I opened the door. Lilly. Diane.

Diane was glaring at Lilly as if she intended to melt her down to a wet puddle; I wouldn't have expected it, but Lilly was staring back. Her heavy face was impassive and tight, and her eyes little black slits.

The tension was heavy enough to touch.

"I told you that I'd take care of it," said Diane through gritted teeth. "Now go back to your room."

"No," Lilly snapped. "I'm not going. Not until I see Celestine."

"Celestine's resting. Go back, Lilly."

I didn't think either of them had noticed me, but Lilly turned and looked straight at me.

"Sir, would you come?"

I looked from Lilly to Diane, who was clearly giving me a "no" signal. I wasn't feeling particularly inclined to be obedient.

"Sure. Why not?"

"It's not your place." That was Diane, trying to be friendly. "Michael, this is Society business. Let us handle it."

"Fuck you," I said, and nodded to Lilly. She studied me for a few seconds, then turned and walked away, and I followed her. I didn't hear footsteps behind me but I had no doubt that Diane was trailing me, watching. I hoped I was worrying her.

We went down one narrow hallway and into another, passed the vacant sitting room and entered a new hall I hadn't seen before. Three closed doors.

The fourth was open.

It took me a minute to remember who he was; I'd only seen him once, and briefly. He'd been huddled in a coat out by the pool on the first evening I was introduced to the Society.

"Jerry," Lilly said. Her voice was quiet and hollow.

Carl's companion. Jerry lay on his bed, eyes half-open. His arms were at his sides, hands loose. One palm was turned up, one down. He was naked except for a pair of red fleece sweat pants.

He looked like a marble statue. White. Sucked dry.

I bent over and touched my fingertips to his jugular to tell me what I already knew. No pulse. He was cold. When I tried to adjust his arm it resisted.

He'd been dead for hours.

His eyes were cloudy and blank. I tried to close the eyelids but rigor was too far advanced. I settled for pulling a fold of the sheet over his face.

On the other side of his neck were two huge gaping holes, ripped there by somebody who was too hungry to care about what he fed on. I touched the dry wounds and raised my head to find Diane standing across the bed, staring at me. Not at the body. At me.

"This is none of your business," she said. I looked around for Lilly, but she'd backed away into the hall. "Get out."

"Why? Something about this you don't want me to know? Like maybe the fact that one of you sucked him dry?"

"Get out," she almost screamed, and her eyes flushed red.

"Does Celestine know about this?"

Diane's hand flashed out and closed around my wrist, fingers like steel bars, nails like razors. She squeezed lightly with the nails. Just a warning.

"Go," she said again. I shrugged and stood up, and after one last tug she released me.

She slammed the door behind me, leaving me in the dark, quiet hallway with Lilly. Lilly leaned against the wood paneling, face averted.

"He was a good boy," she said, very softly. "A good boy."

She pushed herself upright and started walking away, back straight.

I followed her.

She stopped at a door that looked just like all the others. Just like mine. She didn't look back, but she put her palm flat against the wood.

"Celestine's room," she said, and then walked on. I watched her go out of sight around a corner, then turned the knob. It wasn't locked; I hadn't thought it would be. Celestine was so arrogant that it never occurred to her that anyone might not do exactly what she wanted.

She was sitting on her bed, legs curled underneath her. Her head turned toward me as I came in and closed the door behind me, and I saw her face clench for a second before she smoothed it out into a smile. Anger? Regret?

"Michael," she said. She didn't sound surprised. "How nice."

"There's a little problem down the hall."

Her head turned a little away from me. She shrugged. "Jerry's been ill."

"Not anymore."

She knew, all right. Knew and didn't care. She lifted her hand to tuck a strand of dark hair behind her ear, and her fingernails glistened like steel. I had to look away.

Right into the eyes of Carl Keenan, who'd come up next to me without a sound. I stumbled backward a step and turned to face him; he looked drugged and lazy and amused.

"Carl is going away." Celestine's voice was hard enough to strike sparks. "Aren't you, Carl?"

Carl's kindly-grandfather face smiled. What looked at me out of his eyes didn't.

"Yes."

Stuporous satisfaction, in those eyes. Dreamy lust.

"Sit down, Carl," Celestine commanded, and Carl glided over to a small armchair.

"What are you going to do about this?" I asked her bluntly. She drew idle patterns on the flowered bedspread with one fingertip. "Jerry's dead, Celestine. Killed. By one of your oh-so-noble Society members."

She didn't respond. I glared at Carl, and he laughed, a low rattling sound deep in his throat.

"I've been faithful," he said. His voice sonorous, hypnotic. "He was bled out, anyway. Dead in weeks. I just—indulged."

Celestine flinched, and her fingernails ripped into the bedspread. She was hard on the upholstery. I didn't have any trouble identifying the emotion that moved across her face.

Loathing.

"Sounds to me like your Society isn't any better than William," I said, and Celestine's head came up with a snap.

"Not true."

"Then you tell me something good about it. You treat Lilly like a slave. Jerry was just meat on the hoof. Carl here, he's a real prince, and Diane's in there acting like the fucking Phantom of the Opera. What do you want from me, Celestine? You want me to *like* what you are? Any of you?" I smiled through clenched teeth. "Little Marquee de Sade and her friends. You guys are pathetic."

"Enough," Celestine snapped. *"That's enough.* What do you know about it? Do you know where we came from, what we've survived? *We don't kill,* Michael."

"Yeah, Jerry's proof of that."

She stood up and crossed over to me in two steps, fastened her hands around my wrists as Diane had done down the hall. But somehow, even after what she'd done to me, I didn't feel threatened.

Maybe it was the blind concentration on her face, the yearning.

"I don't *want* to be like this," she whispered. *"I don't. None of us do, you must believe that."*

I felt her trembling. When I didn't say anything, she let go of me and stood there, head bowed, unmoving.

"Carl was wrong," she said. "He made a mistake. The Society will punish him."

"I'm scared," Carl said indifferently from the corner.

"They'll make a decision about whether to discontinue his membership. If they do—"

"They won't," he said. She shouted over him. *"If they do, he'll be killed."*

Carl didn't have a comeback for that one. When I glanced

at him, he was relaxed, eyes closed, head thrown back. A drunk.

I had the feeling that he wasn't too worried about the punishment of the Society.

"How many times has the Society withdrawn membership?" I asked. She shook her head. "How many?"

"I don't—"

"How many?"

Her silence was eloquent. Carl chuckled, a rumble of rocks in his throat.

"Never happened, Mike," he whispered. "Will never happen. You know why? 'Cause they're all afraid that once they kill, they'll *like* it. And killing your own kind—why, if they liked that, they'd have to face the fact that killing was fun."

"Stop," Celestine whispered. Carl shrugged and folded his arms over his chest. "It's not true."

"Don't matter," he said. "You'll never kill me."

Silence. Somewhere in the hall, boards creaked. Hearts beat. I wondered where Lilly was; she'd known Carl was here, that's why she hadn't stopped. She'd been smart not to.

"I'm going home," I said, and had my hand on the doorknob when Celestine spoke again.

"Where?" she asked. "After last night, Michael, where is home?"

I'd known it, but I hadn't *known* it, not until she put it into words. My stupid measly apartment, with its cable TV and green shag carpet and spare socks; that was gone. History. I could never, ever go back there.

I hadn't expected it to hurt so much.

"There is no home for us," she said to my back. "There's only each other."

"God help us," I said, and let the door click shut behind me.

Lilly was waiting just around the corner, pretending to straighten a picture. She rubbed her thumb over the gilt frame and avoided my eyes.

"You should go," she said. It was barely a whisper.

"Yeah, I'm thinking about that. What's going to happen to Jerry?"

"To the body?" She pushed the frame a little to the right, then the left, searching for some elusive balance point. "I don't know. When I go back, it will be gone."

"Has it happened before?"

She didn't answer.

"Often?"

A shrug.

"One every few years. Some die—quickly. Some not."

"Why not you?" I asked, and saw that she was crying, tears sliding silently down while she stared at the wall.

"I wish I knew," she said, and took a deep breath. "Will there be anything else, sir?"

I felt a sudden surge of rage for this place, for the vampires, lazy wolves among sheep-like humans. For myself, for allowing myself to be seduced and violated and sucked dry of everything that had made me feel human.

"Yes," I said. "I want to see Adam."

"You can't. He's locked up."

I reached out and touched her chin, turned it slightly toward me—not enough to make her fear I was trying to control her.

"Lilly, he's my friend. I have to try to help him. You have the key, don't you?"

I couldn't tell, from her impassive face, what went through her mind, but after a few seconds she reached in one pants pocket and brought out a small silver key. She turned it in her fingers, watching it catch the light.

"Jerry was my friend," she said, and held the key out to me.

I kissed her hand, very gently, and was startled to see her blush. I hadn't thought she was capable of it.

"He's in the room next to yours," she said, and pointed. "That way."

When I looked back, she was straightening the picture, right, then left.

She was still crying.

No one was in sight when I guided the key into the lock, turned the knob. The house was quiet.

There were no lights in Adam's room. The light from the hall made a soft yellow square on the heavy carpet, and it took a few seconds for me to begin to pick out shapes in the darkness. A heavy bed, too massive to be comfortable; a dresser that looked menacing with its bat-wing curves. A picture framed on the opposite wall, masked by the glare of the light on its glass.

The air stank of unwashed clothes and old blood.

"Adam?" I called. Something moved in the corner, a twitch of rags. He raised his head from the carpet, and his glasses flashed circles of yellow at me.

His face was chalk-white. He held up a hand to shut out the sight of the light, and I swung it partly closed. I found a lamp and switched it on.

He looked like an animal, crouching in the corner. He turned his head away as I came closer.

It was only then that I saw the chain they had around his wrists and ankles. Links heavy enough to hold a ship at anchor. He was secured to a thick ring set in the wall, and though it was bent a little, it was intact.

"Fucking *bitch*," I hissed, and was glad that Celestine wasn't there, because I would have cheerfully ripped her arms off. "Hang on, man, I'm going to get you out of here. It's going to be okay."

He didn't answer me. I touched his hand. Cold, cold skin. I remembered the night he'd brought me into The Life, blood flowing from his veins into my mouth, remembered his strength, dragging me back from death. I hadn't wanted to come.

I still wasn't sure it had been worth the trip.

Silence. The house shifted a little, like a nervous animal. I remembered the terror in Lilly's eyes, so carefully hidden. The Refuge was like a giant stomach, digesting us all slowly down to nothing.

"Adam?" I asked. He shifted a little, and his eyes glinted brown behind the glasses. Weary. Beaten.

"Sorry." The voice was a rusty scrape. His lungs creaked as they inflated again. "Sorry."

My turn to be sorry, for his lover Sylvia's death, for Adam's destruction, for bringing him into this hell. I couldn't even begin to say it, so I just sat, looking at him. His lips twitched in something that wasn't quite a smile.

"You look terrible," he said.

"I've had better weeks. Are you—okay?" What a stupid question. He blinked as if he thought so, too.

"William? I can't feel him now. I feel better." Adam's eyes blinked again, slowly, human-brown and dazed. "Did I dream it?"

"What?"

"The killing." He searched my face for his answer and closed his eyes against it. "I tried not to do it."

"I know," I said. I tried the key Lilly had given me in the manacles, but it didn't work. Seen closer, he looked even worse, bleached white and worn thin. "Rest. Everything'll be okay."

The silence was long, I don't know how long. There were no clocks, no heartbeats to measure by. After a while he opened his eyes and stared at the ceiling.

"I killed Dicky," he said. "And some others."

I touched his hand again, and this time he moved his fingers to touch mine. His chains clicked like dried bones.

"I've got to find the keys," I said, and gripped his hand tightly for a second. "Hang in there, buddy, I'll be back."

"You won't find them. They're going to starve me out."

"No! "I whispered. "No, I'll get you out. I'll take you home. I swear."

His head turned, just slightly, and for the first time I saw him smile. It looked forced and thin, but it was his smile, not William's, not the Society's.

"You can't solve everything," he said reasonably. Brown eyes steady. "I can't leave here yet, in any case."

The door creaked as it opened. I looked over my shoulder and saw Celestine standing there, and Carl. Paul and Diane behind them.

I looked away from her beautiful face, from the terrible sick feeling it gave me.

"Come away, Michael," her voice said. It sounded like she was right behind me, close enough to touch. To destroy. I closed my eyes.

A cool hand closed on mine, and when I looked I saw Adam, eyes narrowed, staring intently at me. He saw something in my face, something he didn't like. Maybe it was temptation.

He let me go, and I got up and walked toward the Society.

"Celestine." Adam spoke quietly, leaned against the wall and managed to look somehow as if it were a position he preferred instead of something they'd forced on him. She flinched at the sound of his voice. "I'll make you a promise."

"I'm not interested in your promises," she said, and held out her hand toward me. I was about to take it when Adam spoke again.

"If you hurt him again, I'll destroy you."

We all knew it was an empty threat. But the look on Celestine's face—guilt? Rage? Fear?

She dropped her hand to her side and clutched Carl's arm. He gave me a syrupy-rich smile, and led her away. Paul held out his hand for the key. I dropped it in his palm.

Adam held my gaze until the door closed between us.

Interlude:

Maggie

Maggie was numbed, by the time they left Joseph Vico's apartment complex. Not by the cold, she was past feeling that.

She had betrayed her partner, herself, everything she believed in. She'd found a storm drain and emptied the cold red plastic baggie into it, then thrown the baggie down. She'd torn the Polaroid to little black-backed bits and tossed it into the communal dumpster, where pieces had swirled like confetti and disappeared. She'd told Jody Lynn Whitfield and her brother not to say a word about her friendship with Joseph Vico, and that was suborning a witness.

She was still numb, and hot, and scared.

"Ready?"

McDonnell wasn't talking much. Still pissed. She nodded and got out of the car.

They were in the 'burbs. Big lawns in front and back. Neatly trimmed bushes. Brick houses built close enough together to rub walls.

The house they walked toward had early spring flowers frozen in the beds, and the brown grass was thick and neatly trimmed. The doormat said BLESS THIS HOUSE, and Maggie absently tapped her toe on it while McDonnell rang the doorbell.

Ellen Franischi was a small woman, 5'5" or under, built like a dancer. Her graying blond hair was held back in a simple ponytail, and she gave them a smile as she opened the screen door to let them in.

A sweet smile, Maggie thought. Lying bitch.

Cynicism was a wonderful thing.

"Mrs. Franischi, sorry to bother you—"

"Don't be ridiculous, detectives, I'm happy to see you again. Please, come in. I have some hot tea in the kitchen. Wouldn't you like some?"

"Well . . ." McDonnell shot a look toward Maggie, and she shrugged. "Sure. That sounds great."

The house was warm and pleasantly cluttered with crafts and handmade things, Maxfield Parrish prints in economical K-Mart frames. Bright-colored toys dotted the carpet like land mines. Three other children in the house, Maggie remembered. An older girl and two boys who were younger than LaDonna.

One of the two boys looked up from coloring as they came into the kitchen; he gave them a wary look and slid off his chair to hold up a drawing to Ellen. She studied it seriously and gave him a big hug. The drawing went on the refrigerator under a magnet that said JOEY'S BEST STUFF.

Joey gave Maggie another distrustful look and ran off into the living room. Ellen sighed and took down three mugs from hooks over the sink.

"He's very shy. A gifted boy, though. Really smart."

"I'm sure." He'd drawn a perfectly recognizable picture of a tyrannosaur gobbling up a man with a safari hat. "Mrs. Franischi—"

"Ellen."

"Ellen, we may have gotten new information about LaDonna's case. A friend of a teenager named Benito—everybody called him Two-Pack—said that Two-Pack was interested in LaDonna. Do you remember seeing anybody around her with that name?"

"I've already told you, I don't remember seeing anybody around her. She never said anything about it. She was a very talkative little girl, I can't imagine why she wouldn't have told me if something made her nervous or unhappy. Or happy, for that matter," Ellen said, and poured the tea. She took down a squeezable bottle of honey shaped like a bear. "She didn't say anything, and I didn't see anybody who shouldn't have been there."

She set a steaming cup down in front of Maggie, and delivered McDonnell's. The honey bear went in the center of the table as Ellen seated herself. The tea smelled faintly of oranges, and Maggie breathed deep to distract herself from a generally depressing feeling.

I'm not buying into this homey crap, she thought, and reached for the honey and stirred in a thin stream of gold.

"We brought a picture. Would you be willing to take a look?" McDonnell asked. Ellen shrugged.

"Why not? But I'm telling you, it won't do any good."

Maggie got the picture out of her purse and handed it over. It was a picture of Gerald. Ellen gave it a short look and handed it back.

"I've never seen him."

"How about this one?" She passed over a picture of Two-Pack, before his ventilation.

"Nope. Listen, I wish I could be of more help, I really do. It's just that—well—I've been through it, and through it, and there's just nothing else for me to remember, you know?"

Ellen looked earnest and disturbed. She looked at the photo of Two-Pack again. "I wish I *had* seen him. Maybe that would have helped. But I didn't."

Maggie accepted the picture back and tucked it in her purse, face-to-face with Gerald's. She hadn't expected anything else.

"Would you mind if we talk to the other kids for a few minutes, just to show them the pictures?" McDonnell was the right one to ask the question—respectful and warm and soothing. Ellen was nodding even before he finished asking.

"Well, Ben and Darla are at school, but maybe Joey—"

She left. Maggie sipped her tea. It was very good, warm and sweet and thick from the honey. She let it seep over her tongue and down her throat.

"I've never been able to shake the feeling that she's not being straight," McDonnell said quietly. He blew on his tea and took a sip, made a face and set the cup down. "You?"

"Yeah. But until now I never thought it was anything criminal. Baggies of pot in the underwear drawer, that kind of stuff."

"Now?" McDonnell asked. She shrugged and felt her shoulder muscles twinge with tension.

"I don't know."

Ellen came back, steering Joey with both hands on his shoulders. The corners of his lips had drawn down, and his eyes were wide and scared. Ellen boosted him up in her chair. He immediately reached for her tea and drank.

"Hi, Joey," Maggie said, and smiled at him. His lips twitched, but that was it. He looked to Ellen for a cue. "Joey, honey, there's nothing to be scared about. We're not going to hurt you. We just want to ask you a question, okay? It's an easy one. I'm going to show you pictures of two men, and you just tell me if you ever saw them before, either around LaDonna or around here, okay?"

" 'Kay," he murmured. Ellen patted him on the head and straightened his hair with expert little flicks of her fingers.

Maggie slid Two-Pack's picture over. Joey picked it up and stared at it.

He looked at Ellen. Then back at the picture.

"Have you ever seen him, Joey?" Maggie asked. He put the picture back down.

"No."

"Say, no, ma'am," Ellen prodded. Joey hung his head.

"No, ma'am."

"That's okay. Now here's the other picture."

It was the same routine. *No, ma'am.* But he looked at Ellen first. Maggie couldn't tell if she was giving him signals—might have been, under the table—but she didn't like the feel of it. She shuffled the pictures back together.

"Thanks, Joey, you've been great. Mrs. Franischi, can we see the other kids?"

"I guess you can come back after they get home."

"Darla and Ben go to a private school, don't they? Which one?" Maggie asked. Ellen looked surprised.

"Why do you want to know that?"

"Which one?"

"Uh—the Moon Lake School. It's over on Preston Road. But I really wish you wouldn't disturb them at school. It's been a very hard year for the children, and I'm trying to get their lives back to normal, as much as possible."

"We'll bear that in mind. Thanks for your time, Mrs. Franischi," Maggie said, and downed the last of her tea. McDonnell solemnly shook hands with Joey.

Outside, on the neat sidewalk, they exchanged a long look.

"Moon Lake School. I've never heard of it."

"LaDonna wasn't old enough for school."

"Let's go take a look. Just a little one."

McDonnell shrugged.

When she looked back, Maggie caught a glimpse of Joey, face pressed against the window, watching them go.

Moon Lake School had big, closed gates. It was in an exclusive section of Preston Road, heavy with bushes and fences and signs that said TRESPASSERS WILL BE PROSE-CUTED. There were no parking spaces.

McDonnell pulled into the driveway of a mansion down the block and stuck the revolving red light on the dashboard.

"Coming?"

"Sure," she said, and slid out. "I've never even walked through this neighborhood. Wouldn't miss it for the world."

What she could see through the bushes looked impressive—ivy-covered brick, fountains, lush grounds. The gates were very serious, at least fourteen feet high and topped with spikes that looked big enough to scare an elephant.

There was an intercom at the gate. McDonnell pressed the button.

A hiss announced the other end had been turned on.

"Yes?" someone asked.

"Moon Lake School?" he asked. There was a brief pause.

"May I ask who's calling?"

"Police. Open up."

"One moment, sir," the voice said, and the hiss stopped. McDonnell grinned at Maggie, and stuck his hands in his pockets. He took a deep breath and breathed out steam.

"This is getting better all the time," she said.

"You bet. Notice they're not cracking the gates."

"I hope they have a bathroom." She sighed, and rubbed her hands together. "I hope they let me use it."

"Maybe in the servant's quarters. Hey. Somebody's coming."

The gates buzzed and one of them swung open just about one foot. A woman in a green business suit squeezed through the opening. She looked like a magazine ad for corporate success, hair carefully cut, makeup perfectly done, body aerobicized to within an inch of its life. Sensible but stylish shoes that had probably cost a small fortune at a store whose name Maggie couldn't pronounce.

She studied McDonnell's shield carefully.

"May I help you, lieutenant?"

"Detective, ma'am. Detective McDonnell."

"I'm Christina Delfin. I'm the administrator of the school. And you are . . ." She gave Maggie a comprehensive, dismissing look. *Nobody,* the look said.

"Detective Bowman."

"How nice." A patronizing smile, displaying orthodontically perfect teeth. "Would you care to state your business?"

"I'd rather not state it out here on the street," McDonnell said, and gestured pointedly at the gate. Ms. Delfin smiled.

"I'd be more than happy to show you inside but we try to disrupt our classes as little as possible. Unless you have some kind of a warrant—"

The afternoon got very quiet. Ms. Delfin's smile faded, as if she sensed what Maggie was thinking.

She looked at McDonnell and saw it in his eyes, too.

"Now, why would you say a thing like that, Ms. Delfin?" he asked pleasantly. "A warrant? Is there some crime being committed?"

"Well—I assumed—" Ms. Delfin was aware she'd stepped in it, and couldn't think of a dignified way to shake it off her shoe. She decided on the I-Meant-That approach. Maggie gave her points for effort. "I think I'm perfectly within my rights to demand a warrant if you intend to intrude on private property. I hardly think it's out of line, as you seem to suggest."

"We'd like to talk to a couple of your students."

"I'd have to obtain permission from the parents before I could allow you to do that," Ms. Delfin said. Her teeth flashed in a smile. "I'm terribly sorry."

"Yeah, me, too," McDonnell said. He looked like he actually meant it. "We'll see you again, ma'am. Real soon."

Maggie touched an imaginary hat brim and followed McDonnell back down the sidewalk. Christina Delfin watched them until she was sure they were past the fence, then shut the gate.

"Friendly," Maggie said.

"You know," McDonnell said, rubbed his neck, "I think we should wait for Ben and Darla to come out. What do you think?"

"I think I need a bathroom."

Darla was tall for her age, with that olive-gold complexion that models go to expensive lengths to fake. Long black hair, crimp-waved. She came out of the gates holding Ben's hand—he was black, about eight years old, sweet-faced. She stopped suspiciously when she saw Maggie coming toward her and looked back as if she wanted to run back inside the gates.

"Darla? Darla, it's Maggie Bowman. We met before, last month, remember?"

"I remember," she said, and shifted from one foot to the other. "We need to catch our car pool."

"Why don't you come with me and my partner, and we'll drive you home? I just need to show you some pictures. It won't take long."

"I—I shouldn't—" Darla bit her lip. "Okay. I'll tell Mrs. Carson. Ben, you stay here with the lady."

Ben, coated and gloved and scarved half to death, waddled over and took Maggie's hand. Darla took two steps and looked back before running around the corner.

"How you doing, Ben?" Maggie asked. She squatted down to adjust his scarves.

"Okay." His big brown eyes studied her. "You're pretty."

"Why, thank you. That's nice of you to say so. How was school, Ben?"

"Okay."

"What did you do today?" She was watching the corner. Darla didn't reappear.

"Spelling. I got an A. And reading."

"What are you reading?"

"Suzy's Family."

Maggie made an absent uh-huh kind of sound. She kept scanning the corner for Darla.

"You're tryin' to find out who did things to LaDonna," Ben announced. She looked into his small face, and smiled.

"Yes, sweetie, yes, I am. You want to help me do that, don't you?"

His smile disappeared.

"We aren't supposed to talk to you," he said. She stared.

"Who said so?"

"Miss Delfin. And Miss Ellen. They said the police already know too much."

"Ben—"

No more time. Darla appeared at the comer. Three adults followed her; one of them was Christina Delfin.

Maggie stood up and locked gazes with the other woman, Ms. Corporate Poster Child. *I knew it,* she thought, and felt a fierce pulse of joy. I knew you were a lying bitch the minute I saw you.

"Problem?" she asked.

"Detective, you're pushing it. I told you, you're not welcome here."

"They're out of school."

"They're on school grounds. Benjamin, come here," Ms. Delfin ordered, and he waddled over to her with a guilty frown. "Ben, did she ask you any questions?"

"No, ma'am. Just about how school was, and stuff."

"Good. Darla, take your brother to the van and go home. Be sure to tell your mother what happened." Ms. Delfin stared at Maggie. "We are not at all happy with your conduct, Detective. How would you like me to make a formal complaint?"

Maggie reached in her coat pocket and found her shield. She held it out.

"Got a pen and paper? Wouldn't want you to get the number wrong."

Ms. Delfin didn't think it was funny. She gave Maggie a long glare and marched the other way, herding Darla and Ben before her. The other two adults stayed where they were, watching her.

"Can I help you, gentlemen?" Maggie asked them brightly.

"Turn around and walk away. You're trespassing."

"Want to see the inside of the jail for interfering with a police officer?"

A short but pregnant silence. The two men exchanged glances.

"We'll wait," the taller one said. The shorter one crossed

his arms. She lounged against the wall and watched to see
how long they'd stand there.

Ms. Delfin came back around the corner, out of breath.

"Where's your partner?" she demanded. Maggie gave her
an innocent look.

"Partner?"

"Damn it! See if he got inside. Find him and get him out
of there."

A horn honked from the next block down. Maggie turned
and glanced over her shoulder.

"No need, there he is. Well, thanks, folks. It's been real
interesting." She turned her back on them and walked back
to where McDonnell had the car idling.

"Happy bunch," he commented when she slid inside and
shut the door. She fumbled with the seat belt.

"Absolutely. You get a look inside?"

"Looks like a school. Smells like a cult."

"Anything specific?"

"I saw a nice little book for the upper grades called *The
Family's Way.* Whatever they're teaching in there, it doesn't
look like a state-approved curriculum."

"So what do you want to do?" she asked. McDonnell
sighed.

"Win the lottery. Find Joseph Vico. Close the file on
LaDonna Bedford." He eased the car into gear and checked
over his shoulder for traffic. "You up for a little stakeout?"

It was, she thought, a poor choice of words.

"Not tonight, dear. I have a headache." She was only half-
kidding; she was exhausted, her back ached like she been
carrying a fifty-pound load, and her feet felt twice their normal size. "Tomorrow. I promise."

She leaned her head back against the headrest and let the
motion of the car lull her into a light doze.

Silence.

"Hey. Sleepyhead." Someone tapped her on the shoulder, not too lightly. She fumbled her way out of the dark. "Sorry. We're here."

"Shit." She started to rub her eyes and remembered her mascara in time. "Man, I'm really beat."

McDonnell looked tired, too—face too lined, eyes too red. He shrugged.

"Go in, take a shower, relax. I'll pick you up at seven in the morning." She groaned. "Cheer up. I'll let you sleep first in the car."

"Oh, what a treat," she sighed. "See you."

There was no one waiting for her by the door, no Michael, no insurance guy, nobody. She couldn't find her keys; they'd slipped to the bottom of her purse.

Tired, she thought. *Way too tired, and scared.*

She dropped the keys and had to grub around in the icy dirt to get them.

Her door whispered open, welcoming her home. *Shower,* she thought. *Nap.*

She dropped her stuff on the couch and shed clothes on the way to the bathroom.

Sleep crawled on her as she lay face-down on the bed, dressed in thick warm sweats. She had to set the alarm, because McDonnell would show up early and she'd still be asleep, and there was nothing more embarrassing . . .

She was with Michael. It was a warm day, and the sun was out, and she was kissing him. He laughed at something she said.

"You're in danger," she tried to tell him, but he didn't hear her. He undid the buttons on her shirt, but they kept somehow hooking back together, so he had to keep coming back to the top. "Mike, please listen, you shouldn't be here."

He was still laughing at her. She reached out to touch him and his skin started to smoke. *Sunlight,* she thought, and screamed. He burst into flame, still laughing.

She came awake with her heart pounding hard in her ears. Her hair was still damp.

Quiet. Dark.

Had she slept that long? She squinted at the clock, and it said twenty past midnight. Even McDonnell didn't show up *this* early.

Her heart was still pounding, too hard. She laid back down on the bed and tried to take deep, slow breaths. Nothing to fear. Everything was under control.

She thought it was part of the dream, at first. A white face, glowing where it picked up the reflected moonlight. It sat in the corner, staring at her.

A woman's face, not Michael's. A woman's face with dark hair around it.

Her eyes looked red.

I'm dreaming, she thought helplessly. *Got to wake up.*

The woman stood up and glided toward her through the dark. Quick. Graceful.

As the cold fingers touched her face, it occurred to Maggie at last that it wasn't a dream at all.

It was too late to scream.

Ten

Choices

The Refuge was a cage. For me, for Adam, for the human companions. Maybe even for the Society vampires.

I hated cages. I stared at the darkness outside of my window and thought about taking a diving run through the glass. Could they catch me?

Yeah. Probably.

"Want something to read?" Paul sat near my door, feet up, looking insultingly at home. He was leafing through a magazine; I couldn't be sure, but it looked like *People*. "No sense in just sitting."

I didn't say anything. He had an accent straight out of Vermont, fall-crisp and broad as a freeway. I wondered if it was his natural speech, or something he'd put on just for my amusement.

Pages rustled. Apart from that, the house was quiet. It was mid-evening, at least so far as I was concerned; I'd heard a clock strike a sonorous one about twenty minutes before. I'd heard a car outside, leaving and returning.

That was the excitement for the evening. That, and Paul.

"Go to the movies much, Michael?" he asked. The accent

was thick as paste. Fake, I decided. He was trying out a new one.

"No."

"Wondered if you'd seen this one. Looks interesting." Paul chuckled. "I haven't been to a movie in, oh, twenty years. Life's been passing me by, hasn't it?"

I stared out the window and waited for some plan, *any* plan, to spring to my mind like Superman to the rescue.

"What were you before?" he asked me.

"Before what?"

"Before."

I glanced over at him and saw him leaning forward, watching me.

"A surgeon," I answered. He raised his eyebrows.

"Can't go back to that. Too bad." He lost interest in me and went back to his magazine. "Got plans for anything else?"

"I think I'll be a lifeguard," I said. He looked at me warily, as if he wasn't sure it was a joke.

"You ought to consider the Society, friend. We can help you. We want to."

"Yeah, right," I sighed. He shrugged. "How's Ciaran?"

He was surprised by the question. "Fine. Why wouldn't she be?"

"I just thought having Jerry sucked dry might have disturbed her a little bit. Made her think."

"Ciaran knows how things work."

"Do you?" I asked, and for just a second I saw a flicker of doubt in his eyes.

He opened his mouth to return the volley, but turned his head and looked at the door a second before the knock came. He twisted the knob and looked through the gap before opening it.

Diane looked us over; I didn't like the wet glitter in her eyes.

"We're in the library," she said, and walked out. Paul put his magazine aside and stood up. He looked at me expectantly.

"Coming?"

"Do I have a choice?"

"No." He smiled, sharp-edged. I thought about making them drag me, but I figured that was more like a temper tantrum than legitimate resistance. I got up and followed him out.

Narrow dark hallways, light fixtures cream-yellow with age. He took me through the dining room—the skeletal candelabra bristled protectively on the table—and past it into the library.

It was a big room, too big to take in all at once; books in rising concentric circles, a staircase that spiraled up into the dark like a beanstalk into giantland, a feeling of age and disuse. The carpet under my feet was a faded Persian that puffed invisible dust into the air where I stepped. The lights were dimmed to a comfortable, shadowy glimmer.

Celestine curled catlike on a big red velvet couch. Diane, stood behind her, arms folded. Carl, with the devil laughing behind his eyes, sat in a wing chair nearest the door.

And Adam stood facing them. They'd allowed him a bath and clean clothes, at least, and there weren't any scars from the manacles. But then, there wouldn't be, on the outside. Only on the inside.

Adam's eyes fixed on me, and when Paul stepped past me to go sit beside Celestine on the couch, it left me in the no-man's-land between Adam and the others. Prisoner, and jailers.

I leaned against the wall near him.

I heard Lilly's breathing and looked up to see her standing in the doorway, staring at me. Her eyes were wide, and I had the feeling she wanted to tell me something.

"Lilly." Celestine's voice was a whip crack. "Close the door, please."

Lilly averted her eyes, stepped back out of the room, and pulled the sliding doors shut. The click of the lock engaging sounded sharp and clear as a gunshot.

Silence. Celestine stared vaguely in our direction. She was smiling a little, and it might even have been a sad smile.

"Well," she said. "Nice to have you both here with us."

Adam and I exchanged a look. No time for strategy; we both knew there wasn't any that would be successful. He was weak, and I was young, and they had us outnumbered. So we waited.

"It's been a long time, Adam," she continued. His shoulders tightened.

"Not long enough."

"And I thought you'd be grateful. If it weren't for us, you'd still be following William like a puppy on a leash." Her smile turned cruel. "Of course, it may be that you prefer that."

Silence. He wasn't going to let her bait him. She swung her attention to me.

"You haven't been a very gracious guest, Michael. Adam, I can understand. He has a history of being—well—difficult. But you . . . I had such hopes for you."

I took a cue from Adam. The silence got uncomfortable.

"Can't we be civilized?" she asked. "Have a reasonable discussion?"

"About what?" Adam's voice sounded surprisingly normal. "I called on you *four months ago,* Celestine. Where were you?"

"I was busy. I came as soon as I could."

He shook his head. His hands clenched at his sides.

"You've been here," he said. "You've been watching. What were you waiting for? Him to kill me?"

"I was waiting," she replied smoothly, "for the opportunity to help you. It only came last night. Be that as it may, Adam, this situation is entirely of your making. You're the one who chose to leave the Society and live wild. You're the one who chose to interfere with William and attract his interest."

Adam took a step or two in the direction of the door. I wasn't surprised when Carl Keenan rose to stand in his way.

"I didn't have any choice," Adam said, still staring at Carl. Carl smiled. "He was killing my friends. I had to try to stop him."

"Friends." Celestine made an elegant, silent-movie gesture of disgust. *"We're* your friends."

"Get to the point." Adam turned back to face her, and she smiled at nothing, blind eyes staring past him.

"All right. The point is, Adam, that we're willing to help you, for a price. The price is that you become a useful member of the Society." Her smile disappeared. "There is an alternative, of course."

"Of course." He walked back toward me and took a leaning position against the wall next to me. "There always is."

He didn't say anything. Celestine's lips parted, and I saw the white glint of fangs.

"It's very simple. If you don't agree, we make certain that neither of you leaves this room."

I looked at Carl Keenan, his lazy lusting eyes; at Diane, whose expression was frozen in a hard mask of hate. Paul alone seemed disturbed—just a little.

When Adam didn't answer, Celestine lifted a hand and gestured. Diane slid the door aside and left the room.

"Now what?" Adam asked. She shrugged.

"Now you choose the alternative."

"Thanks," he said. "No."

"You're endangering all of us," Carl said. Adam turned his head to look at him, and his smile was bitter.

"Am I? I remember you. Weren't you the one who killed three children in Boise in 1964? Was that making the world safe for vampires? Have they been telling you their little religious dogma? It's bad to kill. Evil. But it's good to raise children for no other purpose than to suck them dry, year after year, until they waste away." Adam's smile revealed fangs, this time. "How long did your last one survive, Carl? Four years? Five?"

"I don't see that my personal affairs are any of your business."

"Five years at the most, dying slowly. Rotting. And then, when there's nothing more to be gotten, you throw them away like yesterday's chicken bones and go harvest a new one from your foster homes. You disgust me."

"Carl has killed one human in five years. How many do you have to your credit, Adam?" Celestine spoke, unerringly slicing for the jugular.

"It's not to my credit," he snapped. "At least I didn't torture mine before I killed."

"That's insulting! Untrue!" Carl shouted. He came out of his chair, and Adam glided toward him, taller and thinner and as dangerous as any vampire I had ever seen, except for William.

"Boys," Celestine said, clear as a drawn sword. "Sit."

Carl did. Adam paced.

"These distinctions are meaningless, because I don't intend to go through this debate with you again, Adam. The Society is what it is, and we do what we do, and we're happy with it. We are *not* happy with you and your kind, living wild in the streets like dogs scrounging at the dump. You have a choice to make."

"I've made mine," Adam said.

"I've made yours for you. A family has been established for you here in Dallas. You're going to join the Society."

"No."

"I'm not offering you a *choice*," Celestine said, and stood. The others stood, too. Adam stopped where he was, a white shadow touched by the yellowish lights. His eyes glittered like sparks.

"No," he said. "I see that."

The door slid back with a metallic grinding sound. Diane returned, holding the arm of a girl who couldn't have been a day over eighteen, not even legal enough to order a beer. She was pretty, dark-haired, dark-eyed. She looked nervous as she looked us all over.

"Adam, this is Janine. Janine has asked to be your companion," Celestine said. Adam shook his head in mute stubbornness.

Diane pointed at Adam and nudged Janine. The girl smiled a little shakily and let go of Diane's arm to walk to Adam. She held out her hand to him.

He turned his back on her and walked over to where Celestine sat, went on one knee facing her.

"Don't," he said. It was so soft that I could hardly hear him, and knew none of the others could. "Please, Celestine, you know what this means. I can't. Don't make me do this."

"It's your choice, Adam. Life or death," she said, and withdrew her hand. "She's a very sweet child. You'll like her."

"I don't want to like her."

"Then you don't have to. You simply have to use her."

He kept staring at her, face tight and giving nothing away.

He got up and came back to where Janine stood, waiting. She tried a smile again, but it faded away when he didn't smile back.

"Michael," he said, turning his head slightly in my direction. I took a step forward. "I'm sorry for this."

He reached out and took the girl's hand, drew her forward into his embrace. She melted against him, awkward and unsure but welcoming; she was tall enough to reach to his shoulder, and she brought up her hand to brush his auburn hair back from his face. He held on to her for what seemed a minute or more, and then tilted her head up.

Celestine made a sound deep in her throat, hunger or satisfaction or lust. The others were as still as statues, but their eyes glittered with excitement and desperation.

Adam jerked the girl's head up and back. A sound like cracking sticks echoed in the quiet room, and she made a sound like a sigh, and went limp in his arms.

Adam slowly lowered the girl to the floor and straightened her head to a lifelike angle. Her eyes were still open, dark and gently surprised. He closed them and sat down next to the body.

Maybe I was the only one who saw the agony in his face.

"I'll kill every one you bring me," he said in a voice so low it sounded like the random hiss of the fire. "Every one, until you let me go."

"You're mad," Celestine said. She sounded shaken. "You killed her in cold blood."

"It's all I have," Adam answered, and looked down at his open hands. "Cold blood."

"Do you think destroying yourself has accomplished something?"

"No," he whispered. "Not yet."

Celestine gestured again, and Diane left the room. I felt a chill settle over me.

"Perhaps Michael will be more reasonable," she said, and I heard footsteps approaching. Diane. Holding the arm of another woman, this one blond, blue-eyed—

Maggie.

Interlude:

Maggie

Whatever they were doing to her, it *hurt*. The feeling of invasion was unbearable, nauseating; she fought to say *get your fucking hands off of me,* but all she could do was wait. She was walking along, out of control. A passenger. The woman—no, the *vampire* woman—had her arm in a grip like steel, but even if she hadn't Maggie knew she couldn't have resisted. Drugged? Had they drugged her? Was this how it felt—

She felt a scream bubbling up inside, like blood. *Jesus, Jesus, Jesus, please, Mike—*

He wasn't here. She knew he wasn't here. He wouldn't have let this happen.

An open doorway spilled dim light out on the faded carpet. Maggie stopped—or was allowed to stop—and tried to take in what she saw.

Michael, standing frozen a few feet away. Adam, sitting on the floor next to a young woman who was lying too still to be alive. More of them, three more.

Michael. His face went from blank to shocked to absolute fury in the space of a heartbeat. He lunged forward, and the woman holding Maggie's arm gripped it tighter and said, very clearly, "I'll break her arm if you try."

He stopped where he was. Maggie stared at him, helpless to say a word, and watched him struggle with his anger.

"Welcome, Margaret." That was the other woman, the dark-haired one on the couch. Her eyes looked strange, but it might have simply been due to the low lights. "I've heard a lot about you."

She patted the velvet sofa next to her. Maggie took a step forward—still fighting—and sat down between the woman and a chubby-looking man wearing wire-rimmed glasses.

She wanted to scream. Her heart was hammering in her ears, deafeningly loud. They knew she was scared.

They all knew.

Adam raised his head and looked at her, then at the woman beside her on the couch. His eyes had taken on a reddish luster.

"Stop it," he whispered huskily. "Don't do this."

"Do what?" The woman smiled and showed fangs. They gleamed in the dim light like smooth strange jewelry. "Margaret, my name is Celestine Vaughn. These are my friends—Diane you've already met, I think. That's Carl, and this is Paul." She ignored the presence of Adam and Michael. "And you are Mrs. Michael Bowman. I'm so pleased to make your acquaintance."

"Celestine, let her go," Michael said. Maggie tried to get her breath, to tell him it was okay, but she couldn't force a sound out through whatever it was that held her. The other woman continued to smile, and laid a hand lightly on her shoulder. Steel-hard fingernails touched the skin of her throat, and she shivered. That was all she could do, shiver and scream inside. "I'll fucking kill you if you hurt her."

"Your husband loves you very much." Celestine's voice

was a whisper of air next to her ear, too close. The hand at her throat felt as cold as a corpse's. "You realize what kind of danger that puts you in, don't you?"

Like William, Maggie thought. *Playing with her food.* She fought to slow down her breathing, the panicked thudding of her heart.

"If he doesn't kill you," Adam said, "I will. Let her go. She's not part of this."

"She's very much part of this," the woman corrected. Nails scraped lightly over Maggie's skin, around to the back of her neck. She was watching Mike's face and saw him flinch. "Such an amazing turn of events. The rest of us have had to adopt our families, or use children from our foster homes. Michael is so lucky to already have a family of his very own."

The only thought that came to Maggie's mind was *The baby not the baby.*

She heard Adam make a sound that was not quite a hiss, not quite a scream. Not a human sound at all, but thick with rage.

"Well, she *is* his wife, isn't she? His companion for life. For the remainder of *her* life, anyway." Celestine's voice had turned cruel, and Maggie felt bright hot spots of pain as nails dug into her skin. "Stop, Michael. If you move again I'll kill her."

"So much for all your preaching," Michael said. His voice sounded as if it had been flayed. "You're just a killer. Just like William."

Celestine smiled, or snarled.

"No," she said. "No, I'm afraid I'm much more dedicated."

The pressure went nuclear inside Maggie's head, expanding, tunneling, destroying. She went rigid and knew that in a matter of seconds it would all be over, all dark.

God, she hated losing.

Her vision had dissolved to sparkles when she felt something happen, threads snapping in her head, a twinge like a muscle spasming. The pressure—disappeared.

She jerked, and her body moved with her.

Now that she was able to blink again, and move her head, she found she was looking at Adam. He was staring at her with an intensity she found strangely comforting.

"You can get up," he said, and she felt strength rushing back into her legs. "I won't let her stop you."

"Stop interfering," Celestine snapped, and Maggie felt something brush cold against her mind like wet spiderwebs.

Again, the threads snapped, and this time they felt whippy and lashlike. It was Celestine's turn to flinch, and Maggie gasped for air that tasted old and chilled and found her hands pressed tight against her head, as if she could keep everything out that way. Her stomach lurched, and she swallowed hard to hold down a bitter rush of churning coffee.

"Maggie," Adam said, and she looked up at his face, the compassion in his eyes. "Get up. She can't stop you."

That was fine for him to say. He didn't have fingernails like steak knives pressing into his neck.

And then Michael reached out a hand to her.

It was one of the hardest things she'd ever done, but she leaned forward and felt his fingers close over hers; his strength pulled her up and then she was in his arms, and she didn't care that he was cold, didn't care at all.

The back of her neck felt frostbitten.

It took a minute or so of shuddering for her to feel in control again, ready to push away from Mike and stand on her own. He didn't want to let her go; she saw it in his eyes, and squeezed his hand to let him know she felt the same.

But apart, they could fight.

"Who the *fuck* do you think you are?" she asked; she'd been waiting for more than an hour to say it. Just hearing her own voice steadied her. Adam's head turned slightly toward her, though he kept his eyes on Celestine.

"This," Adam said, "is the Society. Don't be too impressed."

"Yeah, well, don't worry, I'm not." The girl, on the floor. Dead. *I can't deal with it,* she thought. *I can't deal with anything but staying alive.*

Oh, God, it was just a kid. She glanced at Michael and saw that he was scared to death, scared to have her in the way. She worked hard to keep the fear out of her voice.

"My partner is going to pick me up soon at my apartment. When he gets there and I'm gone, things are going to get ugly."

"That's hardly a problem," Celestine smiled. "I'm not worried about the police."

Maggie cast a significant look toward the dead girl.

"You should be. Your little vampire suburb is going to set up residence in a six-by-nine cell. With morning exposure." Maggie was still trembling, but she clenched her fists to hide it. "I'm going to make sure you get a nice even tan."

"I've been here in this city for nearly twenty years, Margaret. Why ever would I worry about the police?" Celestine raked her fingernails casually over the sofa arm, with a sound like Velcro ripping. Her eyes were milky-white. Maggie could just barely see the outline of pale blue, long faded, and the brownish dots of iris.

Her fear disappeared, because now instead of the all-powerful vampire she just saw a cockroach like the ones she hunted for a living. An arrogant cockroach.

Celestine had given her the last pieces herself—the foster homes, the families. Time to tell her what she'd done.

"Because I'm going to see that you fry, you bitch. But mostly because I know about the Franischi house. And the Moon Lake School."

Celestine's eyes widened. Color misted into the white irises like red fog, swirled and grew bright.

Diane and Paul and Carl got to their feet. Their eyes were shining, now. Red stars in the dark.

"You've been busy," Celestine murmured. "Too busy, little girl. What else have you been digging in?"

"LaDonna Bedford. You killed her because she was talking about your little Society."

Celestine's face closed up for a few seconds, became the face of a corpse with wide, wild eyes. Then she smiled, and Maggie thought, *she's still a corpse.*

"No, we didn't. We just didn't stop it from happening. It's not the normal course of events, I assure you; if one of the children shows—bad judgment—we simply change their memories and put them back in the foster care system your own people have so excellently designed. We don't keep any children who don't display the right characteristics."

"Like obedience? So they'll sit up and beg when you want them to?" Maggie was glad she still had the anger, glad that it poured out in an angry rush. "That's your great Society? Your little cults of slaves? God, I don't have to arrest you. You're too stupid to survive."

"Mind your manners," Celestine whispered, and flicked a finger at Paul. "Bring her here."

Paul stood up and took a couple of steps forward; Michael

stepped in the way, and she found herself stepping back from what she saw on his face. Paul paused, too.

"I *want* her," Celestine hissed, and the hesitation went out of Paul's face. Diane started forward, too.

Goddamn it, she didn't even have a *gun*.

In the sudden hush, Adam stood up. Maggie thought he would go to Mike's defense, but he moved like a haze of mist, a smear of color that suddenly was behind the couch. White hands closed around Celestine's throat and lifted.

She flailed wildly, choking. Her fingernails slashed wildly at the velvet and opened white wounds that poured cotton stuffing.

His face was tight and anguished, but his eyes were very bright.

"Mind your manners," he told Celestine, and shook her like a rat. Diane and Carl started closing on him, and he squeezed tighter, and Celestine made horrible gagging sounds. "Don't. You know I'll cheerfully rip her head off, and won't that be a mess. Back away."

Paul lunged forward, reaching for Maggie's arm; she knew she couldn't move fast enough to avoid him, but before she'd even tried Michael had come between them. His hand closed around Paul's wrist and slammed him to the floor. The fight was a blur, white skin, fangs, red eyes.

Diane started circling slowly toward Maggie, a wolf picking out the undefended sheep. *Fuck this,* Maggie thought. Instinct had always been her best friend; she let it guide her now, let it catapult her in a shoulder roll across the floor toward a spindly-looking antique table no longer than her arm. As her hand closed around it, Diane appeared over her, fangs fully extended, eyes burning red.

Maggie swung the table. Diane was fast, *real* fast, but

Maggie hadn't intended to hit her. The table hit the wall and splintered in a spray of wood.

The end she held had a jagged wooden leg on it.

Diane started to move on her, stopped when Maggie brought the makeshift stake up to chest level.

"All right," she panted. "Now we're even."

Diane hissed at her and Maggie felt a cold touch in her mind, but she shut it out, looked away, kept the stake between herself and disaster.

Celestine stopped struggling. Adam lowered her back to a sitting position on the couch; Carl hadn't moved from where he stood, and Paul was just shaking off the blow that had landed him on the floor.

"Now," Adam said softly. "Let's be friends. Celestine, you're going to let us leave now."

Fat chance. Maggie thought, and from down the hall heard the cold clear sound of a scream. Carl turned toward the sound. Adam's eyes went blank.

"That was Ciaran," Paul whispered, and clawed his way up to his feet. "Ciaran!"

"She's dead," Carl said. It didn't stop Paul; he slammed the sliding door back with a screech of metal and disappeared into the hall.

For a few seconds there was no sound at all except for Maggie's quick breathing, and then there was the sound of glass breaking, wood snapping. Voices cried out.

"He's here," Diane whispered. "Oh my God, he's in the house."

"Adam!" Mike said urgently. "Adam, let's go. Come on."

And, ever so slowly, Adam's eyes turned the color of dried blood, then fresh blood. Celestine lifted her head to look at him, and her expression was bitter and terrified.

"I'm sorry," he said. "I never really had a choice."

The door slid open with a long grating groan.

Something crawled over the threshold, dragging its legs uselessly behind it. Firelight glittered on smashed glasses as it raised its blood-smeared face.

"Paul," Carl said, and took a step forward.

There was a smell in the room now, old blood and decomposing flesh; Maggie coughed and felt Michael's arms go around her, holding her tight.

The thing Carl had named Paul crawled a few more feet and laid quivering on the carpet.

"Help him!" Diane screamed. Carl hurried over and reached down to take Paul's hand.

Paul's hand snapped out and fastened around Carl's wrist with unbelievable speed, yanked hard. Carl tumbled, off-balance but already twisting to regain it.

Too late. The smashed glasses tumbled off the face. The eyes were wide, ice-blue, void.

William rolled over on top of Carl and pinned him down while he raised his other hand, and the stake he held in it.

He stabbed Carl through the heart.

"Carl!" Diane screamed, and was almost drowned out by the sound of blood jetting, flesh tearing. William tore open Carl's throat and began to noisily feed.

Maggie felt herself get weak and had to cling to Mike for support. This wasn't real, couldn't be real. The way he moved—the way he—

It was all just a blur. Eyes like frosted ice, and a cold creeping over her that she couldn't shake away. Mike, falling away from her, knocked away into the darkness. She saw him get to his knees to come to her and there was a white shadow between them, grinning.

Nothing between her and death, now. Nothing but the piece of wood in her hand.

She lunged. William stepped out of her way and put his arms around her from behind, and it was like being in a grave, cold and damp and rotting, and dark, so dark, so dark.

It hurt. Oh, God, it hurt so bad.

Eleven

Wounds

I was dreaming of death. It was dark, and painful, and it didn't go away. Something brushed over my face that smelled like dust.

Someone was moving out there in the dark; I felt the vibrations through my back, like ripples in a pool. I couldn't hear anything.

The thing over my face dragged free, leaving a film of dust over my lips and tongue. I wanted to swallow and couldn't. My eyes were shut and I couldn't make them open.

Death was pain, and the pain went on forever. It burned at me, hotter and hotter until there was no place to hide, no place to go. In a second I would be gone, a spark snuffed out in the dark.

The pain reached its peak and dimmed. Cooled. It ceased to be the universe and became only nine-tenths of it.

My eyelids fluttered like nervous moths and flew open.

There was light, ghostly, coming from the open window. No, the *shattered* window; jags of glass stabbed in toward the center, held tight in the splintered frame. The curtains billowed over my face like the touch of ghosts.

I slowly, slowly rolled over on my side.

Maggie lay within touching distance, curled toward me. Hair spilled over her face in a tangled golden stream, and sight of her face through the veil first comforted and then frightened me.

Dead. Oh God no, no, please—

A breath puffed out of her mouth and disturbed a few strands of hair. Her eyelids flickered.

I crawled toward her, every muscle on fire, and a shadow fell over her face, and over mine.

"No!" Adam whispered, and crouched down next to me. He reached out to smooth Maggie's hair back from her face and realized what I already had. "She's alive."

And then he stopped, eyes riveted. I sat up and, from that height, saw what he did.

A livid bruise on her neck.

Two punctures.

Wounds running thin red.

My first lungful of air came out in a rush, just sound. Adam's hand braced me, or I would have fallen over. I was careful as I gathered her in my arms; she felt cold and fragile, and I couldn't warm her. Her head rested on my shoulder and the puff of her breath whispered on my collarbone.

She was still alive. I held on to that like I clung to her, and thanked William, thanked him, for this one small mercy.

If it was a mercy. It wasn't like him to give that kind of thing.

For the first time, I looked at Adam; he looked as drained as Maggie, and there were burns on his hands that could only have come from wood. No wounds; he'd healed.

Celestine was gone. Diane had run, of course; she was a coward at heart. Paul and Carl were both dead, heaped on the carpet along with the poor undisturbed corpse of the girl named Janine.

Just Adam and me, and Maggie.

"Where—" I couldn't even finish the question. He read it in my face.

"Gone. It's nearly sunrise." His voice, like mine, was thin as thread. "He's had his fill tonight."

He smoothed Maggie's hair again, comforting himself and her. The wounds on her neck—raw, horrible, invading. I felt rage well up again and swallowed it. No time now.

The sky outside was blue-gray, and I was tired.

"Have to get her home," Adam's voice scratched, and he stood up. His hand pulled me up, too, and I settled Maggie in my arms. She slept, but I heard her mumble something that might have been my name.

I stepped over Carl's body and tried not to notice what had been done to him. Adam led me into the hall and almost lost his balance; he caught himself with a hand flat against the wall.

"Is there anyone else?" I asked. He didn't answer me. "Lilly?"

I didn't expect him to answer, and he didn't.

Lilly did.

She came out of the dining room and stared at us in dull shock; her black shirt and pants were smeared with dust, and I wondered where she'd found to hide during the long night. She would've seen it all by now, I supposed. More than I had.

"We've got to get her home," Adam repeated. I shook my head. "We have to," he said. "She's lost too much blood. She needs a hospital."

"No," I said. "No, he'll find her—"

Adam's hand closed over mine, crushingly strong. His eyes were wide.

"He'll find her *here*, Mike. Send her home."

I didn't want to give her up but the sun was spinning closer and Lilly came out of her daze enough to find the keys to one of the cars; I carried my wife out to a big gray Lincoln and laid her gently on cold velour that reminded me of caskets. Her color was ashy.

Adam leaned in the driver's side window to lock eyes with Lilly.

"Don't take her all the way home. Get to a pay phone and call a cab for her, put her in it. Her partner is going to be waiting at her house. He'll take care of her from there. If the cabby asks, say you found her wandering on the street."

I'd forgotten about her partner. She'd said he would be waiting.

I touched her cheek one more time; it was cool enough to be my skin. Her eyelids fluttered, and I saw a quick glint of blue. She murmured my name.

Lilly started the car. Adam tugged me toward the house, and the sunrise bathed the east in party colors.

I collapsed in the hallway, and knew I couldn't get up again. My lungs were full of water, my muscles turned to lead.

A line of morning sunlight crept across the carpet toward me.

Adam's hands tugged under my arms, and I watched the sunlight recede past my shoes. Into the darkness.

I never even heard him shut the door.

Interlude:

Andy McDonnell

The drive was a blur of cars that looked too shiny and brake lights that drilled into his skull like lasers. It felt like a hangover, but he hadn't deserved it; his good night's sleep had dissolved into dreams that woke him every five minutes, and half of them had to do with Maggie.

Why the hell would he dream about Maggie's dead husband?

Right turn, left, left. Lights. An automatic reaction, stop for red, go for green. Hit the gas for yellow. He took another left and looked around, blinking, suddenly wide awake.

Maggie's apartment complex. The autopilot controls still worked.

Another cold morning, and the wind had an edge like a papercut. He pounded on Maggie's door and waited, shuffling his feet, for her to let him in.

A woman came out of an apartment six doors down, wrapped in scarves and a coat with more colors than the rainbow. She started her car and left it running, hurried back up the walk and slammed the door.

He thought about going over and trying the car door, just

to see if she'd been stupid, but it was too cold and he was too tired. It was too cold for car thieves.

Maybe she hadn't heard him. He knocked again and shoved his gloved hands in his coat pockets. A big pot of coffee, that was what he needed. Maggie was the right one to come to for that.

There was no sound from her apartment. He felt the back of his neck prickle and tried the knob. Locked.

Her car was still sitting innocently in the parking lot. He went around to the side, but she'd drawn all of her curtains. Nothing to do but knock again.

He was considering kicking the door in when he heard the lock turning, and the door swung open to let him in. It was dark inside, and it was a couple of seconds before he noticed anything really wrong; the way she clung to the back of the couch, the dazed look in her eyes.

He caught her just before her knees let go.

He found a thick blanket in the closet that looked like cotton candy; he wrapped her up in it, and her face looked hollow and old in the middle of pink fluff. She hadn't said a word, and neither had he. He reached out for the phone and pulled it across the coffee table to his side and dialed 911.

She sat huddled in the blanket, and didn't look at him. There was a darkening bruise along her left cheekbone, and her hair was tangled and dull. The rest of her was invisible in the cotton candy.

"You okay, kid?" he asked. She looked past him, and he felt his heart clench in his chest. *Somebody's been here,* he thought, and tried not to think of the word *rape.* "Come on, Maggie, you're scaring me. Say something."

"I'm okay." It didn't sound like her—lifeless, shell-shocked. She blinked and met his gaze. "It's been kind of a long night, that's all."

Hollow. It was like dropping a rock into a well and never hearing the splash.

"Sounds like a pretty good story," he said, and tried to smile. "Let's hear it."

She rocked a little, back and forth. The couch springs squeaked like fingernails on a blackboard.

"I don't know where to start," she said. Not stalling, he thought. Confused. "Where do you want me to start?"

"I dropped you off last night. What did you do then?"

"I took a shower. I fell asleep on the bed and when I woke up there was a woman in my bedroom."

"What woman?"

Maggie's eyes blinked and seemed to focus on him for a second. Just a second.

"Her name's Diane. About five-seven, long black hair, dark eyes."

He dug for a notebook, wrote it down in letters that were tighter and deeper than he usually used. *Easy,* he told himself. *She's alive. Anything else we can fix.*

He said that a lot to victims.

"What happened then?" he asked, to stop himself from thinking about it. *We'll get there. We'll get there together.*

"I don't know. She took me someplace, but I don't remember the drive. I just—woke up—in this big room."

"Can you remember anything about the room? Sounds? Smells? Anything outside the windows?"

"Dark. The furniture was—old. The house felt old. I couldn't see much. There were bookshelves, a sofa, some chairs. I couldn't see anything outside the windows except bushes." She hesitated and sipped coffee. "It was expensive, though. The furniture. The house. A high rent district."

"Okay. Okay, who was in the room besides you?"

"The woman, Diane, the one who'd brought me. There was another woman there, Celestine, and two men. One of them was named Carl, he was black."

"And the other one?" Andy had gone way down behind his shields, now, steady and calm. He watched her face, waited for some sign of the dam breaking.

"I don't remember his name."

"What happened in the house, Maggie?"

She sat in silence, staring straight ahead. Her face was empty but tight, every muscle iron-hard under the skin.

"I think they're all dead," she said, and her eyes filled up with tears. "I think."

He waited for more, but she just sat, and the tears rolled out and down her face.

"Sweetheart, you have to help me out. Did you have your gun? Did you fire your gun? What happened?"

"I don't know," she said again, and began crying in earnest. "I remember him saying—Michael—"

As she bent forward to put her face in her hands, he saw blood on her neck. He got up and leaned over, pulled away her collar. She tried to bat him away, but he held her arm and took a look.

"You've got a bruise on your neck," he said. Two nasty punctures. She'd been drugged.

She stopped struggling. Her muscles trembled under his hand like wires stretched to breaking.

"Yeah. Yeah, I know," she whispered. The trembling got worse. "Let me up."

"Where are you going?"

"I think I'm going to throw up." She looked the part, face yellow and eyes gone dead. Her hands felt ice cold.

As she stood up, she lost her balance. She grabbed for the

chair and gasped; he steadied her and her nails dug deep in his arm.

"Kid?" She turned her face in toward his jacket and clung to him. Another spasm ripped through her, he felt it like an earthquake. "Maggie, Jesus—"

She gasped, couldn't form any words. Andy lowered her carefully back to the couch. Something icy settled in his stomach when she started whispering. He couldn't understand the words.

"Is it the baby?" he asked. She shuddered and reached out for him.

"Get Mike," she whispered in his ear. "Please, get Mike."

He couldn't think of a thing to say, just felt a sick falling sensation in his stomach. As he eased her back on the cushions, he glanced down.

The crotch of her blue jeans was soaked through. The cotton-candy blanket was turning bright red underneath her.

"Lie down," he said, and was surprised his voice was so steady. "Lie down flat. You trying to scare me or something? I've seen worse than this when my niece gets a nosebleed. Come on, sweetheart, lie flat."

"I don't want to die," she said, and it sounded quiet and distant. He took a deep breath against a pain in his own chest.

"What's that, a joke? You aren't gonna die. Help me out here. Lie down."

She finally let him ease her back to the cushions. Her hair spread out over his hands like tangled silk as he held up her head to put a pillow underneath.

"Better?" he asked, and knew it was a stupid question, but he had to keep her talking. Her eyes stared straight ahead, gradually going blank.

"Sure," she whispered. And caught her breath, once. The scream fought its way out of her throat, a wild sound like an animal caught in a trap. She reached out blindly for him, grabbed his hand and held on to it. Squeezed hard enough to make his bones grind together. *Please, just let her lose the baby.* he thought, appalled. *Just let her lose it.*

After her scream faded, something took it up, a shrieking in the parking lot. He leaned close and smoothed the hair back from her forehead.

"Ambulance is coming," he said. No more jokes, now. She stared at the ceiling, pale as a corpse. "Come on, kid. Help me out. Talk to me."

"They're vampires," she said, or he thought she said. He blinked.

"Who?"

"In the house. Where she took me. They're all vampires."

The paramedics burst in with clattering stretchers and big red boxes, and he had to move. She looked worse from farther away, barely alive.

Vampires. Jesus Christ.

He turned away so that nobody would see his face.

Twelve

Cold Comforts

Four bodies in the Refuge. Carl. Paul. Janine. I found Ciaran after sunset, butchered on her bed. Her eyes stared up at a blank ceiling, and her mouth was open a little as if she were about to ask a question. There was very little blood. I touched her fingers and found them cold and stiff.

I closed Ciaran's door behind me and continued down the hall, opening one door after another. Empty. No signs of struggle. Adam had been gone when I woke, and I hadn't found Lilly; the Refuge had turned into a cold mortuary, and I was the only ghoul still walking.

Toward the end of the hall I saw something move, a shadow, a flash. Nothing but my imagination, probably. But—

I kept walking. After the first few steps, I realized that I was hearing something, too.

Thuds. Regular, whispered thuds.

A heartbeat. Somewhere.

"Lilly?" I said, and my voice echoed from dark wood and blank walls. "Lilly, are you there?"

In addition to the thuds, I heard the watery sound of lungs

filling and emptying. I slowed and stopped, turning in a slow circle. Did the house have hidden panels? Hidden rooms?

I was so intent on the human whisper that it almost cost me my life. I felt her approach at the last possible second, and managed to avoid the sharp pointed stake she'd meant for my heart. I got it in the arm instead, a burning, scorching invasion that made me scream in pain and stumble weak-kneed right into her. She fought me off and dropped the stake; her hand was swollen almost twice normal size, burned an angry red.

She backed off as I held out a hand to stop her. I gritted my teeth and waited for the pain to wash away; it took a horribly long time.

"It's okay," I said. "Diane, it's me. Michael."

Diane looked much the worse for wear, hair tangled over her face, clothes torn. Her eyes were red and wild.

She made a feint for the stake again and turned at the last minute to close with me. The back of her hand smashed into my face and snapped my head around; she got a grip around my throat with her other hand and slammed me back against the wood paneling, one hard impact, then another.

When she let me go I slid down to a sprawled sitting position, head aching, body stunned into submission.

Then she picked up the stake.

A shadow formed behind her in the dimness, smoke and white skin. Adam's hand caught her wrist and twisted until she dropped the weapon.

"Bastard!" she screamed, and scrambled for the stake. This time, when her fingers closed around it, they spasmed so badly she dropped it. She tried again, blind with rage, but her fingers curled uselessly away from the source of their pain. Smarter than she was.

I tried to sit up and flailed like a puppy on a waxed floor. My arms and legs were too numb to use.

"Easy," Adam said, and pulled me to my feet and steadied me until my legs started tingling back into reality. "Have you found Celestine?"

"No."

Diane was still trembling, staring at me as if I had grown two heads and seven tentacles. I had the feeling that she might go for the stake again, if either of us made any sudden moves.

"You," she spat. "I'll kill the both of you."

"I think there's been enough of that," Adam murmured. He kicked the stake away when she tried to pick it up again. She looked up at him and the expression on her face went beyond hate.

"Your bloodline has to be destroyed, all of you. You're corrupt. You're evil."

Adam just cocked his head and looked down at her.

"The Society will destroy you," she said.

He smiled.

"Well, they've certainly tried before. Don't be stupid, Diane. I didn't let William in the house, I was with you. He came in through Ciaran's window, which means that he got control of her, not me. I'm not his creature, at least not now." His smile thinned into a straight line. "But I think Celestine may be."

"Celestine is strong! She'd never submit to him!" Diane spat. She stood up and took a step away from Adam into the darkness of the hallway. "She's not weak, like you."

Adam just watched her. She turned and walked away.

"Where's Keith?" I asked; I hadn't found her companion's body. Adam lifted a hand to silence me and waited until he was sure she was out of earshot.

"Come with me," he said.

We went the opposite direction from Diane, down the hall into a section of the house where I'd never been, storage closets piled with dusty boxes and locked cabinets, empty rooms whose doors yawned open like sleepy mouths. A hundred hiding places. I still heard the faint thud of heartbeats, but nothing else.

"Lilly and Keith?" I asked.

He nodded. There was dried blood on his torn shirt, smeared in a broad brown streak. There was a wide stain of blood on the right side of his collar, too.

"I wanted to let them have a little peace."

I thought of Lilly's strong, wounded face, and nodded. Peace for all of us would be nice, but if we could give it to Keith and Lilly, just for a few hours, that would do.

"What happened to Maggie?" I asked.

He hesitated, and that wasn't like him; he looked away, and my fear got even thicker in my throat. "Lilly followed the cab. Maggie got home all right."

"But?" The fear had gotten hold of me and choked, and I fought to get words past it. "What else?"

He turned to face me, and I felt my skin tighten at the unhappiness in his eyes.

"Her partner got there, and Lilly was about to leave when she heard the ambulance."

"Ambulance?" I repeated numbly. "Is she hurt?"

"Lilly didn't get close enough to see." Adam was desperately uncomfortable now, and I knew I didn't want to hear what he had to say. "Has she told you about the baby?"

I was sure I hadn't heard him right. He read the answer in my numb expression.

"I didn't think she had," he said miserably. "I'm sorry."

I couldn't think of anything to say; he stared off past my shoulder at a blank dusty wall.

"Baby," I finally heard myself say, and had a flash of physical memory, of Maggie's skin soft under my hands, of her face alight with love, of how I'd promised her . . . I tried to speak and there was no air in my lungs. I pulled in a breath and tried again. "That's not possible."

Adam continued to look at the wall.

"She was pregnant when you—died," he said. "I guess she's about four months along now."

I turned away from him. There was a metal storage cabinet leaning wearily against the wall behind me, and I rested my hands flat on the cold metal.

Maggie.

Maggie.

She hadn't told me. All this time and—

"You could be wrong," I heard myself say. "How do you know? Did she tell you?"

"She didn't have to," he whispered.

Vampire senses. I'd heard it, too, the ghostly echo in her heartbeat, and I hadn't known what it was.

"So why did they take her in the ambulance?" I asked, though I already knew. The metal bent under my hands with a sound like a whine.

"She was bleeding," he said. He didn't have to say the rest, I knew it. My fingernails dug into the thin metal and scraped long screaming gouges out of it, silver curls like party bows breaking loose and spiraling down to the carpet.

There was something wrong with me. I should have felt something, anything, because I understood very clearly what he was trying to tell me. I should have felt something.

But I couldn't feel anything. When I rummaged around

for something, anything, all I could think of was the fact that she hadn't even tried to tell me about my child.

"Do you know what hospital?" I asked him. He nodded. "I need a phone."

I must have stopped walking on the way to the phone, because I found my forehead resting against cool white plaster that smelled of century-old paint and rich rotten dust. Adam's hand rested on my shoulder, then went away.

Something shattered inside of me, and the grief was almost unbearable. To lose Maggie, that was terrifying. To lose this baby I'd never even known about—

When I was able to look up, Adam was standing several feet down the hall, facing a dusty window. His face was tinted red by the sunset like a Chinese demon mask.

"Let's make the call and get out of here," he said. At the other end of the hall I saw Diane, watching us. Adam raised his head and turned to face her. The look they exchanged was hot enough to melt steel.

She turned and stalked away, toward the sound of heartbeats. Toward Lilly and Keith.

"I've made them a promise," he said to her stiff back. "Keith wants to go with you, and I can't stop him, but I promised him that he could find me if he ever wanted to leave you. Do you understand?"

She kept walking, passing into the shadows.

Adam kept watching, as if he could still see her. "Take what's yours and go, Diane. Lilly stays here."

The shadows were inhabited after all; she stopped, and now I saw the outline of her pale face turn toward us. I couldn't see her well at all, only well enough to identify the hate.

"Next time I see you, either of you, your blood is mine," she said. In another blink she was gone, the shadows empty.

Adam went back to staring out the window. I found the phone, and the receiver felt heavy and cold and impersonal.

I'm sorry, Mr. Bowman—

I dialed the number Adam had given me.

I'm sorry, Mr. Bowman—

We had to get out of the Refuge, but I refused to do what Adam wanted. I wouldn't leave Dallas. That only left one house for us to use.

It was haunted.

A metal FOR SALE sign creaked on the lawn. Adam led us around the side of the house, through the gate and into the backyard. A dog began a raw-throated barking two houses away, until a gruff old-man voice yelled at him to shut up. The house next door was dark, too; its for sale sign looked newer and more hopeful.

I didn't see him touch the back door but suddenly it was yawning open. I felt the terrible sadness, the loneliness, the grief that breathed out at us, knew Adam felt it, too.

Sylvia had died here.

"Your house?" Lilly asked Adam. He didn't answer, just walked on into the living room. The furniture was gone, leaving only a big cold room with a wooden floor. They'd replaced the boards in a square roughly where the couch had been; I wondered why until I remembered lying there, on the floor, while Sarah Foster aimed a gun at my head.

Boom.

I turned in a slow circle, remembering how William had leaned over me, laughing. Adam had been upstairs, trying desperately to breathe life into a woman too dead to return.

It was a haunted house, all right.

Adam took a few steps up the stairs and stopped, looking

up. His face was blank, his eyes blind. His hand tightened on the railing.

It must have hurt worse than anything I could imagine. He took a quiet breath and went up another step, then another.

He didn't look into her room as he passed it, just kept walking. I looked. It was just a room. All the blood was gone, but I thought I smelled the lingering odor of it.

Sylvia's ghostly perfume, sad, so sad. Her kindness had deserved so much better.

The secret door at the end of the hall clicked open. Adam disappeared inside. I looked behind me and saw Lilly's pale, stolid face; the only sign of her distress was the strength of her grip.

We'd all lost something, someone to William. That steadied me a little.

Adam shut the door behind us, and clicked the lock. He'd turned on the closet light, and the warm yellow glow washed out over thick carpet and two twin beds, piles of blankets and pillows. Books, still stacked haphazardly in the corners where Adam had abandoned them.

No one had touched this room. No one even knew about it, or so we hoped; it was an emergency bolt hole, one that we were both desperately uncomfortable with. Tomorrow we'd move.

I knew Adam well enough to know he'd never come back again.

We picked our spots silently; Lilly sat on one of the beds. I sat where I was most comfortable, in the middle of a pile of books.

Adam just paced, back and forth. His glasses were smeared with something; he took them off and cleaned them absently on his shirttail, then realized his shirt was filthy. He stripped it off and tossed it in the corner; he found another in the closet and shrugged it on over tense shoulders and star-shaped scars in his ribs. Lilly glanced at me, but neither of us spoke.

I picked up a paperback from the pile and started thumbing through it. The words blurred in front of my eyes, but I kept pretending to read—it was something to do other than stare at Adam.

The hospital had given out no information. She was in "guarded" condition. At the last minute I'd realized I couldn't say I was her husband—her partner would have told them I was dead. So I'd had to fumble and substitute "cousin" and they hadn't bought it.

She was alive. I knew that much.

"How's the book?" Adam asked. I glanced up at him, startled. He appeared to be concentrating hard on buttoning his shirt, one careful move at a time. I wondered if the fabric still smelled like Sylvia. Most of my clothes still smelled like Maggie, at least in my mind. His voice was almost normal, just one thin dark thread running through it. "I confess, it was never one of my favorites."

I turned it over and looked at the cover. It featured a vampire, complete with dripping fangs and cape, cringing in fear from a wimpy-looking college-age kid while a half-dressed young woman draped herself artistically over a tombstone.

"It's a classic," I said. "Any ideas about what we do now?"

Adam's smile was brief and bitter, and I saw the glitter in his eyes. "Killing him sounds like a good plan, if we can manage it."

"Do you know where to find him?" I asked, and he nodded.

"Sure." He settled his back against the wall and crossed his arms across his chest; the closet light caught on the metal frames of his glasses. "I was there for four months. I ought to know it."

I spared a glance toward Lilly and saw that her eyes had drifted shut; she looked drawn and exhausted. "Then I guess we just go and do it."

He laughed, a thick, painful sound.

"Be serious. We tried that four months ago, and it ended up with me on his line and you almost dead. In case you've forgotten, he has Celestine now. If she's completely his, he'll be able to use her against us."

"What about Diane? Do you think she'll help us?"

"An excellent question," he said, and sat down on the carpet across from me, legs crossed, relaxed. "I wish I could answer it. Ultimately, of course, she believes what she said at the Refuge—that William's legacy has to be wiped out. That includes me, and you, and Celestine, though I doubt Diane's willing to face that at the moment."

He paused and allowed his eyes to close.

"I think she's probably right, too. Our blood is bad, Mike. Tainted. I've always felt that, and I never intended to pass it on to you. Funny how these things happen."

"You think you're tainted?" I asked. His lips twitched, not quite a smile.

"I would think the answer is obvious."

I waited. His faint smile went away.

"Did Celestine tell you how William amused himself with us? Sometimes with her, sometimes with me. Mostly with me, for some reason. I suppose he liked me better."

"I don't—"

"Don't want to hear it? No, I wouldn't either. This isn't the self-pity hour, Michael, this is information you need, so listen." Adam's eyes opened, and they looked human, tired, disillusioned, compassionate. "I know Celestine hurt you that night at the Refuge; I heard it through the walls. She put me in the room next to you so I could hear very clearly. That—that is what William's done to us. Celestine is a sadist. I—am—something similar. It's very hard for me to watch it happen to you, too."

I stayed frozen where I was, staring at him, one finger still marking my place in the ridiculous book I had pretended to read. On the bed, Lilly's breathing regulated to a deeper, slower rhythm—asleep, and at peace.

"I will not watch it happen to you," he amended, very softly. "You're my blood, Michael, whether I intended it or not. And you must know, I may have to kill you to protect you from him."

I couldn't think of any reply at all. He shook his head and stood up, opened the door, looked out. The hallway beyond was thick with darkness and ghosts.

"We aren't safe here, are we?" I asked. He continued to stare down the hall, toward Sylvia's room where she had died and he hadn't been able to save her. I looked away and found myself staring at a photograph of her; she'd been happy in the picture, laughing. The silver frame had begun to turn black with tarnish.

"We aren't safe anywhere." Adam closed the door, locked it, and sat down again. "We can run, you know. It won't save us for long, but we can run."

"We fight," I said. "I have something to protect."

I knew he understood.

Interlude:

Andy McDonnell

He'd spent the day at the hospital. Funny, how most people hated the places. He'd never minded them much, a miracle, considering that his father had gone in and out of Boston Memorial seventeen times. Heart. Colon. Prostate. You name it. George T. McDonnell had always come back better than he went in, until he popped off from an aneurysm at the age of seventy-four while mowing the backyard. Andy had no prejudice against hospitals.

Except—just maybe—this particular hospital.

"Can I get you something, dear?" a sweet-faced granny asked; she was pushing a cart full of candy and cold drinks and magazines. Her apron was bordered with cheerful little hearts and she wore a button that said GOD MADE MY DAY. Her eyes were small and kind and the color of a hot summer sky. "Something to drink?"

"No," he said, and had to clear his throat. His mouth felt like a rat had nested there during his nap. "No, thanks. What's the time?"

She checked a heart-shaped watch hanging from a red ribbon and frowned far-sightedly at it.

"It looks like—nine o'clock, dear. Are you waiting for your wife?"

"No, ma'am, just a friend."

"Ah," she said, and smiled. "I hope she's doing well."

"Yeah, me, too." He nodded to her and watched her squeak her cart away, spreading a little warmth to other harried-looking men and women in the waiting room. McDonnell had chosen a corner seat, one where he could keep most of the hallway in sight. There was supposed to be a guard outside of Maggie's door, but that wasn't possible until she had a room, and for hours now she'd been shuffled from one lab to another, one room to another, while the doctors pissed around and waited for somebody to tell them what to do. He wished he had a cigarette and caught the eye of a woman across the aisle who was fishing a Marlboro out of a full pack. There was a big stern NO SMOKING sign over her head, which they both silently agreed to ignore.

As he drew in the first lungful, he thought, hell of a time to fall off the wagon, but that didn't stop the smoke from feeling warm and thick in his lungs. Whatever happened to the good old days when people smoked because it was good for the lungs? They'd all died off, he guessed, and blew a ring toward the ceiling. It was slightly off-kilter, wobbling like a jammed tire as it spun. He took another drag and tried again. Goddamn it, he was going to get it right if it killed him.

As he achieved his third perfect ring, he saw the evening nurse waving at him from the station. She was a big woman, heavy-hipped and big-breasted, attractive, with a smile that could light up the city for a week.

"How's she doing?" he asked. Her name tag said G. N. Davis, R.N. He wondered what the G. stood for.

"Sir, you really have to put out that—"

"Come on, don't give me the bullshit. Is she okay?"

She hesitated and took a quick look around, then leaned across the desk toward him. She smelled like clean soap and antiseptic, with a little hint of perfume thrown in.

"She's okay."

"What about the baby?"

"Well, there was a lot of hemorrhage, but they got it under control. She'll probably be able to carry it to term, but she's going to have to be a lot more careful. If her blood pressure goes up, they'll confine her."

He hadn't actually realized how tense he was until he felt the muscles in his back let loose. The relief left him monumentally tired.

"Can you get me in to see her?" he asked. The nurse narrowed her eyes at him, and he smiled. "Come on, be a pal."

"Five minutes," she said, and shoved an ashtray at him. "Put it out before I put you out."

He'd forgotten the cigarette. He took one more guilty puff and crushed it out in a bowl of orange ceramic, and followed G.N. Davis's gently swinging skirt down the hall.

Maggie looked frightening pale, lying on those white sheets. The bruise along her cheek had turned a rich lemon-yellow around the edges, and eggplant purple toward the center. As the door shut behind him, her eyes fluttered open and focused on him.

"Andy," she said, and he felt a flush of warm pleasure at the sound of her voice. Jesus, so close. So Goddamn close.

"Hey, kid, how are you? They tell me you're going to live to chase the bad guys again."

She rewarded him with a transparent smile and winced when it pulled at the bruise.

"Yeah, that's what I hear. Jesus, you have some luck with partners, don't you? First Frank, now me."

"Frank took a bullet," he shrugged. "You, you just scared the shit out of me."

"Did I?" Those blue eyes, twilight-blue. Narrowing. "You came in—and I told you about the woman coming to my place—"

"You told me about being taken to a big house, and you said that you thought everybody was dead. You remember that?"

"Yeah," she said, but her face had closed up on him. "Yeah. I mean, I think there was a fight. I don't really remember."

"You remember telling me they were all vampires?"

Her pupils expanded in panic, contracted again.

"Did I say that?" she asked, and laughed. "Jesus, I must have really been out of it. Vampires. Can you believe it?"

He didn't say anything, just looked at her. Her smile faded.

"You couldn't remember anything else about the house then. How about now?"

She told him pretty much what she'd said the last time, vague details, nothing that would help him track it down. It sounded like a hallucination, but the bruises were real, and so were the wounds in her neck.

He thought she was lying to him, and that bothered him. A lot.

"They say the baby's going to be okay," she said, and her right hand made a gentle circle on her stomach. "Some luck, huh?"

"You bet, kid," he said. "Some luck. You got anything else to tell me?"

She did, he knew it. It was all there, floating around behind those eyes, ready to come out.

But she just smiled.

"Take another look at the Franischis yet?" she asked. He shrugged.

"Drove by it once. Haven't had much of a chance, what with all the excitement you've caused. Why?"

"I think it would be a good idea to keep an eye on them."

"Why?" He looked at her sharply, and she closed her eyes as if she were too tired to talk anymore. He knew it was a dodge. "You think they're related to this?"

"I think they're in it up to their eyebrows, Andy. That's my professional opinion, if it's worth anything. And I can't go do the legwork myself right now. Hows about taking it on for me?"

He rubbed at his chin, felt the wire bristle of a day without a shave. Jesus, he probably stank, too, not to mention the ripe cloud of cigarette smoke he'd brought in with him.

"For you," he said quietly, "anything."

Outside, in the hall, he thought about the way she'd evaded his question. *Remember telling me they were all vampires?* She'd said, *did I say that?*

She knew she'd said it.

He hunched his shoulders against a sudden shooting pain in his back and headed for the nurses station. G.N. Davis was typing something at the computer but got up when she saw him coming.

There was something about her smile. He cruised closer to the counter.

"Good night, detective," she said, and he liked her voice, too, one of those deep-in-the-throat voices. "Be careful going home."

He slowed up and looked her right in the eyes.

"G.N.," he said. Her cheeks turned a little pink. "What's your first name?"

"Gloria. Gloria Naomi Davis."

He smiled and tipped an imaginary hat to her.

"Top of the evening, Gloria. Be seeing you."

He was whistling as he got on the elevator, dead tired but lighter than he'd felt for days. Gloria Naomi waved at him from the counter, still smiling.

And damned if he wasn't smiling, too, all the way down to the parking lot.

Stupid, he thought, and sighed. His breath made little circles in his coffee. The coffee was too strong, too hot, and too old, scraped off of the bottom of a pot at the convenience store down the street. That reminded him of Joseph Vico. He needed to get on those reports in the morning.

Ten more minutes, he promised himself, and checked his watch. Nine-fifty. At ten, he was on the road and heading for at least six hours of decent sleep.

Across the street, the home of Ed and Ellen Franischi glowed like a middle-class icon of purity. A carefully kept lawn. Flower borders marching in line like good little soldiers. Smoke drifting out of the chimney.

Home sweet home. He checked his watch again.

"What the fuck am I doing here?" he asked himself, and took a scalding sip of coffee. Christ. If he wasn't careful, doing favors for Maggie would get his ass busted. She was contagious. He watched the Franischi house and thought that he'd rather be in there, in front of a nice fire, than be here in this piece-of-shit department car with no heat and a bad cup of coffee.

Three more minutes down, while he waited for the coffee to cool. A car turned down the road and pulled into a driveway six houses down. Two people got out.

He probably wouldn't have even noticed if he hadn't been so goddamn bored, but the two people walked around *behind* the house, not up to the door. He waited, but didn't see any lights coming on inside.

Anything? He wondered. Nothing to do with the Franischis, that was sure. But a robbery—

Yeah. Maybe. Or maybe a couple of kids sneaking in the back so they wouldn't wake up Mom and Dad.

He checked his watch. Three more minutes, and he was gone.

Lights went on in the Franischi house at T minus one minute. Lots of lights. He saw Ellen Franischi dart by the kitchen window and head for the back of the house, then return with the youngest boy in her arms. Joey, that was his name. Joey the artist.

The older girl, Darla, passed by, too, pulling on a coat. Were they going somewhere? On a school night?

Ellen Franischi was talking to somebody, somebody he couldn't see. She looked confused at first, then scared.

Then defiant. Andy put his coffee aside and leaned out of the window to watch.

Ed Franischi, tall, tufts of red hair still clinging to his scalp, blundered by one of the den windows and went toward the kitchen. He looked shattered and scared.

A pair of hands reached out to Ellen. She stepped back, holding tightly to Joey.

"Shit," he murmured, and opened the door. "One more fucking minute—"

Ellen Franischi backed away, out of the window. Another woman came into view. She had long dark hair, shot through with silver. Her skin was pale—really pale. The front door opened while he was trying to catch a good look at her face.

Ed Franischi came out on the doorstep holding the second-oldest kid, Ben. Ben was bundled up in a heavy coat and gloves, and he was crying.

Another guy came out of the door, young, maybe twenty. He was coatless and shivering; he took Ben away from Ed and bounced him nervously as Ben started to wail in earnest.

Darla came out on the porch, still pulling on her gloves. She took Ben and quieted him.

"—too young! You can't take him!" Andy heard Ellen saying. "Please, just leave him! We can take care of him here!"

Andy got out of the car and let the door click shut, no slam. He'd gone about halfway across the street when Darla spotted him. Her mouth opened in a round O of dismay.

He put a finger over his lips and kept coming.

It would have worked if the dark-haired woman hadn't chosen that moment to come out of the door carrying little Joey, who was screaming like the blue devil. Ellen Franischi followed, crying, and Ed had to grab her and hold her while the dark-haired woman and the younger man started down the walk with the kids.

Andy pulled his badge out and held it over his head. The dark-haired woman stopped and slowly lowered Joey to the ground; the kid collapsed where he was put and stayed there, howling.

Andy didn't like the look on the woman's face, not at all.

"Police, ma'am. Let's have a little chat," he said.

And that's when the world went to hell.

Ellen Franischi screamed, a sound that would break glass, and the dark-haired woman turned into—something. Something with red eyes that moved very, very fast. Andy just had enough time to get his gun free before she was in his face, and her eyes were red like blood and Jesus, she was strong, fingernails like claws, and the teeth, Jesus, teeth—

"Diane! No! For God's sake, stop!" That was the man,

yelling loud enough to raise the whole neighborhood, and asphalt slammed into Andy's back and a weight stood on his chest and the teeth, the teeth—

He shot her, point-blank. Powder choked him and stung in his eyes, made an acid-burn ring on his cheek.

Nothing happened.

"Jesus Mary Mother!" he screamed, as fast as he could get the words out, and pulled the trigger again. The noise was louder than a howitzer going off inside his head.

Her *eyes*—

He saw a face over her shoulder. The kid, Darla. Darla dragged at the thing's shoulder, pounded at it with her fists. He took his finger off the trigger, half afraid he was going to shoot again because he was so goddamn scared.

Dead, he thought. *I'm dead.*

The eyes and the teeth went away. So did the weight on his chest. He groaned and heard a rib creak, and rolled weakly over on his side. The woman—was that what she was?—had already crossed to the sidewalk again, had picked up Ben and the screaming Joey, and now she was running. The man ran behind her, legs windmilling wildly to keep up.

Darla hesitated, looking at him, and started to take off, too. He got up and forced his legs to work, to pump hard. He caught up with her and grabbed her from behind, lifted her off the ground in a bear hug.

She screamed and struggled, but he held on.

She wasn't going with—whatever that was.

No way in hell.

Thirteen

Home Improvements

"Do we need a cart?" That was Lilly, whose normally yellowish complexion looked downright lemony in the orange wash of sodium parking-lot lights. Adam looked around and found a stray. We began pushing it toward the big orange awning and the cart made an unholy racket of rattles and jingles and squeaks. "Do you have any money, sir?"

"Yeah," I murmured. I'd stopped at an ATM and pulled out the maximum of two hundred dollars. The account was in the name of Gregory Dunlap, and I was now Gregory Dunlap, according to my identification. That wouldn't last long; Greg was a paper shell, just designed to give me enough cover to last until I could set up a firm new identity. Maggie's idea.

Thank God.

"What we need shouldn't cost much," Adam said, and looked over at Lilly as we marched across the blacktop like a flying wedge. "You don't have to do this, you know. I'd rather you stayed at the house."

"No," Lilly said simply. "Not as long as Celestine needs me."

The parking lot looked like an anthill; irregular lines of people carried or pushed or pulled things from the store to the car, from the car to the store. Workers ants in big orange aprons patrolled the parking lot and nabbed stray carts that tried for a quick getaway.

This was my idea. I was no longer sure that it was a good one, but it had been the only constructive one we'd had.

Vampires in Home Depot. I was reasonably certain that not even William would have anticipated this move.

Somebody on the loudspeaker blared a call for assistance in kitchens and bathrooms. I shoved the cart ahead of me like a bulldozer, carving a way through the confusion. We passed windows, caulking, pesticides strong enough to burn the lining of my nose even though I was careful not to breathe. Phones. Lights. A whole glittering cave of chandeliers.

"Where the hell is it?" I asked nobody in particular; Lilly shrugged, and Adam concentrated on keeping his head down and not looking anyone in the eye. He looked as ill as I felt. Finally, out of desperation, I flagged down a worker ant in an orange apron. His name was Fred, and Fred looked like a sun-dried out-of-work jockey with a square toupee. He gave the three of us a strange look, but his smile never even wavered.

"Help you folks with something?" he said. He talked like Mr. Rogers on helium. I looked around.

"We need ten wooden stakes, about, oh, this long. Round ones, if you can find them."

"Oh." Fred chewed his lip and checked a tattered list in his apron pocket. "Hmm. We have garden stakes, you know, the square ones, but round ones—we'd have to turn them on the lathe. Might be tomorrow before I can get those for you since it's almost closing time. Ya in a hurry?"

"Kind of." William wouldn't hang around forever, waiting. He'd come.

"Well-l-l-l, let me check in the back. Ya'll hang on right here, I'll be back." He wandered back through an aisle that looked like God's storage closet, if God were not exceptionally well organized. Lilly dumped three big hammers with rubber grips into the cart, followed by three pairs of heavy work gloves.

"Wood burns you," she said, by way of explanation. "Why not wear gloves?"

I pulled the thick fabric over my fingers and picked up a raw piece of lumber. I got a faint tingling sensation in my hand, nothing else.

"Lilly," I said, "you're a genius. What else?"

"Sawdust," Adam said. His voice sounded thick and damp. "Hurts."

There was a light haze of it all over the aisle where we stood. He was right; it burned when I breathed it in. I imagined those little motes of wood dust hitting the lining of my lungs and exploding into sparks. As an experiment, I reached down and gathered up a handful.

It burned like holding a handful of fire ants. I dropped it and rubbed away the sting on my pants.

Fred ambled back our way, chewing on a pencil stub.

"Sorry, folks, no round stakes. I can get you the square ones, though, or can fix up them round ones tomorrow for you."

"Give me ten of the square ones," I said, and pointed to the drift of sawdust under the wheel of my cart. "Hey, do you sell this stuff?"

Fred frowned. His face wrinkled up like a prune.

"Wheels?" he guessed.

"Sawdust."

"Sawdust?"

"Yeah. Do you sell it?"

I got a long look, this time. And then the smile came back. It looked anemic.

"Mister, you want it, I'll sell it. How much you want?"

I turned and looked at Adam.

"Oh, I think a pound ought to be enough."

"A pound," Fred repeated. "You want a pound of sawdust. Regular old sawdust."

I slapped him on the shoulder.

"In a plastic bag, Fred. Thanks."

"Anything else?" He said it quickly, hoping there wasn't. Adam reached out and put a fingertip on something I'd missed—a big bamboo stick, pointed on the end, with a reservoir for oil at the end. A beach light, or whatever they called them. A backyard torch.

"Yeah," I agreed. "One of those."

"Just one?" Fred was hopelessly lost, his smile set in concrete. He just wrote it down and didn't try to argue me out of it. "Want some matches with those?"

"No, I want one of those little fireplace lighters. The long kind."

By the time we'd finished the list, a cheery voice was telling us it was time to make our final selections and proceed to the checkout counter. Fred dropped the stakes in the basket with the sawdust and beach torch, and wedged the fireplace lighter down in the middle. I slipped him a ten for his trouble, and he gave me a grin that showed brown, horsey teeth.

Definitely a jockey.

Outside, the three of us donned work gloves and moved the purchases into the trunk of Celestine's black limousine, which was big enough to hold a Volkswagon and an extended family of clowns. Our purchases looked pitiful in the midst of all that carpeting. I looked at Lilly as we surveyed the arsenal, and she returned my look, unsmiling.

"What do you think?" I asked her. She shook her head. Not much of a cheering section.

We pulled out onto the street and the streetlights began to whip by like comets. Adam went about five miles, then pulled the block-long limo over to the side in the parking lot of a gas station. We weren't parked near the pumps, and I shot him a questioning look.

He handed me a quarter.

"Try the hospital again," he said. My fingers closed around the hard metal and I squeezed hard enough that I thought it bent a little in my fist. Maggie.

We couldn't go there, I knew that, but I had to talk to her at least once, tell her—

Tell her how sorry I was.

My fingers had memorized the number. I let them punch it in and heard the machine swallow my quarter; double buzzes on the other end, and after nine rings I got a human voice.

"I'm checking on the status of a patient," I said. "Margaret Bowman."

Silence. I hated the silence, because I knew what she was doing—checking the computer, reading the updates, editing it for me. Never give them too much, that was the policy. In case things change suddenly.

The caution infuriated me.

"She's in room 638, sir. I'll ring you."

I caught myself about to protest. My God, was I that scared of talking to her? Did I think she'd tell me that she hated me? Never wanted to see me?

Yeah, I was that scared. I fought the urge to hang up as the phone began to buzz again.

"Hello?" Her voice. I closed my eyes and listened to it; she sounded drowsy and relaxed. "Hello?"

"Hi, baby," I whispered. My throat felt rusty and tight. "It's me."

God, I hated the silence.

"Mike?" she asked, a breathless whisper. And then she started to cry, a slow quiet weeping that made me want to bang my head against the lemon-yellow concrete wall I faced. "Oh, God, Mike, I was so scared."

"Sweetheart, I tried to call before—"

"It's okay, it's okay. I'm okay."

No, she wasn't. Fear cut me, and I bled tears that I wiped away with my shirtsleeve.

"I didn't want to let you go." It sounded so weak.

"I know," she said. "You had to, Mike. The sun was coming up."

The sun always came up, a hard hot wall between us. I heard plastic crack and relaxed my grip on the phone.

"Adam said you were—are—"

Another silence, and this one really hurt. I heard her draw in a deep breath and let it out.

"We're going to have a baby, Mike. Our baby. Yours and mine," she said. Her voice sounded thin and weak, but it was still there, and I loved her with everything in me, I wanted to crawl through the phone and hold her. "It's going to be okay. The baby's okay."

"I love you," I whispered. I didn't know what else to say— that I was glad? Was I? I hadn't had time to think about it. A baby. I was something out of nightmares. What kind of father was I going to be?

"I've got to go, they have people coming in here every three minutes. Mike? Be careful, won't you?"

"I will," I promised, and heard her sniffling. She'd always hated crying, hated how her eyes swelled and her nose turned red and her sinuses drained. "Joe Vico loves you."

"Joe Vico had better get the fuck out of town, Mike, and I'm not kidding. It got very close. *Very* close. Use the interim ID until you can pick up new ones from Guillermo down on Pine Street. It'll cost you, and you'd better clean out your account quick. Use an ATM, don't go to the bank. Then ditch the card." She took a deep breath. "You shouldn't have kept my picture in your apartment."

"I know." The phone line had picked up a buzz, and her voice was drifting away from me. "I had to. I needed you."

Drifting away, years away, miles away.

"I love you, Mike," she said, and her voice was almost covered by static. "Goodbye."

"Love you, too," I said, and hung up the phone before I could think of something else to say. I kept my hand on it for a few seconds, letting the pain run its course, and then got back in the car. Adam and Lilly stopped talking and looked at me.

"She's alive," I said. "The baby's alive."

Adam put the limousine in reverse and pulled us away into the night, away from that dimly lit phone and the last human contact I might ever have.

"Then you'd better stay alive, too, hadn't you?" he said.

I wasn't sure where we were going until we'd parked the limo, and even then I thought maybe I was wrong. But Adam took Lilly's arm and led her forward, up to the fence with razor wire on top. There was a big chain and lock on the chain link gate, and Adam stood there for a few seconds staring through the links to the darkness beyond.

"We have to break the lock?" I asked. Adam shook his head and dug in his pants pocket. He came up with a shiny silver key.

The lock gave way with a meaty thunk, and the chain slithered away to pile on the ground at our feet. Adam picked it up and motioned me through the opening. I took Lilly with me.

Adam locked up behind us. I took a good look at the dark booths ahead, the skeletal shapes of rides, the spiderweb-shape of the Ferris wheel looming overhead.

"I remember this place," Lilly whispered unexpectedly. "It was so nice. All kinds of rides and things for kids."

"What happened to it?"

"It went bankrupt, I think. Nobody came."

Past the empty windows of the concession buildings, a winding track that must have been used for mini race cars wandered through whispering grass that had grown waist-high. One security light glowed on the fence nearest the free-way, and apart from Styrofoam cups rustling in the wind and papers fluttering, there was no sound at all.

We might have been on another planet, and we'd taken only a few steps off the main street.

"I don't like this," I said, and adjusted the Home Depot apron around my neck. Lilly had stuck them in at the last minute, day-glo orange burlap with big pockets. Wooden stakes clinked and jabbed in mine. I carried the big beach torch and couldn't shake the feeling of being ridiculous, a Monty Python skit. "He could be anywhere. Maybe he didn't come here at all."

"He's here," Adam said. There were clouds tonight, low clouds that caught the sodium freeway lights and bathed everything in a dim pink tint. "He likes it here. We just have to make him come to us."

"What a plan," I said. "We dress up like the Three Stooges and wait for him to come kill us."

Adam dug his work gloves out of his pocket and slid them over his pale hands. I already had mine on.

"At least we get to make a fight out of it," he said, and the shadows swallowed us up.

Some of the rides had been carried off in the bankruptcy—there was a big empty circle with a sign that said TILT-A-WHIRL, and the skeletal remains of another ride that was only half dismantled. The Ferris wheel loomed like a skyscraper, and the baskets creaked softly in the wind. A drift of old greasy wrappers and smashed cups lay against most every building. From the shadows red eyes blinked and tiny hearts thumped out a frantic syncopated rhythm. Rats. Lots of rats, nesting undisturbed.

Lilly made a throaty sound of distress as we passed one of the toilet buildings; the smell was rich and ripe, fermenting to levels that made it torture to have vampire senses. Probably wasn't so bad for her, of course. Mildly disgusting.

"I thought you said this place wasn't open for long," I said. She nodded.

"Three, four months at most. Maybe vagrants stay here."

"Wonderful."

I tried to snort the smell out of my nose, but it coated my tongue and slid down my throat like syrup. I gagged and wished I had something to throw up. I hadn't fed. It would have meant feeding from Lilly, and I wouldn't do that, not even in necessity. Adam was right. We had to make choices.

That wasn't my choice.

Our footsteps sounded like wind whispering through the

fence. Adam kept us to the shadows; he and I scanned the horizons, watching, waiting.

William knew we were here. I had no doubt of it. The question was, would he come for the bait, or would he wait until we came for him?

He didn't like being cornered, I knew. We had that much advantage.

The folded carcass of the Spider leaned to our left. To our right, a haunted house painted with cartoonishly unfrightening witches and devils. An accordion-style iron gate protected the entrance.

"Well?" I asked.

"He stays a lot of places. That's one of them," Adam said. He pointed to the toilet we'd passed, the one with the smell.

"You're kidding," I said. I wished he was, but I knew differently. There was a certain expression he had when he was thinking about William. Hate that ran that deep was hard to conceal.

"I'll go," I heard myself say, and fished around in my apron pocket for a stake. "Will I be able to see in there?"

"Not without a light," Adam said. "He likes to lay under the sinks sometimes. That's where he kept me chained."

I found the fireplace lighter and clicked the trigger. A thin stream of flame shot out. Enough to see by, provided I was careful and my hands didn't shake too much. I didn't want to take the torch—in close quarters it would be almost useless—so I held a stake in my gloved left hand and the lighter in my right.

Armed for battle.

"Wish me luck," I said, and ran across the open ground to the deep shadows near the toilet entrance. The sign that said MEN flapped in the wind; I saw Lilly and Adam watching. Waiting.

I emptied out my lungs and left them empty, and stepped into the bathroom.

There was nothing under the sinks but a lone rabid-looking rat gnawing at a discarded hamburger wrapper. The stall doors were half-closed, and I kept the lighter burning while I opened them, one by one. A dark fetid mess floated in one bowl. Dead insects in another. The third lid was down, which was probably for the best.

I opened the last stall, and the door creaked slowly back. The firelight flickered on white porcelain and smooth water. Nothing.

Something fell into the toilet and splashed, legs thrashing. A long hairless tail whipped like a tentacle as the rat scrambled for purchase and paddled to stay alive.

Naturally, I looked up to see where it had come from.

William hung there above me like some evil angel, and his eyes were wide and blind with pure pleasure. His lips split into a grin that went too far across his face.

"Oops," he said. "Sorry 'bout that."

I flung myself backward, and couldn't seem to let go of the trigger of the lighter; in the flickering light he floated down and took one long, disjointed step toward me. I took a breath and gagged on the unclean taste of rot, and jabbed the lighter at him. He stopped.

"Mike," he said, and the grin got wider. "You got balls, boy, I give you that. How you like the place? Got *atmosphere.* You know, I used to keep Adam right over there, under the sinks. Got me some chains that were thick enough even he couldn't rip 'em open."

I took a step back. He was too quick, I couldn't outrun him. All I had was the ridiculous little lighter and a pocketful of stakes that seemed completely useless now.

"Want to try it out, Mike? The sinks, I mean?" He was

coming, I knew it. The stake in my left hand felt warm even through the glove.

I slashed blindly at him, and saw his face loom close to the lighter's flame, eyebrows throwing black winged shadows up over his forehead, skin glowing red.

Then the light went out. Something cold touched my mouth, and I gagged and slashed again. Nothing. Nothing there.

I clicked the lighter frantically two, three times. It came to life with a belch of flame.

Except for a couple of rats squeaking anxiously, I was alone.

Interlude:

Maggie

The night shift floor nurse had taken quite a shine to Andy McDonnell; she asked a lot of questions about him—the one about his wife had been buried pretty deep, but Maggie hadn't been made a detective for nothing. She'd told the nurse that Andy was divorced, which was certainly true. She didn't mention Mary Lee, the bartender at M.L.'s, because she wasn't supposed to know about her, anyway.

The nurse had gone away happy. Maggie read a dog-eared paperback and tried not to think about how Mike had sounded on the phone, so quiet, so far away. He'd tried to protect her.

That meant—everything. Everything.

Her door swung open with a hiss of weather stripping, and the nurse's smile announced the visitor like a loudspeaker. Maggie marked her place in the book and started to say hello.

The look on his face stopped her. McDonnell stripped off his raincoat and tossed it on a chair; he looked scraped and stretched and flat-out exhausted. None of that explained the look, though. She'd only seen something like it on his face

once before, when he'd had to draw his gun on a kid of
twelve who was holding a pump shotgun. It was a look of
absolute concentration, absolute horror.

"Sit down," she said, and he shoved papers and magazines
to the floor and dragged the chair very close to the bed. The
smell of sweat and stale cigarettes trickled over her. She
raised her head and saw the nurse still hanging around the
open door; one look was enough to convince the woman to
swing the door shut. "What the hell—"

"What are they?" McDonnell barked, and when she
started to ask him what he meant he grabbed her arm and
held it tight. "No fucking around, Maggie. You know, and I
have to know. What the hell are these people?"

"I don't know what you're—"

"Goddamn it!" He let go of her arm and shoved himself
out of the chair; he stalked to the window, hands jammed
into his pockets, head down. "Just tell me. Just do that much
for me."

She took in a deep breath. It didn't help. Caught in the
middle, again, between what she wanted and what she needed
and what everyone else deserved. Andy deserved the truth.
He deserved her honesty.

And she could not, absolutely *could not,* be honest.

"Tell me what happened," she said. *Give me time to think.*

He told her, in a flat tense tone, about the fight on the
street in front of the Franischi house. About the eyes. The
teeth.

About Darla, who was sitting in the waiting room with a
patrolman to keep her from running off.

The Franischis were downtown, waiting for interrogation.

"So you tell me, Maggie, what the fuck have we gotten
into here? You knew, didn't you. You knew the whole time,
and you didn't tell me."

He was more than angry. He was scared, and scared people did unpredictable things. He had the Franischis, but Maggie didn't think they'd ever talk. He had Darla, who might.

He had a memory of something he couldn't explain and couldn't live with.

"I saw her, Maggie. Right up close. Right in my face," he said when she didn't speak. He stared out of the window into his own reflection. "I'm not crazy."

It wasn't a question. He pulled a pack of Marlboros from his coat pocket and lit up; his hands shook a little, hardly enough to see. He took a long, vengeful drag and breathed smoke at the windowpane.

"You going to answer me?"

"I can't," she said, and his head turned and his crazy eyes looked into hers. "Andy, you're asking me for something I can't give you."

"I've *seen* it. I can't forget it."

No, she couldn't either. The first sight of Michael, with his bloody eyes and pale skin and the way he moved—she couldn't forget.

"Let the Franischis go, Andy. They're not going to tell you a thing."

"I watched this—this thing take those kids. What the hell am I supposed to do about that? I'm supposed to *do* something." He rubbed at the deep gray lines on his forehead.

"Have the Franischis said anything about the abduction?"

He made a short barking sound that didn't qualify as a laugh. "They say the kids went camping. Camping. With Ellen's brother and sister."

"They won't change the story. The Franischis weren't chosen by accident. They were picked because they could be managed."

A knock came on the door, discreet, firm. A crack in the

door admitted the nurse's Cheshire smile, which faded at the sight of the smoke drifting from McDonnell's cigarette.

"You can't smoke in here," she protested, and advanced on him. "Really, detective, you should know better. If you care about your partner at all, you'll have to make more of an effort."

She took the cigarette away from him; he let it go without a struggle and watched her carry it off like a dead rat. The door bumped gently shut behind her.

"Maybe you'll have to make more of an effort, too, Maggie, because I'm going crazy here, and I'm not kidding around. I saw what I saw. I just don't know—" He jammed his hands in his pockets again, and cellophane crackled; he pulled out the Marlboros and looked at them as if they'd grown there on their own. "See this? I stopped smoking ten years ago. Ten years, never wanted a cigarette. I've smoked a pack and a half in the last seven hours."

Maggie's room faced west, and the sky was still black. The stars glittered white and cold. *Day,* she thought. *Maybe I can talk in the daytime.*

McDonnell pitched the Marlboros at the trash can; they scattered like pick-up sticks. He turned back to face her, and she felt cold and frightened at the look in his eyes.

"I need to know what they are, Maggie. For God's sake, please. Please."

There was no easy way. She looked up at the ceiling and wished herself gone, dead, away.

"They're vampires," she heard herself say.

And kept talking.

When she was done, McDonnell was back in the chair, head in his hands. His hair was thinning on top, and through the gray his scalp looked pink and vulnerable.

"You're completely nuts," he said. He rubbed at his forehead and propped his chin on one hand; the lines in his face looked unhealthy, now, deep slashes like wounds. His eyes were spiderwebbed with red. "Nuts."

"You've seen them," she murmured; she was too tired to talk, too scared by what she'd just done. Maybe if she slept, it would all end up a dream . . .

"Yeah, I've seen them," he said, and reached out to take her hand in his. He studied her short fingernails with too much concentration. "Makes me nuts, too, I guess."

"The Franischis don't want to press charges against anybody, they just want to go home. Let them work it out with you."

"Maggie, I fired my gun. Twice. How the hell am I supposed to put that in a report when it's all just a big mistake?" He swiped his hand over his face again. "No matter how you look at it, it's a fuck-up the size of Cleveland."

"The Franischis won't say a word about the shots. If you don't, it doesn't become a departmental issue, just a misunderstanding."

He gave her a long, considering look, and she wished she could just sink under the bed, down a few floors, to someplace dark and quiet.

"How far is this going to go?" he asked. "Cover this up, and what're we going to cover up next? How about the murders at the JiffeeMart?"

He'd figured it out. She wasn't too surprised.

"I'm not trying to cover anything up, Andy; as soon as I can find out from Michael what happened—"

"He's one of *them*."

"He's my husband, damn it. He'll tell me what happened. Look, if it is a vampire thing, then there's no point in going much further because even if we get somebody we're going to look like lunatics and be off the job in a matter of days. Isn't that so?"

He nodded. She reached for the glass of orange juice the nurse had left on the table and took a thick, sweet mouthful.

"So we play it by ear, Andy, that's all I'm saying. And we make sure that we do what we can, everything we can, to stop them if they're killing. But we can't put that in a report. Ever."

He kept nodding, but she wasn't sure he agreed with her. It seemed more like he'd just forgotten how to stop his head from moving.

"What about the kid?" he asked.

"What about her?"

"You expect me to turn her back over to the Franischis, like there's nothing wrong? Like they won't hand her over, too, the minute the bitch shows back up to collect? I can't do it, Maggie. I can't."

It was all shadows and fog, this far into the gray. Nothing seemed solid anymore, nothing to hold onto except her feelings, and what they told her was right and wrong. Trying to fill out a report on the Society, that was wrong. Giving Darla back to the Franischis, that was wrong, too.

"How old is she?" Maggie asked. "Sixteen? Seventeen?"

"Sixteen. Jesus, I'll never forget hearing those kids crying, never."

Darla. Awkward, shy, afraid. Brainwashed. If given the chance, she'd go over to the vampires and be happy about it.

"Don't let the Franischis take her," Maggie said, and he looked up. "Tell them you're placing Darla in protective custody."

"Then what do I do with her?"

"Find her a home." She shivered, and pulled the thin blanket up around her shoulders. Cold in here, or maybe it was just her body telling her it wasn't ready for all this. "Or let her do what she wants. Anyway, it's a better chance than she's got if she goes back with Ed and Ellen. At eighteen, she'd be collected by some vampire and end up a slave. Twenty-five, at the most, she'd be dead. That's what she's got to look forward to if you don't do something, Andy. So do something."

She was glad he didn't ask what. The warmth of his hand on hers made her drift, and she was almost gone when she heard him whisper, "Okay."

She dreamed of red eyes and teeth, and a pain in her womb like something slashing from inside. When she woke up, he was gone.

Do something, she'd told him. She hadn't told him what.

She didn't have any idea of what to do, herself.

Interlude:

Andy McDonnell

"How long have you known?" Darla asked. She scraped chocolate pudding from one side of the dish to the other, lumping it into shapes and then mashing it flat with her spoon. Andy took a sip of coffee and tried to think of the answer. *Ten minutes* didn't sound confidence inspiring.

"A while."

She sighed. Her dark brown eyes flashed up and away; she would have like to have stared, he guessed, but she didn't know how.

"You won't do anything to Ed and Ellen, will you? I mean, they're all right. They tried real hard to make us feel like their kids and everything. Ellen, she was real good with Joey."

"Tell me about LaDonna," Andy said. His mouthful of toast tasted like slightly charred cardboard; he took another sip of coffee to soften it up and looked for jam. He found grape jelly the consistency of curdled milk.

"LaDonna," Darla sighed again. "Everybody wants to talk about LaDonna. I mean, I'm sorry she's dead and everything, but she was—crazy, you know? She kept saying she was going to run away, or that she was going to tell everybody. That was crazy."

"You never thought about running away?"

A sidelong glance. She made a round hilltop in the pudding. "Maybe I thought about it but I never told anybody."

"Where would you go? If you ran away?"

"Why?"

"Just curious," he said, and she stared at him for a full three seconds before blushing and looking down at her pudding again. "You sure you don't want any food?" he asked her.

"No sir," she murmured. "Alaska."

It took him a second to figure out what question she was answering.

"Alaska. Pretty cold up there."

"I don't mind the cold."

"Of course not, you're young. So why Alaska?"

Darla shifted in her chair and looked around. The cafeteria was deserted except for a hollow-eyed man sitting near the door, and a woman with two young children trying to choose between red and green Jell-O in the serving line.

The room felt cold and unwelcoming. Even the chairs were hard. Andy added that to his mental list of things he didn't like about the hospital—for a relatively new list, it was getting long quickly.

"Mountains," Darla said. "Lakes. Stuff like that. I've never seen that."

"Snow, ice, polar bears," Andy added.

"I've *seen* those."

"You've seen polar bears?" he asked, surprised. She gave him a withering look.

"We got the Discovery channel."

"Why'd you do that, back at your house?" he asked her. She frowned.

"Do what?"

"Try to get that woman off of me."

Darla took her time answering; she sculpted something tall out of her pudding and finally took a bite from it.

"You didn't do anything," she said in a low voice, muffled by the pudding. "She didn't have to hurt you."

"Has she hurt people before?"

Darla didn't answer. He sipped at his coffee and pushed it away, so he wouldn't be tempted to try it again.

"Darla?"

"Yes," she finally said. "She hurt this guy, I don't know his name. She's nice most of the time, I mean, really, she's not bad at all. It was just that he—he got in her way."

"Like me."

"Yeah." She put her spoon down and took a drink of orange juice; the idea of chocolate pudding and OJ made Andy feel a little sick, but she seemed to enjoy it. "You guys were real nice when you were at the house. I didn't want you to get hurt."

"Thanks." Boy, that sounded lame; a sixteen-year-old kid had thrown herself on a crazy woman (vampire) and saved his life, and he couldn't think of anything to say but "thanks." "I've got to ask you a question, Darla, a real serious one. Do you want to go back with Ed and Ellen?"

He saw the flicker of fear in her eyes.

"Sure," she said. "Why wouldn't I?"

"Maybe because you don't really want to be part of this family they're talking about. Because you don't want to end up with people like this Diane. Right?"

"They've been good to me." Her voice got softer, almost inaudible. "Nobody else has ever been nice like that. If I leave there where do I go? I mean, they'll take me and put me in another foster home. I don't want that."

"Is that all?" he asked. She looked up, right into his eyes.

"No," she said. "No, I don't want to go into the Family. But I don't have a choice anymore. I'm one of them now. They'll come back for me."

Diane, she meant. Diane would come back for her. Andy remembered the kids, screaming. He pushed his plate out of the way.

"Darla, if you don't want to go, I'm not going to let anybody take you. That's a promise from me to you, okay?" It was a promise he didn't have any clue how to keep. "You want to go up and see Maggie?"

"Isn't it past visiting hours?" she asked. He stood up and grabbed his coat from the chair. She struggled into her ski jacket and pulled her hair out of the collar with a practiced swing of her head. "Aren't we going to get in trouble?"

He just grinned.

Gloria Naomi Davis was on duty.

Gloria frowned at the sight of Darla, but Andy explained that the kid was a material witness in a crime and he couldn't leave her sitting around by herself. He also made a date for Friday night, for Chinese food.

Darla dug an elbow in his side as they went down the hall.

"Not a word," he warned her, and she looked offended.

"I'm not a *kid,*" she said, and gave him a look from under long dark eyelashes. "I have a boyfriend. His name's Ron."

"Ron." Andy chewed the name like a lump. "How old is he?"

"What are you, my dad?"

"How old?"

"Twenty."

He pushed open the door to Maggie's room and let her walk in first.

"Twenty's way too old—" he started, and in the space of a second the room clicked into cold focus.

Maggie, asleep on the bed, turned away from him. She was curled on her side.

On the chair next to her, the woman. Diane. The vampire.

He heard the hiss of the door closing behind him and thought about yelling, but he didn't know who he'd be yelling to, or what they'd do if they came. He reached out and found the silky fabric of Darla's ski jacket and pushed her into the corner. She hadn't made a sound.

He drew his gun and slid the safety off, but he didn't raise it.

The woman—Diane—watched him without any expression at all.

"I wouldn't recommend that," she said, and he was surprised that it was just a normal voice, a little on the soprano side. Her eyes looked dark just now, but he wasn't ever going to forget the color they'd been the last time. "You know you can't hurt me with it. And there are two other people in this room you could kill with it. I could do a lot of damage in a hospital if you make me angry."

"What are you doing here?" he demanded, and she smiled a little.

"Taking care of problems. There have been a lot of problems lately. LaDonna, you, Darla—quite a list." She watched his face intently. "I didn't have anything to do with LaDonna's death. You do understand that?"

"Yes."

"I have reason to believe that this woman won't talk—she has enough motivation to keep quiet. You, on the other hand—you're quite a problem, detective. You don't know what you've blundered into."

"I know," Andy said. He made sure he stayed between Diane and the kid. "You haven't said why you're here."

"Darla." Diane raised her eyebrows. "I can't let her go, not now. She belongs to us now, and she has to come with me."

"To die?" Between the eyes, he decided. He stared at the place he would have to shoot. "No, I don't think so."

"Not to die. To live." Diane's eyes moved left, to focus on the girl. "You understand, don't you? The Family will protect you. We will always protect you. Come here, Darla. I'll take you home."

It wouldn't work, Andy thought. The kid thought about Alaska, about running away. Security didn't have any charm for a kid like that. Security was for adults.

So he was surprised when he heard the whisper of her ski jacket scrape over his arm as she passed him. He made a grab for her and missed; Diane reached out, and Darla took her hand.

Diane turned the kid's hand palm up and pushed up the sleeve of the ski jacket. She turned the arm slightly so that Andy could see the puncture scars in Darla's wrist.

"She's Family now," Diane said, and Andy brought his gun up and took aim. Between the eyes.

"Detective?" He couldn't afford to take his eyes off of Diane, but he did, just a flick, to see Darla staring at him. Her face was pale and set. "Sir, please don't. You can't change this. You can't."

"Don't you want to go to Alaska?" he asked through gritted teeth. His blood was pounding in his ears. "Get over here."

"I can't. I'm sorry." He did look at her then, and saw the

tears shimmering in her dark eyes. "I wish I could. But I can't. It's too late for that."

Diane's hand went around her shoulders and squeezed. The kid turned her face toward the woman and cried.

Andy slowly lowered the gun.

"See?" Diane said, and she was no longer smiling. If anything, she looked resigned. "I can't leave her. She needs us now."

There was nothing to do, nothing at all. He swallowed a mouthful of rage that tasted like vomit and put the safety back on his automatic. He holstered it and went over to the window. Still dark and cold. The night lasted forever.

"Detective," Diane said. He looked at the reflection in the glass and couldn't see her, just Darla. The impossibility of that made him dizzy. "Detective. One more thing."

He turned around and her eyes blazed red. He tried to move and couldn't.

"I should kill you."

"No," Darla murmured, and turned her face away, balled her fists up near her temples.

"Shh, child, I only said I should. A dead policeman will only cause more trouble than he's worth, anyway." Diane's hand stroked the girl's long hair, and the red in her eyes faded to a distant emberlike glow. The crushing pressure in Andy's head eased. "The killer of LaDonna Bedford is dead, detective. That's all you need to know to close your case. The Family, the children, Darla—these are things you will not remember."

"The hell I won't," he said flatly. Diane's smile was sharp and sad.

"Hell," she told him, "is a relative term. I can make the process quite painless, if you cooperate."

"No."

Diane's hand left Darla's hair and stretched out to touch the exposed white skin of Maggie Bowman's throat, just about where the eggplant-colored bruise began. Her nails gleamed like steel.

"No?"

Andy pulled in a deep breath, held it, let it out. He took a step toward Diane, closer and closer until he could see the faint blue flush in her skin, and feel the chill from her.

He'd known from the moment he'd seen her that there would be no choice.

"Wise of you," she whispered, and her eyes were red, deep enough to drown him.

Fourteen

Amusements

The pirate ship creaked in the wind. A nylon sail caught the cold breeze and flapped, and when I set foot on the wooden deck I felt the tingle of danger through my shoes. On the freeway, less than a football field away, car headlights blazed by in a stream. But here, on the pirate ship, there was just shadow.

Lilly's hand clutched my arm; she was blind here, and I smelled her fear even through her thick wool coat. Her face looked ghostly and strained.

"It's getting late!" She was trying to whisper but it was as loud as a shout to a vampire; I put a gloved hand over her mouth and felt her nod through the thick fabric. I put my lips close to her ear.

"I know. Keep hold of me."

William was in a game-playing mood; after his little creep show in the toilets he'd gone on a frenzied spree through the park, always a minute or two ahead of us, close enough to taunt. Adam had seen him on the gangplank to the pirate ship; I'd only seen a shadow, flickering among other shadows.

Adam was in front of us, his white shirt billowing in the wind. He climbed up a short flight of steps to a higher level and stood there silhouetted in the moon. A ghost ship, I thought, a ghost captain, and almost expected to hear the timbers creak as the waves washed against her. They'd have to be ghost waves, of course; the ship was set in concrete, surrounded by a shallow little lagoon of stagnant water.

The skull and crossbones snapped in the wind overhead. I looked up and saw something in the rigging. It might have been a shadow. Might have been.

Adam saw it too; he jumped down toward us just as something hit the deck next to him. A bottle. With a burning rag—

He lunged to his feet and shoved me and Lilly out of the way as the bottle exploded in a wave of blue flame across the wood.

Up in the rigging someone laughed, low and vicious.

"Don't like it, do you?" William called. "I didn't like it when you tried to burn me up, boy. Turnabout's fair play."

The wood had been baked dry through the Texas winter; I heard the hiss as the fire took hold. Adam pointed me toward the gangplank where we'd come on board and gave me a shove to get me started. His head stayed tilted up, waiting for William's next move.

"Where's Celestine?" Adam shouted. I got a glimpse of William, crawling like a white spider from one rope to another. Maneuvering to get directly above Adam.

"Wouldn't you like to know?" I saw the spark of flame as William lit another Molotov cocktail. It fell like a comet.

Adam jumped up, grabbed the rigging and started climbing. I tugged Lilly toward the gangplank; she found her footing more easily now, because the night was turning violent orange behind us. I put a foot on the slanting board with a sense of deep relief.

It slid out from under me and flew away into the darkness.

Celestine stood below us, teeth bared, eyes red. She beck-oned to me with long, sharp, glistening nails.

"Come on, Lilly. There's nothing to be afraid of," she purred, and I felt Lilly's shiver as if it were my own.

"That's not her," she said. Celestine's grin looked as sharp as her teeth.

"No, it *is*. This is what I really am, isn't it, Michael? It's just that I don't have to hide it anymore."

I looked up and saw Adam high up in the rigging. There was no sign of William. I could jump down, of course, and maybe I could fight her; maybe I could even beat her.

But what about Lilly?

I dragged her in the other direction. Celestine loped around, following the sound of Lilly's footsteps, and when we got to the rail she was there, waiting.

The fire was a billowing roar behind us, a monster eating up the whole middle of the ship. Somebody would have seen it from the freeway; we didn't have long before the place was crawling with fire trucks. William would get away in the confusion. Kill again.

Kill Maggie and my child, for spite.

"It's me," Lilly said suddenly. "It's me she wants."

"No."

"We've got to do it! It's the only way!"

She let go of my arm and, before I realized what she was doing, dived off the ship into the shallow water below.

I followed. The splash was cold, the water choked with leaves and debris. I got my feet under me and lunged up, out of the moat.

Lilly went under the water with a gurgling scream. Ce-lestine was nowhere to be seen.

Under the water. I saw her hair misting out like a cloud.

She had Lilly around the neck and I remembered the freezing despair of drowning, of cold water swelling in my lungs and my body convulsing—

If I had stopped to think about it, I might not have gone in again, but then the water was cold around my face and body and pressed on my skin like a lover; I wrapped my hands in Celestine's hair and pulled as hard as I could. Her head snapped up out of the water, but in the next second she slashed at me and I remembered the exquisite bright pain she'd shown me. For a second I was paralyzed, and she got in a couple of good cuts on my arm.

Lilly surfaced with a gasping sob that made me remember what I was fighting for. I caught Celestine's wrist and twisted; she cried out and tried for my throat with her other hand. I got a hand flat against her stomach, braced myself and pushed as hard as I could.

She shot out of the water and landed with a thud against the wooden hull of the ship. I saw the red fire go out in her eyes like a burned-out light bulb, and then she flopped forward into the water and sank.

To the bottom.

I grabbed Lilly, who was gasping and choking, and lifted her out of the water before diving down for Celestine. She lay with her arms outstretched, cheek touching the rough algae-covered concrete. Her dark hair waved like a drowned flag.

I grabbed her around the waist and pulled, propelling us back to the surface. Lilly helped me haul Celestine's body out of the pool and onto the cold dry grass.

The pirate ship was burning brightly. As I looked up, a nylon sail dissolved into spiderwebs and cancerous black and sloughed away. The pirate flag had an orange fringe of flame.

Adam had no place to go. He looked down at me, and I beckoned. Urgently.

He landed on his feet, from a distance of more than two stories.

"Did you get him?" I asked. He wiped cinders from his forehead and grimaced.

"No. I never got close enough."

One thing was certain, William wasn't on the pirate ship. It was burning like the Aggie bonfire, and approaching sirens wailed the War Hymn.

"We've got to find him!" I yelled. Adam nodded and scooped up Celestine, balancing her on one shoulder.

"Adam, careful!" I warned. "She's—"

"I know what she is," he said, and to my surprise he sounded sad, not angry. "Believe me, I know better than anybody."

I looked from him to Lilly, who stood beside me shivering; her coat was soaking wet, and if we didn't get inside and warm soon she'd freeze. Time was short and getting shorter.

"It's going to be morning soon," Lilly said. Adam nodded and looked at the horizon, which seemed to be catching fire from the glow of the pirate ship. "Sir, please, we've got her, we can go—"

"Not yet," I said. She gritted her chattering teeth and tugged at my sleeve.

"But—"

"We won't be safe until he's dead, Lilly," I snapped, and she breathed out a white mist of sorrow. "I'm sorry, but we have to go on. Can you make it?"

She nodded, one grim convulsive dip of her head.

Adam led us back down the twisting path, to the haunted house.

"In here?" I said, appalled. He nodded. "But—"

He wrenched open the accordion gate and disappeared through the dangling rubber flaps in the entrance. I pulled my fireplace lighter out of my apron pocket and clicked it.

Nothing. It was too wet to work.

The slide of those flaps over my face reminded me of the dusty curtains brushing against me as I'd lain helpless at the Refuge. Darkness settled over me, close and invasive and choking; even with vampire eyes I could only see shadows, hints. Something loomed up and I batted at it with my free hand; it tore with a metallic shriek.

Just a painted piece of steel. Nothing a child would be scared of.

"I can't see," Lilly whispered, and not all the shaking in her voice came from the cold. "I don't think I can do this. I can't see."

"Just hold onto me. You'll be all right." It was a lie, but I couldn't do any better for her just now. She wasn't safe anywhere—not outside, alone; not in here with me; not back in the hidden room at Sylvia's. There were no safe places from William. "Here."

I gave her a stake. She clutched it in her right hand and kept her left wrapped around my arm. My work gloves were soaking wet, clumsy as mittens, but I found another stake in my apron pocket and got a good grip on it.

I couldn't see Adam, who'd gone on ahead. Couldn't see anything. I felt my way along with my gloved fingers and listened to Lilly's panicked shallow breathing. She was shaking convulsively now, too cold to go on, too scared to stop.

Sirens crested to a frenzied moan outside and stopped.

I heard something moving ahead of me, a subtle change in the air, and reached out, carefully.

A cold hand closed around my wrist and jerked me off balance. Lilly cried out as she was knocked aside; I raised the stake to strike and realized that the hand hadn't pulled me forward as an attack.

It was a plea. I stripped off my glove and reached down in the dark to trace smooth cool skin, sharp cheekbones, long silky hair.

"Celestine?" I whispered. It sounded like she was trying to speak, but I couldn't hear her. I got my hand under her shoulders and propped her up. "Celestine?"

"Help me," she whispered, and no matter what she'd done to me, even to Maggie, it hurt to hear someone so much in pain. "Please, Michael, please, don't let him do this to me. Please. No more."

She wrapped her arms around me and clung; I sat there in the dark and held her while Lilly sat huddled next to us, shivering. My eyes were slowly becoming accustomed to the dark; I picked out the dim curve of Celestine's cheek, the outlines of Lilly's face. The walkway around us was littered with junk and pulleys and wires; we were on a motorized track, but the cars were gone. Up ahead was a long black tunnel that seemed to have no end in sight.

Celestine shuddered against me, and I didn't have to be told that she was struggling to keep William from gaining control of her again. I squeezed her fingers hard and saw her face contract with pain.

"Where's Adam?"

"I don't know. He dropped me—I think he . . ." She ran out of air and had to refill her lungs, a painful, creaking process. "He saw William."

"Up ahead?"

She didn't know. I eased her back against the metal wall and realized that I could see her expression now. It wasn't my eyes that were growing accustomed.

It was getting light. Which meant morning . . .

I felt the first heavy falling sensation. Celestine curled into a ball on her side and Lilly cradled her like a child. I stood up and braced myself against the wall. Outside, I heard voice shouting, fire hoses gushing. It wouldn't take them long to put it out, and then there'd be investigators, police—

We had to get out of here. *Now.*

I started down the tunnel at a walk, then broke into a run. I couldn't see anything, just black, but I couldn't afford to slow down. I held my hands out in front of me to feel the way.

My fingers hit a metal door and slammed it open with a grating scream. I was in a big round room, and the tracks went around and down—

—into the pit. I took a step forward and looked down.

Papier-mache monsters peeked out of caves. Plastic were-wolves lurched out from doorways. A washed out Dracula froze, caught in the act of rising from his coffin. He had an ash-smeared white shirt and auburn hair.

Dracula turned his head, and I saw the glint of glasses. Adam touched his finger to his lips in a demand for silence.

"Welcome," William's voice whispered. It came from no-where, and everywhere, ricocheting off of metal and making me dizzy trying to track it. I lurched back from the edge of the pit and tried to look everywhere at once. "I thought you'd never get here, Mikey."

"Where are you?" I yelled, and I was surprised how much of my hate came out in it. "Come out. You've been waiting for this, haven't you?"

"No, not yet. See, boy, I ain't even started playing with you. Adam, he still owes me a little time. He left me. I don't like that. And he took my pretty little Celestine with him." William's voice lost all of its fake-hick accent; what was left was still and cold and inhuman. "I'll get around to you after I'm all done with them."

"You're done *now*. Finished. I'm not leaving here until I kill you, William, and that's a promise."

"Quit that, boy, you're scarin' me." There was no mistaking where the voice came from this time. Behind me. Close behind. I whirled and sliced with the stake but he was gone. The whisper came from the shadows to my right this time. "You gonna talk me to death, or you plannin' on hurtin' me with that toothpick?"

Something brushed by my arm. I stabbed for it, and his laugh echoed.

"I always live up to my promises," he said, and this time when I turned he was right there, inches away, eyes wide, teeth bared. Before I could use the stake he took it away from me and tossed it down into the pit. It bounced off of something with a dull thud.

I couldn't reach the others I had in the apron. His fingernails scrabbled on the heavy cotton fabric and ripped it loose from my neck. He upended it over the pit, and the stakes and the fireplace lighter rained down with musical thumps and pings. He let the day-glo apron flutter down after them.

"Alone at last," he purred, but there wasn't any playing left in him. The day was dragging him down, and I saw the end of my life in his eyes. "Don't you worry, now. I'll tell little Maggie you said your goodbyes."

Down in the pit I heard something click, a sound that didn't belong there. Fire blossomed orange. William's face, so close to mine, convulsed in rage, and he threw me backward as he approached the pit to look down into it.

Something came up, rising magically, smoothly. I couldn't understand what it was at first—tall, skinny, bamboo. Burning on one end.

Adam had thrown me the beach torch. I snatched it out of the air just as his other present arrived, thrown with perfect accuracy to strike William right in the face.

A plastic bag full of sawdust broke on impact and showered him with tiny wormy curls of wood.

He screamed and leaped backward, clawing at his face, his eyes. Finally hurt, at last.

I raised the pointed end of the torch, meant for ramming into sandy soil. He whirled and saw it coming. His lips parted in amazement as the sharp edge slammed into his chest and parted skin, shoving aside ribs.

And punched through his heart.

His fingernails tore at the bamboo and his screams stabbed at me. I shoved harder, until I saw the point emerge from his back. He didn't have any air to scream with, but I saw it in his eyes. Boundless hate, frustration, arrogance. He opened his mouth and black sooty blood ran out of it to drip down his smeared sweatshirt.

I was weak, so weak. We went to our knees together, like men at prayer. He slashed at me once more, weakly, before he collapsed over on his side, his white hair making a frail halo around his blood-smeared face.

The beach torch was close enough to make my skin sizzle. I sank backward and watched dazedly as his body convulsed one last time, and his hands wrapped around the stake and pulled.

Once, twice. It slid an inch with a noise like pebbles grating.

He met my eyes, and smiled like a skull grinning.

Behind me, two voices cried a warning—Adam's, too far away, and Lilly's. I started to turn but something slammed into me, threw me forward toward William, toward the burning torch. His arms opened wide to catch me and draw me to my death.

I twisted and threw myself flat on the ground, inches away from the fire. A weight climbed on my back, and icy fingernails tore at my shirt. I turned my head and saw Celestine stab downward with one of the stakes I'd left with Lilly.

Adam's hand shot out and grabbed Celestine's wrist; the wood bit me, but shallowly, only an inch or so. Not too bad, just bad enough to make me wish I could die and get the pain over with. I twisted around to face William and saw that his eyes were still open, not quite blank yet. Going—going—

Gone.

Adam shoved Celestine away, into Lilly's outstretched arms. His hand steadied me as he pulled the stake out. Slightly more painful than dying.

Just slightly.

I heard the stake hit the bottom of the pit, and collapsed back into Adam's arms.

"Sleep," I whispered. His face looked like polished aluminum; pale and shiny and inhumanly hard.

"Can't sleep here," he rasped. "Get up."

I couldn't. Morning dragged at me like an anchor.

Adam got up and snapped the beach torch in half, leaving the stake portion in William's body. He picked the body up and stumbled over to the far corner. A door. I saw the glow of morning coming in around it.

"Don't!" I whispered, but it was too late. He turned the knob and went outside, into the sunlight. He dragged William's body behind him, all the way into the full morning, going to his hands and knees before he made it back to the shelter of shadow.

William's body began to smolder. As I watched, it burst into blue-white fire.

Adam collapsed on the floor beside me and vomited up a thin string of red bile. His skin smoldered then bubbled into painful blisters.

"We can't stay here." That was Celestine, somehow able to talk. "We must get up. Walk out."

"We can't," I said.

"Dead if we stay," she murmured. "Must go."

I hadn't thought I could fight any harder, but somehow I made it to my feet. The effort blinded me. I found Adam and tugged him up to a leaning position; his arm went around my shoulders, mine around his. Lilly helped Celestine to stand.

The car was only fifty feet away, on the other side of the fence.

We were burning within twenty feet.

I thought I was beyond death by the time the limousine's clown-car trunk slammed shut on our pain, and cut off the blinding, mutilating sun. The car lurched into gear and began to move; I heard shouting, sirens. Lilly's driving tossed us from side to side. We attained the freeway and for a few seconds there was only the sound of our skin sizzling, and then Adam made a sound I will never forget.

He was laughing.

As Celestine's limousine carried us away into the rising sun, I was laughing, too, even as daysleep drowned me again.

William was gone.

Epilogue

A car's lights flickered through the trees as it wound up the drive to the cabin. I lit a cigarette and watched our visitor's progress.

"Want me to stay?" Adam asked; he stood in the shadows near the door, arms crossed. I shook my head. He was wondering, I supposed, whether or not I was depressed enough to be suicidal.

It was a fair question. I'd asked it myself several times in the last few days.

"Go on and finish up. I'll see you in a few minutes."

He was packing for the trip. We'd agreed—as much as any of us agreed on anything—that Dallas was no longer safe. Celestine was going back to the Society, and Lilly with her. Diane was still out there, somewhere, with a deep grudge.

Adam was leaving town.

Me, I was still thinking.

The car pulled up in the drive, and a man got out. A snappy dresser. Well-cut red hair. Bookish glasses. He came up to within a few feet of the steps where I sat, and stopped.

"Mr. Bowman, "he said. Tension hummed in his voice like bees. "My name is Kurt Cadell. I've come a long way."

I didn't say anything, just contemplated him, then my cigarette. He shifted from one foot to the other.

"I have a check for you," he continued. "Well, actually, for Mrs. Bowman. Maggie."

He could have been fishing for confirmation of a guess, but I didn't think so. The tension was coming from fear—he was scared to death, and still standing there, waiting. I let him stand.

"It's fifty thousand dollars." He cleared his throat. "Your life insurance payout. I knew you were still alive. I followed your wife for a while, traced her bank withdrawals. You were living under the name of Joseph Vico, and depositing money under the name of Gregory Dunlap."

The cabin behind me was dark and quiet, but I knew Adam was listening. Waiting to save me, if I'd let him. I let out a lungful of heavy, warm smoke.

"You're good," I said. No reaction from him. "So, you want money?"

"If I did, I wouldn't be giving you a check for fifty thousand dollars."

To prove his point, he dug an envelope out of his coat pocket and handed it to me—plain white, no writing. I opened it. He hadn't been joking.

"So?" I asked. Cadell's pulse raced faster, loud in my ears. He tilted his face up to the moon, to the stars unobscured by city lights, anything to look away from me.

"I want to be like you."

I sat without moving for a while, then stubbed out my cigarette in the ashtray next to me on the steps. A chilly breeze riffled the grass and whispered the leaves, and Cadell shivered. Over his shoulder, the landing lights of Dallas glowed like eyes.

"Why?" I asked. I meant it to sound cold, but it only sounded despairing. Cadell looked surprised, as if he hadn't expected the question. "What have you got to live for?"

His face tightened in anger, or pain.

"Nothing."

My smile felt sad and bitter.

"Welcome," I said, "to the club."

Of all the things I was bad at, goodbyes seemed the worst. I'd had months to think it out, to tie my loose ends, to be ready.

I wasn't ready.

I paused in the door of Maggie's room. She lay in a tangle of covers in shapeless pajamas that could have been mine. There was a small frown still etched between her eyes, as if she lived with a deep and constant ache. Her gun was next to her, on the nightstand.

I went to the next doorway, and looked in the crib, where my daughter slept. Andrea Marie.

"Daddy's here, sweetheart," I whispered and lifted her in my arms, rested her wobbly head on my shoulder, listened to the steady thump of her heart. When I swallowed I tasted Kurt Cadell's blood at the back of my throat, warm as unshed tears.

Andrea's tiny hand balled in a fist near my chin. I stroked it with one finger.

I heard the bed creak as Maggie got up. I kept my back to her until I heard the metallic click of her gun coming off safety, then turned. The fear in her face slammed into my chest as if she'd actually shot me.

"Put her down," she said. I didn't move.

"You know I wouldn't hurt her." My voice was as unsteady as hers. "Jesus, Maggie, you know that."

Whether she did or not, she thumbed the safety back in

place and put the gun down on the changing table next to her. A few blocks away, a police siren keened and faded.

The look in her eyes hadn't changed.

"You should have told me you were coming."

The nursery was cheerful yellow and powder blue. It smelled of creamy talcum and diapers. I imagined how it would glow in the sunlight, and imagined Andrea's face lit that way. So many things I had to regret, these days. I could hardly even remember them all.

"I couldn't just leave." There was a mirror on the wall, and it showed Andrea hanging in empty space. I exerted will and saw my body ghost into existence around her. Startling, how normal I could still look.

"I never asked you to leave," Maggie said; there was something dark in her voice, something defensive. "I never did that."

I eased Andrea back into her warm nest, covered her with the fluffy yellow blanket. My fingers brushed her soft cheek.

"You didn't have to." I looked up, and she flinched. "I got the message loud and clear."

Her mouth opened, closed. Her face went rigid. I left Andrea and came to stand next to her, only a foot away, closer than I'd been in so many months. The smell of her washed over me and drowned me in misery.

I took the check Cadell had given me out of my pocket and put it in her hand. She never looked down at it, never looked away from my face.

It was hard to turn away, harder than dying. I passed through the doorway, into the darkness of the hall where the shadows waited.

"Mike?"

The sound of her voice was a knife in my heart. I'd made her cry, again. I stopped and waited as she walked toward me, moving through the shadows. Her arms reached out and wrapped warmly around me.

"Don't go."

I looked out the window to where Adam waited, a tall pale statue in the moonlight. He was turned away from the house, maybe listening, maybe not.

"Goodbye," I said to him, and Maggie's body felt fever-hot against me, arms desperately tight, holding me to life. "I'll see you again."

He must have been listening after all, because he turned and met my eyes across the distance, and I felt rather than saw the smile.

"Goodbye, my friend," he said, and walked away, out of sight. I waited until I heard the sound of his van pulling away before allowing myself to turn in the circle of Maggie's arms and hold her.

No more goodbyes.

Roxanne Longstreet is the author of three previous novels: RED ANGEL and THE UNDEAD for Zebra Books and STORMRIDERS for Iron Crown. She cleverly disguises herself as a mild-mannered office worker in daily life. Roxanne, her husband—fantasy artist, Cat—and pet iguana—Iggy—live and work in the Dallas, Texas area where they are active in science fiction, fantasy and horror fandom. She is a graduate of Texas Tech University, a member of the Greater Dallas Writers Association and ORAC, and is a card-carrying Wednesday Weirdo.

HAUTALA'S HORROR AND
SUPERNATURAL SUSPENSE

GHOST LIGHT (4320, $4.99)
Alex Harris is searching for his kidnapped children, but only the ghost of their dead mother can save them from his murderous rage.

DARK SILENCE (3923, $5.99)
Dianne Fraser is trying desperately to keep her family—and her own sanity—from being pulled apart by the malevolent forces that haunt the abandoned mill on their property.

COLD WHISPER (3464, $5.95)
Tully can make Sarah's every wish come true, but Sarah lives in teror because Tully doesn't understand that some wishes aren't meant to come true.

LITTLE BROTHERS (4020, $4.50)
The "little brothers" have returned, and this time there will be no escape for the boy who saw them kill his mother.

NIGHT STONE (3681, $4.99)
Their new house was a place of darkness, shadows, long-buried secrets, and a force of unspeakable evil.

MOONBOG (3356, $4.95)
Someone—or something—is killing the children in the little town of Holland, Maine.

MOONDEATH (1844, $3.95)
When the full moon rises in Cooper Falls, a beast driven by bloodlust and savage evil stalks the night.

YOU'D BETTER SLEEP WITH THE LIGHTS TURNED ON!
BONE CHILLING HORROR BY

RUBY JEAN JENSEN

ANNABELLE	(2011-2, $3.95/$4.95)
BABY DOLLY	(3598-5, $4.99/$5.99)
CELIA	(3446-6, $4.50/$5.50)
CHAIN LETTER	(2162-3, $3.95/$4.95)
DEATH STONE	(2785-0, $3.95/$4.95)
HOUSE OF ILLUSIONS	(2324-3, $4.95/$5.95)
LOST AND FOUND	(3040-1, $3.95/$4.95)
MAMA	(2950-0; $3.95/$4.95)
PENDULUM	(2621-8, $3.95/$4.95)
VAMPIRE CHILD	(2867-9, $3.95/$4.95)
VICTORIA	(3235-8, $4.50/$5.50)